Books by James R. Callan

THE CRYSTAL MOORE SUSPENSE SERIES

A Ton of Gold, A Crystal Moore Suspense, Book #1

Silver Medallion, A Crystal Moore Suspense, Book #2

Political Dirty Trick, A Crystal Moore Suspense, Book #3

THE FATHER FRANK MYSTERY SERIES

Cleansed by Fire, A Father Frank Mystery, Book #1

Over My Dead Body, A Father Frank Mystery, Book #2

Plot for Murder, A Father Frank Mystery, Book #3

Murder a Cappella, A Sweet Adelines Mystery

Written with Diane Bailey

Y2K, The Novel

NON-FICTION TITLES

Character: The Heart of the Novel

How to Write Great Dialog

Y2K and You

Computer Literature Made Easy and Fine

Bits, Bytes, Apples and Mice

A Plot
for Murder

A Father Frank Mystery

A Plot
for Murder

A Father Frank Mystery

James R. Callan

Pennant Publishing

Copyright

Cover Design: Nada Orlic, Erelis Design

ISBN 13:   978-1-7321227-3-4

Pennant Publishing

Dedication

This book is dedicated to Earlene, without whose help neither this book nor its author would be here today.

Consider joining my email list and I'll send you a free short story that's just fun. Email me at:

jim@jamesrcallan.com

and say, "Send me a free story." I won't spam you, and I will never sell, rent or give your email address away.

A Plot for Murder

Chapter 1

"KILL HER. NOW." He was almost yelling. His dark eyes burned into her.

"But, I like her."

"That makes no difference."

"But..."

The man let out a long breath. "It's her life - or your career." He put his hands on his hips and fixed her with a disgusted look. "Why am I bothering with you?"

The woman twisted her hands together, looked down at the floor. Lines of anguish creased her face. "Okay. If I have to."

"You have to."

She fixed her gaze on his hands. "How?"

The angry man now looked puzzled. "How what?"

She took a quick glance at his face, then averted her eyes again. "How should I kill her?"

He shook his head as if he couldn't believe this. "I don't care how. Just get it done. Quickly."

She forced herself to look at the man towering above her, pleading with him. "But my readers love her."

Rod Granet shook his head. "Don't you know anything about writing, about producing a great book? It's the story." He paused. "Your story, at least as you've described it to us, demands that the character gets killed." The tall, handsome speaker shrugged. "*Something* is going to die: either this character, or your book. Make up your mind which is more important."

* * *

Maggie DeLuca felt sorry for the young woman standing at the front of the auditorium with a hundred and fifty writers watching her. She looked like she wanted to sit down or hide, but there was no place to hide. At this point, the woman - Maggie guessed she was in her early twenties - probably regretted asking the self-centered, egotistical Rod Granet about her novel. Maggie had made the same mistake three years ago and look what it got her. She stood up and quietly walked out the back door. "The scumbag," she muttered.

"Who's a scumbag?"

Maggie looked over at a middle-aged woman sitting on a bench outside the auditorium. She hadn't noticed the collection of people gathered under the shade of a giant hickory tree.

"Rod Granet," Maggie answered.

"And why is he a scumbag?" asked another woman in the group.

"He stole my story, that's why."

"He did what?" said the first woman. And several others gasped.

"Took my story and published it under his name."

An African-American woman leaning against the tree said, "Plots are often similar. You're saying his story was very much like yours?"

"Not similar." Maggie's anger was not dissipating. "Exactly. Scene for scene."

A short, plump woman said, "That's hard to believe."

"Hard to believe? How about this? I created a new word for a poison: mertetrocide. There is no such word in English. But I used it as a poison. Granet used that word in the same sentence as I had. Is that enough for you? He copied my book."

"He'll have to pay for it in the end," said the first woman.

"Yeah." Maggie shook her head. "Maybe sooner than he thinks." With that, she turned and headed for the women's residence building. She needed to cool off before she made everybody avoid her.

Just then, the doors to the conference arena opened and a crowd of writers poured out. Among them - Rod Granet.

The woman who had been sitting on the bench stood up. "Mr. Granet." He looked in her direction. "That woman over there--," She pointed at Maggie. "She said you stole her novel. Is that true?"

For an instant, Granet looked startled. Then a big smile came over his face. "No. I never stole an idea. Never needed to."

His denial stopped Maggie in mid-stride. She turned to face Granet. "Yes you did. I showed my manuscript to you when you were here three years ago. And now it's a bestseller. But it has *your* name on it."

Granet smiled, and gave a nervous laugh. "Ridiculous. I don't even remember you or your book." He looked at the writers around him. "Must not have been very memorable." He delivered the last sentence as a joke, following it up with a thin laugh. Two or three people gathered around him laughed also. But the majority turned to look at the woman who had just accused the *USA Today* bestselling author of stealing her book.

Maggie was never one to back down from a fight. "Memorable enough that each chapter, each scene is the same." Maggie's eyes were blazing. "You moved it from Pittsburgh to Kansas City. You changed Ursula to Jenny. But you didn't even check to see if mertetrocide was an actual word, before copying it. The book is mine."

Granet was no longer smiling. "If you continue this kind of libel, I'll have my lawyer deal with you."

"Not libel. Slander. It isn't in writing. Yet."

Now Granet's face was red and his voice hard. "Either way, you'll end up paying for it."

"And you might end up paying dearly for stealing my story." Maggie abruptly turned and marched off toward the center's housing.

Chapter 2

THE PINEY WOODS Writers Conference, or PWWC as most people called it, had started ten years ago as a half-day workshop for twenty writers, held in the rarely used banquet room at a local restaurant.

Today, it was a full four day conference that drew nearly two hundred writers and would-be writers paying two hundred and fifty dollars each to hear published authors, agents, editors and publicists tell them how to write a good book, get it published and then market it. Some even promised they would deliver the secrets to make a successful career out of writing.

Instead of the barbeque smell that had permeated the restaurant, now the PWWC had moved to the park-like setting of the Lakota Retreat Center nestled under tall southern pines and ancient hickory and oak trees. The lovely Lakota Lake wrapped itself around three-quarters of the fifteen acre Retreat Center. The neatly maintained grounds helped provide a peaceful, quiet, park-like atmosphere.

The large, well-equipped auditorium could easily manage a crowd of two hundred and fifty, and several meeting rooms allowed breakout sessions to handle the growing number of sessions the conference offered. To accommodate private consultations with editors, agents or other faculty members, eight smaller offices were available.

But among the many advantages of the center, none was more appreciated than the accommodations. Situated ten miles from a small town, the ability to provide housing for many of the attendees and the faculty was a strong drawing point. Individual cabins scattered along the shore of the lake provided housing for the faculty. This kept the speakers on site for interaction with attendees beyond the scheduled sessions.

Two residence buildings contained many small bedrooms suitable for one or two attendees, available at a very modest fee. This allowed attendees to stay onsite, providing more opportunities to meet with the faculty and network with other writers. A large cafeteria provided tasty meals at a reasonable price.

The move to the Lakota Retreat some five years ago had been a huge success and many believed a contributing factor in the growth of PWWC.

Maggie was a bit surprised J. R. (Rod) Granet was on the faculty. First, he had been here three years ago and PWWC rarely had repeat speakers. And second, Granet had received the prestigious Austin Benedict Award for Best Plot of the Year for his latest novel, *A Garden Variety Murder*, the book that made him a *USA Today* bestseller. With his awards, he could pick which conferences he appeared at. PWWC must have shelled out a hefty honorarium.

* * *

Until a few days ago, Maggie had not read *A Garden Variety Murder*, its price too steep for her budget. But shortly before the conference, she decided she needed to read his book before attending, just in case she got an appointment to meet with him. By the time she finished the first three pages, her anger had reached the danger zone.

Today's first session offered attendees the choice of hearing J.R. Granet speaking on plot development in Room 101, an agent discussing what should be presented to an agency in Room 102, or a marketing manager outlining the power of an engaged email list in Room 103.

A good night's sleep had quieted Maggie's anger. She decided to skip Granet. If she attended his lecture, she was certain another confrontation would result. She headed over to the marketing session. She was a little late. The soft rain during the night had made all the foliage look freshly washed and gleaming. Beautyberry bushes seemed to flourish beneath every pine tree. Last night's rain had turned each deep purple berry into a glittering globe that caught and reflected the morning sunlight.

Scattered throughout the area were stunning Nandina plants with their large clusters of cherry red berries.

    The morning was just too glorious to rush. She felt certain nothing important would be covered in the first ten minutes. She was reaching for the door when she heard a woman running in the hall.

    "Have you seen Mr. Granet?" she called to Maggie.

    "No." *And I don't care to either.*

    "He's late for his session. He's not in the cafeteria. And the room is crowded with people. Some are getting annoyed."

    "Can't help you," Maggie said.

    A minute later, two men burst out of Room 101. "...probably just overslept," Maggie heard one of them say. From what I've heard, he probably had a late night private consultation." They both snickered. "Let's bang on his door and drag him over. I paid good money to hear him."

* * *

    Forty minutes later, Maggie almost wished she attended Granet's talk. The expert on email marketing had droned on about how important it was, without giving any helpful suggestions on how to increase your email list or how to write an engaging email. As she stepped out of the building, she saw four police cars racing up, red and blue lights flashing, tires screaming to a stop opposite the building.

Chapter 3

"PRINCE OF PEACE Church, this is Father Frank. How can I help you?"

"Frank, this is Maggie. I need—"

"I recognize my sister on the infrequent times she calls. How's the conference going? Are you learning anything?"

"One of the speakers has been killed. Some of the writers here are freaking out. You need to come over and talk to some of them."

"Killed? What happened?" *An accident?*

"We don't know. But the police are here and questioning a lot of people. From what little I've picked up, I think he was murdered."

"Murdered? At a writers conference? That doesn't make sense. You're pulling my leg, right?"

"No. I'm serious, Frank."

" Why would someone kill one of the speakers?"

"Because he deserved it. Because he stole things. I don't really—"

A hand clamped on to Maggie's neck and another grabbed her cell phone. She jerked around, ready to strike out at the person only to be looking into the face of a burly policeman.

"What do you mean he deserved it?" asked a second policeman tall enough that Maggie's eyes were level with the Timber County Deputy patch on his shoulder. Her phone was lost inside his fist.

Maggie, rarely at a loss for words, stared at the muscular man in the brown uniform, her mouth hanging open, but no words coming out.

The man's intense eyes bored into Maggie. "Why did he deserve to die?"

"Ah, well, ah, he wasn't a nice man." *That was lame.*

The deputy kept his laser focus on Maggie, but said nothing.

"Ah, what I mean is, since he was kind of a jerk, probably someone ... well, I can imagine he might have done something to cause ..." She tore her focus away from the deputy's face and looked down at the ground. "I don't know what I mean."

For several seconds, he continued to study Maggie. Then, without taking his focus off her, said to his partner, "Take her over to the room Ellison set up for questioning." Then back to Maggie, "What is your name and where do you live?"

"My name is Margaret DeLuca and I live in Dallas."

"Officer Worthy will take you to a room where we can talk. I'll be over shortly to get the rest of your statement."

"Can I have my cell phone back?" *Surely he can't just take my phone.*

"Possibly after we talk." He motioned with his head and Worthy took Maggie's arm and guided her across the open area, into the conference building and into a room. Another deputy and two other people Maggie recognized as conference attendees were already there.

No one was talking. Everybody, from police to conference people, looked worried. Maggie regretted saying Granet deserved to die.

Chapter 4

FATHER FRANK GAZED at the phone in his hand. He played back their brief conversation in his head. Maggie said he deserved it. He stole things. And then she was cut off when someone grabbed her phone. Surely it was a deputy.

He had managed to pick up a few words here and there, but he couldn't make out the questions or her answers. Before the sound became almost totally muted, the policeman had said something like, "What do you mean he deserved it?" *So he must have heard Maggie's statement about the victim deserving it. Not good.*

Since she did not come back on the phone, Father Frank had to assume they had taken his sister into custody. What on earth was going on?

The priest looked at the financial books in front of him. He'd planned to work on his report to the parish council next week. But it sounded like Maggie was in trouble and might need his help. The conference was only fifteen miles away. He pushed away the books and grabbed his car keys.

Twenty-five minutes later, he pulled up to the entrance to the Lakota Retreat Center. He was stopped there by a young officer whose uniform indicated he was part of the Timber County Sheriff's department.

"Hi. I'm Father Frank, minister at Prince of Peace Church. I'm —"

"I don't care if you're the Pope. The Sheriff said no visitors. Period."

"But my sister's in there and —."

"And you're staying out here. When they finish with her, she'll come out and you can see her then."

"I think there has been a misunderstanding and —"

"But I did *not* misunderstand the Sheriff. No one goes in."
The man turned and walked back to his cruiser, picked up the
phone and began talking. But he kept his eyes on the priest.

Father Frank didn't know what to do. He knew
everybody in the police department of Pine Tree. He'd met the
Timber County Sheriff once. It had not been a good meeting.
And there seemed to be some friction between the Sheriff's
department and the city police chief.

The priest picked up his cell phone, amazed he had
remembered to bring it, and dialed Maggie's phone.

After several rings, a person answered. "Yes?"

"Ah, this is Father Frank. Is this Maggie DeLuca's phone
I've called?"

"It is. And you are calling because?"

"Obviously I wanted to talk to her."

"About what?"

"Are you with the police, the sheriff's department?"
Father Frank tried not to let his impatience show.

"Yes. And right now, we are questioning Ms. DeLuca. So
she is not available."

"I'm her brother and I'm outside the gate of the Retreat
Center. Is it possible I could come in and be there when you
finish questioning her?"

Father Frank could hear that the man had covered the
phone with his hand and was talking to someone, probably his
superior. In a minute, the man was back on the phone. "Yes. You
may come in. We are in the conference center, room 105." And
the man hung up with no further comment.

In less than a minute, the deputy at the gate got out of his
cruiser and approached Father Frank's car. "You can go in now.
Do you know where you are going?"

"Yes."

Without another word, the officer opened the gate and
motioned for Father Frank to drive in.

* * *

When Father Frank parked in front of the conference
center, May Ellison, the conference director, was speaking to a
large group of writers. She was a striking person, with rich,

chestnut colored hair, matching eyes, and a beautiful face that caught everyone's attention. With an easy grace, she commanded attention and respect. As the priest got out of the car, she was saying the conference would continue and the afternoon sessions would be held according to the schedule.

"As I'm sure you all understand, the Sheriff needs to talk with those who were here last night. I've asked Val Monroe to provide him with a list of all those who stayed in conference housing last night. Unfortunately, until we can get that list to the sheriff, the gate will be closed. As soon as he has that list, those who are not staying here - were not here last night - are free to leave. But please, do stay for today's remaining sessions. For those who were on campus last night, you will have to stay until a member of the sheriff's department has had a chance to interview you."

A woman near the front stuck up her hand. "There were nearly a hundred staying here. How long do you think it will be before we can leave?"

Ellison pursed her lips and shook her head. "I can't really say. However, the conference will continue, and I hope you all will stay and finish this great program. Let's just do our best to cooperate with the police so they can move quickly through the interviews."

A man asked about the two morning sessions that were lost and particularly the one-on-one interviews that were cancelled this morning. "See the conference secretary to reschedule any interviews lost this morning. As for the two sessions, we are working on fitting those in tomorrow. Please check the official conference bulletin board. We will be working hard to try to provide all attendees with the best experience possible. The program *will* continue. Please continue with the conference. These sessions are too good to pass up. And thank you for your understanding."

As May Ellison started across the courtyard, Father Frank caught up with her.

"Pardon me. I'm Father Frank, pastor at Prince of Peace Church in Pine Tree. My sister Maggie DeLuca is attending the conference. She called and said some attendees might need help coping with the tragedy. If I can be of help, please call me." He fished a card out of his pocket and gave it to May.

"Thank you. That might be necessary. A few of the attendees here are taking this very hard. Let me talk with some of them and if any need some help coping, I'll call."

She started to leave, but the priest stopped her. "Can you give me any information at all? When did it happen? Where? How was he killed? And who found him?"

Father Frank saw that the barrage of questions seemed to make her suspicious. He changed his approach. "It's just that a few details might help, so I can counsel the best way."

"I don't know much. The police haven't told me anything. But, Rod Granet was found this morning by two young men who were attending the conference. Mr. Granet had not shown up for his morning session and they went to see where he was. They found him in his cabin, over there." She pointed to one of the individual cabins near the shore of the Lakota Lake. "That's all I can tell you. That's all I know. The police haven't said how he was killed, or when. He was at the general dinner last night. I left the dinner about 8:15 and Mr. Granet was talking with a couple of attendees just outside the dining hall then. The two men found him about 9:20 this morning."

"Thank you, Mrs. Ellison. As I said, if I can be of any help, please call."

She nodded and moved on like she had an appointment.

Probably wants to go crawl in a hole until this is over. What a nightmare for the conference director.

Father Frank looked around at the tranquil area. He had visited the Retreat Center a number of times and it always gave him a feeling of calm just being here. It managed to retain a quiet, peaceful, natural feel even as it was neatly manicured. The grounds gently easing down to the tranquil blue lake usually brought a smile to his face and a slower rate to his breathing.

Not today.

Even if Maggie had not said there was a murder, the priest could feel tension in the air. The conference director had obviously tried to smooth things over. But the moment she left, the crowd broke into small groups, usually three to five people, having whispered conversations. No one was smiling. Ellison might work to make it the "best experience possible." But relaxed or pleasant seemed out of reach.

As soon as he stepped in the door of room 105, he was met by a Timber County Deputy.

"Hi. I'm Father Frank. I'm Maggie DeLuca's brother and I spoke on the telephone with an officer here. He asked me to come in."

"Wait here." The slightly overweight man turned and walked through a door. A minute later, he returned. "The Sheriff will see you in a few minutes. He's still interviewing Ms. DeLuca."

"Perhaps I could —"

"You can sit in one of those chairs right there."

"I heard someone at the conference died. Can you—"

"The Sheriff will be with you when he can. Please have a seat." The man turned away and studied the room.

Obviously not going to get any information from him, Father Frank thought as he sat down in a chair near the door he had entered. There were twenty or thirty chairs in the room, arranged in rows facing a podium with a large screen behind it. About half of the chairs were occupied, some by women and some by men. A few of them were whispering. Several had printed materials they were carefully studying. The rest stared at the blank screen.

Who made up this motley crew? Witnesses? Suspects? People who knew the deceased? And where does Maggie fit in?

"Father Frank, I'm Sheriff Sam Bark."

"Glad to meet you, Sheriff. Can I see my sister?"

"As soon as we're through interviewing her." The overweight sheriff raised his head and studied the priest. "Weren't you involved in all the church burnings over in Pine Tree a couple of years ago?"

Father Frank gave a small laugh. "Well, not really involved. But I did go with Detective Oakley when he arrested the young man who set the fires."

"What I heard was you were a lot more involved in the case than that. And last year, with the eminent domain dispute." His voice had been like gravel being washed by water. Now, it became harder, sounding more like pieces of iron being pulled along concrete. "But the point I want to make is this. Do *not* get involved in this case. Even if your sister is implicated. I'm not saying she is. Just stay out of it. Is that clear?"

At the word implicated, Father Frank's smile vanished and his eyes turned dark. "I hear you, Sheriff. But if you decide my sister is implicated, let *me* be clear. I *will* be engaged." He cocked his head to the side and looked puzzled. "I'm amazed you would think otherwise. Do you have any sisters?" He raised his eyebrows. Now the Sheriff's features hardened, but before he spoke, Father Frank continued. "Do you have any reason to believe she might be implicated, as you put it?"

"Do not interfere with my investigation. I will not hesitate to charge you with obstruction." A smirk crossed his face. "And yes we have a reason. She publicly threatened the deceased. And two of my deputies heard her say, 'Because he deserved it. Because he stole things.'" Bark turned to one of his deputies. "Escort the reverend off the property. Now."

Without another word, the sheriff turned and left the room.

The deputy put his hand on the priest's arm and steered him out of the building. Three minutes later, Father Frank was driving slowly back to Pine Tree, his mind turning over the strange events. The police were questioning Maggie. *The sheriff thinks she's involved. He says Maggie threatened the victim publicly.* Father Frank wondered what that was about. And then, two deputies heard Maggie saying the victim deserved it and he was a thief. He stole things.

Father Frank shook his head and pursed his lips. If the victim stole things from Maggie, the sheriff would have the motive. *She's staying in the residence rooms right there at the retreat. And Granet is staying in one of the cabins, so she had opportunity. Means? I don't know how he was killed. If he was stabbed with a knife from the dining hall, Maggie could have the means.*

Dear Lord, please watch over Maggie. She's a good person and certainly did not kill another human being. Please keep Your arm around her. And Your hand over her mouth.

Chapter 5

"PRINCE OF PEACE, This is Father Frank. How can I help you?"

"Get me out of here." Maggie's voice was taut, each word escaping from clenched teeth.

"Don't you have your car there?"

"Yes, I've got my car here. That Nazi sheriff won't let me go. He and his henchmen grilled everyone who wasn't registered for overnight housing and let them go. But those of us who are staying at the Center have to do just that. Stay. No one goes out and nobody comes in."

Father Frank took a deep breath. "First, do not call him a Nazi. And don't call his deputies henchmen. They have a very difficult job right now and are doing the best they can. And since it appears Granet was killed at night, those of you staying there certainly had an opportunity."

"That's what he said. Lakota has security cameras on the only road in. He said nobody came in or out between nine-thirty last night and six this morning. Right now, they think he died around midnight, give or take an hour. They'll know more, he says, when the autopsy is complete."

"Sounds like he's keeping you posted on the progress of the case."

"Then there's not much progress. Time of death. That's about it."

"So, how long does he plan on keeping all of you?"

"'Till he solves the case." Maggie let out a low growl. "I don't know."

"How's everybody - except you - holding up? I can tell you're not taking it very well."

"Most are fine. For some, it's like a slumber party. Get together in a group. Gossip. Ellison is really trying. She's providing more or less unlimited snacks and sodas, games, puzzles, stuff to keep us amused."

"But clearly, you are not taking it well. What's really bothering you, Maggie? Why are you talking to me instead of gossiping with the girls."

"Women. "

"Right. Women. What's bugging you?"

Father Frank could hear Maggie let out a long breath. "What do I call him, if I can't call him a Nazi?"

"How about Sheriff."

"Fine. I think the Sheriff considers me his prime suspect."

"What? How would he —"

"I don't know, but he does. As I said earlier, he concentrated on those who were not staying on site. Except for me. I have rated three interviews."

"Three?"

"Three. One with a hench- sorry - a deputy. Manford, I think. Then one with the Sheriff himself. And then one with a guy who thinks he's Chuck Norris."

Father Frank laughed. "Okay. I understand Deputy Manford. And he thought there was enough to bring in the Sheriff. So who is, or what is, Chuck Norris?"

"A Texas Ranger."

For several moments, neither said anything. Finally Father Frank said, "That's probably good. They're good and will have no agenda. They'll get it right."

"But, why —"

"Lakota Retreat Center isn't in any city or town. And the Sheriff of Timber County probably doesn't have the personnel or the expertise to handle a complex murder case. I'm just guessing." The priest looked out the window. Blue skies, slight breeze, perfect temperature. "It's a gorgeous day, and there aren't many places nicer than Lakota. And you are there for the conference. How's it going?"

Only a grumble came through the phone line.

"Come on, Maggie. Have you gone to any of the lectures since ..., well, today?"

"No. Yeah. I went to one this morning on email marketing. That was before the police arrived. Haven't tried one since. Everyone's jabbering about Rod and what a terrible loss this was to the literary field. I almost threw up. He was a thief. I heard a man say Granet stole his title. Of course, someone said that's not so bad. You can't copyright a title. I wanted to smack her. Since Rod didn't break a law, it's okay? How about stealing a complete plot, scene by scene? I finally just got up and left."

"Did you get the name of the man who claimed Rod stole his title?"

"No."

"I'd write down the name of anyone who had trouble with Rod. Or any kind of a disagreement. What've you done since the questioning? "

Maggie laughed. "Just sulking in my room."

"Well, get out. You said a man had a beef with Granet. Go join every group you can find and listen. Who else had a problem with him? A bunch of writers talking. Who knows what secrets might come out? See what gossip you can pick up. You might find some clues that can divert attention away from you. And if a group is talking about story lines, or whatever writers talk about, go find another group. Find those who want to talk about Granet. From what little I've heard, mostly from you of course, not everybody liked the guy. Was there somebody who really, *really* didn't like him?" He paused just a second. "You won't hear anything sitting in your room."

Maggie laughed. "You're right, little brother. Rod was an ass—, ah, a jackass. I wouldn't be surprised if there was a husband or two who might have been happy to snuff him out."

"Well, if they've ruled out suicide, then someone was angry enough to kill him."

"Okay. You do have some good ideas, every once in awhile. I'll get out and be an info vacuum. Anybody has a beef with Rod, I'll find out. And since I've already told the world I hate his guts, I can use that to steer the conversation in that direction."

"Try not to be too vocal about your displeasure with him."

"Displeasure? Yeah." She gave a quick, mirthless laugh. "That about covers it."

"Be careful, Maggie. You do not want to reinforce your motive, even with the other writers. If you have to use that to 'steer the conversation,' as you said, do it quickly and then back off from your gripe. You'll get information listening, not talking."

"But then, they wouldn't hear my clever repartee."

Chapter 6

IT TOOK MAGGIE less than ten minutes to begin gathering information.

"How do you know that?" A young woman with serious eyes asked the man who was encircled by half a dozen conference attendees. They stood under a huge hickory tree near the conference center. The sun was settling over the lake, sending a narrow but brilliant beam of light bouncing across the water, producing a scene one might see advertising a fantastic vacation resort. Maggie focused on the short, chubby man at the center of the group. She wandered over, trying to look casual.

"I saw them find it," the man answered, nodding to emphasize the veracity of his statement. "One of the deputies reached under a bush and pulled out the knife. He had on gloves. He yanked a bag out of his pocket and put the knife in the bag and sealed it. He looked at his watch, then wrote something on the bag. At that point, he took off jogging over to the sheriff's cruiser.

"What kind of a knife was it?" a petite brunette asked.

The man looked at her and frowned. "Ah, I don't know." He shook his head. "Maybe one of the steak knives they have in the cafeteria here. Like we used at dinner last night."

By now, Maggie had wormed her way inside the group to stand right in front of the man. "You said he put it in a bag. Was that like an evidence bag?"

The man shrugged. "I don't really know. But that's what I guessed it was."

Another man, probably in his sixties, asked, "Did he seal the bag?"

"He folded the top over and pressed it down, all the way across, like you might press an envelope shut. It looked like it stuck closed."

"How close were you?" asked Maggie.

The first man shrugged. "Maybe fifty feet."

"But it looked like one from the cafeteria?" she asked.

"That's what I thought. I mean, I'll take a closer look at the knives tonight. But that's what came to mind when he was putting it in the bag. Course, I wasn't real close."

She looked up to see Sheriff Bark exit his car and head for the cafeteria.

"Hey, let's go on over and eat." The young man enjoyed being the center of attention. He didn't want to give that up." Maybe we can hear what the Sheriff has to say to the cooking staff."

Several of the group started to follow him, but Maggie turned the opposite way. *I've got all I'm going to get from them. Time to look for another avenue of information.*

Dining hall or conference center? She turned right, walked thirty feet and went in the main entrance of the conference center. May Ellison had opened three rooms where anyone could gather to visit or play games. In the first room, Maggie saw a small group watching the television. *No information here.*

She went to the next room. Ten or twelve women were talking quietly.

Maggie entered and all conversation stopped. Most of the group watched her walk over.

"Hey, don't let me stop the discussion." She gave a tiny laugh. "Unless you're talking about me."

"No. Just how strange this year's conference is," said an attractive African-American. "Drag up a chair and join in."

The women, there were no men there, had arranged their chairs in a loose circle. Maggie pulled a chair over and two women moved their chairs to make room for her. She thanked the women.

"My name is Faith. Have you been to the PWWC before?"

I guess I'm not going to be just a fly on the wall. "I've been to a couple, though not for the last few years. And my name is Maggie."

The woman sitting next to Faith said, "Well, I was here last year. It ran very smoothly, the speakers were good and I really enjoyed it."

"And nobody got murdered," said Faith.

For a moment, nobody said anything. Then, a large woman in a light blue caftan sitting directly across from Maggie said, "You're the one who accused Granet of stealing your story, aren't you?"

Chapter 7

MAGGIE WASN'T PREPARED for that. *I should have expected it. A lot of people heard me make the accusation. Well, let them hear my side before the rumors start.* She took a deep breath and sat up a bit straighter.

"I came to PWWC three years ago. Rod Granet was one of the speakers. He wasn't a *USA Today* bestseller then, but he had published several books and gave a good talk. I signed up for one of his one-on-one sessions. I told him I had a finished manuscript and was looking for an agent."

"Did you get one?" asked Faith.

Maggie laughed. "No. Still don't have one. But at the end of my visit with Granet, he offered to read my manuscript and give me his opinion of it, maybe put in a good word with his agent. Well, of course I sent him a copy. Three weeks later, I get an email from him. Instead of telling me how great my book was or giving me his agent's phone number, he was rather brutal. He told me my writing was okay, but the plot was boring. I should scrap that plot line and just start an entirely different book."

"How rude," said Faith.

"What did you do?" asked another woman.

"I started another book. Once I got over his stark criticism, I looked back at the story I'd sent him and convinced myself it wasn't that bad. So I sent it out to another agent. She said it was quite good, but not her genre."

"Is that the book you said Granet stole?" asked Faith.

"Yes. But I didn't figure it out until recently. Since he was coming to this year's conference, I got his bestseller and read it."

"*A Garden Variety Murder*," offered the woman sitting next to Maggie.

"That's the one. *USA Today* bestseller." Maggie gritted her teeth, the anger fresh. "I couldn't believe what I was reading. It was *my book*."

Maggie could hear several of the group take a quick breath. She didn't dare look at them, lest she start crying. Her story. His book. "Oh, the names were changed and the location. But every chapter, every scene was straight out of my manuscript. He didn't even bother to change the order. Not even the year. It wasn't just my story." She paused and shook her head. "It was my book."

The blue caftan asked, "Can you prove it?"

Maggie shrugged. "I have my original manuscript. It has a date on it."

"That's too easy to manipulate," one of the women said.

"I created a word - mertetrocide. It's in his book, in the same sentence as it is in my book. But it's not a word. I just made it up."

A few nodded, but one woman said, "That's only one word in a whole book."

Faith's head jerked up. "You sent it to an agent. That would put a date on it, and before Granet's book came out." She jerked her head up and down, proving what she said was the truth.

"So, what are you going to do?" asked a woman to Maggie's left.

Maggie drew her mouth in a thin line. "I don't know." She shook her head. "I thought I might gather a bunch of the attendees and have my manuscript and his book side by side. Then invite Rod in and start running through the scenes, mine, his. Then ask him where my half of the royalties were?"

Several of the women laughed. But Faith didn't. "If he stole it, you should have all the royalties, and a public acknowledgement it was your book."

The corners of Maggie's mouth turned down. "Yeah. That'd be nice. But that aint gonna happen." Maggie had passed through her angry stage and now just felt like crying. She stared at the floor, wondering if there was anything that could be done. "As Lady Macbeth said, 'What's done cannot be undone.' A big publishing house isn't going to admit it's marketing a novel with the wrong author's name on it."

Several mini-conversations ensued but Faith's strong voice overrode all of them. "Probably not. But what did you mean yesterday when you said to Granet, 'You might end up paying dearly for stealing my story"?

Maggie didn't know what to say. Everyone focused on her. She could almost hear their minds asking, "Did you kill him?" And when she looked at several of the women, they averted their eyes. Others looked wary, not afraid, but suddenly uncertain of this new woman in their circle.

She got up and scanned the group. "I did not kill Rod Granet."

She turned and walked out.

Chapter 8

THE SUN HAD disappeared into the lake, but a rosy glow covered the western sky, letting pink patches show through the stately pine trees. Now that it was late October, the warm temperatures disappeared quickly when the sun set. Maggie wrapped her arms around herself.

Why had she freaked out in there? She should have expected such questions. Certainly the Sheriff had been more direct. *Did you kill Rod Granet?* Had she let that get to her? No. But that was his job. She expected that from him. Probably he asked several conference attendees the same question.

But these women were not law enforcement. They were, well, not her friends, but at least her colleagues. Fellow writers. And surely some of them recognized Granet for the jackass he was. And she had to admit, the question was not unreasonable. *If our positions were reversed, I'd have asked that very question. What did I really mean? How was he going to pay dearly for stealing my story?*

For several minutes, Maggie stood looking at the lake, shimmering through the trees. She wasn't seeing the water. She was trying to answer her own question.

A couple of guys walked past and one of them looked at Maggie. "The sun's gone, and if you stay out here too long, dinner will be gone."

His comment jolted Maggie out of her thoughts. "Yeah. You're right. I'll just follow you two."

* * *

Dinner was served buffet style. Maggie stacked her plate with catfish, fried okra, yams, and salad. She drifted by a group of women about her age and was about to sit down when she caught the drift of the conversation: where to get the best buys on clothes. She abruptly turned and walked by another, somewhat younger group. One comment was all she needed to join them.

"Thank God I didn't take him up on it," said a twenty-something slender woman with strawberry blonde hair. "I'd be the prime suspect."

"Come on, Susan. What did he say?" asked a woman sitting across the table.

Maggie took the only vacant spot at the table and settled in, more interested in the conversation than the food.

"I had asked to talk with him about my manuscript. He said he'd be glad to. Why didn't I come by his cabin around 8:30, after dinner. There was just something about the way he said it and looked at me. My predator meter hit the red zone. I stammered a bit, finally said I was meeting with someone else that evening."

"I'll bet he was disappointed," Maggie offered.

"Yeah." Susan blinked a couple of times. "No. Not disappointed exactly. It was more like ... like angry. Like I'd taken something away from him."

A woman probably twice Susan's age, smirked. "Maybe you had just taken dessert away from him." Her conference badge identified her as Alice.

Susan looked at the woman, frowning slightly. "It wasn't for dinner."

"No, I'm sure it wasn't. But I think *you* were going to be dessert."

"Oh," Susan said. Then her eyes opened wide. "Oh." And her mouth stayed open.

"Ask Val about Rod and his late night ... consultations," Alice said.

"Val?"

"Val Monroe, the faculty coordinator. Ask her why she invited him back."

Maggie waited with the rest of the women to hear how the faculty coordinator was involved.

"He's a *USA Today* bestseller," said Susan.

"She had a late night consultation with Rod three years ago. I think she wanted another."

A few snickers broke the silence at the table.

"But, he is an award winning author," persisted Susan.

"There are lots of other *USA Today* bestsellers who haven't been here before," said Maggie. "Has PWWC ever had any other speaker come a second time?"

A distinguished looking man with silver hair said, "I've been coming to these conferences for at least eight years. I can't think of any other speaker who has been here twice."

"Well, about now, I'd bet Val is not happy we did this time either. Even before Rod got taken out," said Alice.

Maggie frowned. "What makes you say that?"

Alice smiled. "I saw Val and Rod talking Thursday evening. Looked to me like Val was pleading her case. Rod was just shaking his head no."

"Could have been about some special session she wanted him to give," suggested Susan.

"I'll bet you're right. A special session for one."

Susan opened her mouth to speak, but several giggles from the women stopped her.

Alice continued. "Well, let's just say it looked personal. And when Val left, she might have had ... Well, I don't know. But I've seen women who just got rejected. That's what she looked like. Hurt. And angry."

Chapter 9

SATURDAY, FATHER FRANK was trying again to tackle the accounting when the telephone rang.

"Hi, it's May Ellison, from the writer's conference."

"Of course, Ms. Ellison. How are things going?"

"You had offered to come over and talk to a few of the attendees who were having a difficult time dealing with the murder."

"Yes, I did. And I'm still willing to help if I can."

"We now know Granet was killed by having his throat slashed. I'm sure that piece of information has spread through most of the attendees."

Father Frank didn't know how to respond to that, so he said nothing.

"During the last session, one lecturer was discussing murder as a plot element. He, unwisely, used as an example a man getting his throat cut. One of the women burst into tears and bolted from the lecture hall."

"Oh my," said Father Frank. "Not a good choice. Couldn't he have used death by poison?"

"Probably a lecture he's given before and he just didn't think how it might affect some people after what happened yesterday." She sighed. "If your offer is still on the table, could you come over today?" She hesitated only a second. "The sooner the better."

Father Frank mentally ran down his "to do" list. Nothing that couldn't be put off. "I could be there in an hour. Will that do?"

"That would be great. I'll be in room 205 in the main Conference Center. Thank you."

* * *

By 1:15, Father Frank had talked with two women, including the one who had burst into tears in one of the morning sessions. When he didn't see anyone else waiting outside his interview room, he walked over to the cafeteria and grabbed a Dr Pepper. He had walked outside, ice cold soda can in his hand, and was reading a flyer posted on the wall when Ellison approached him.

"Hello Ms. Ellison. I see the entertainment tonight is karaoke. Sounds like fun."

"We usually have a Halloween party and people dress up and it's lots of fun. But I decided, no skeletons or people with knives sticking out of their neck tonight."

"I think not. Good choice. A little singing ought to help."

"And Father, I can't thank you enough for talking to those young women. Both are in a much better frame of mind following their talk with you. I think they'll be fine now."

"I'm glad it helped them. I'm always nervous in this type of situation," Father Frank confessed. "I just say a prayer and hope the good Lord will put the right words in my brain."

"Well, it worked today. So far." She gave a tiny laugh. "There are two others who would like to talk with you. They're ..." She paused, tilted her head to one side and pursed her lips. "I was going to give you my take on them, but maybe I'll not put any preconceived notions in your head. You'll figure them out better than I could anyway. But, Holly Waterton is in the room waiting for you now. And Sean O'Reilly would like a few minutes of your time after that."

Father Frank nodded a couple of times. "I'm guessing Mr. O'Reilly did not burst into tears."

May smiled. "No, I don't think so. He's registered for the conferences, staying in the guest quarters, and had a meeting with Granet scheduled for Friday afternoon. But he doesn't ... " She paused and glanced down for a second, then looked back up at the priest. "Well, I'll just let you make your own assessment."

Father Frank cocked his head to one side. "You have raised my interest." He laughed. "I guess I'd better get over and visit with Holly. Will Mr. O'Reilly be waiting or do I need to find you after Holly and I finish?"

"Oh, I expect he'll be waiting."

* * *

The room had only two chairs and a small table. The chairs faced one another and the table was between the chairs, but slightly off to the side. It contained a box of tissues plus two small pads of paper and two pencils. Father Frank let Holly pick a chair, then he took the other one. Her gaze was down, but her focus shifted constantly.

Father Frank watched for a few moments. He guessed she was twenty, give or take a year, and a striking beauty. "Would you prefer I call you Ms. Waterton or simply Holly?"

Without looking up, she muttered, "Holly." Her left heel maintained a constant beat on the floor.

"Okay. So tell me, how is the conference going? Are you learning some good stuff on writing?"

"Some. Mostly, I wanted to meet other writers and find out if they have the same ... problems I have with writing." Suddenly, she looked directly into Father Frank's eyes, a frown covering her face. "I'm worried about my fiancé."

The priest's eyes opened wide, not sure where this was headed. Did it have anything to do with the conference? Of course, it didn't need to, but then why was she bringing it up? "How so," he asked cautiously.

"I'm not a Catholic, but I know you have this thing about confessions and you can't tell anybody what you hear. Is that really true?"

Father Frank worked to keep a smile from forming. "It is true that what priests hear in the confessional cannot be repeated outside. Not to anyone. Not under any circumstances." He was about to elaborate, but decided that was not the point right here. She just wanted to know how private this conversation was. "But, while we are not in a confessional, and you're not a Catholic, I promise you what you say to me will be strictly between you and me. I will not reveal it to anyone." He paused for a second. "Unless it would save a life."

Holly considered this. She looked back down. The frown returned and the heel picked up the beat. "What if it got someone into trouble?"

"Only if it would save someone's life." He couldn't decide if a smile would help, but decided to remain serious instead. This kind of information was standard to him, but obviously she was trying to process it, and in the context of her own troubles.

For nearly a minute, neither said anything. Finally, Holly put her foot solidly on the floor and again met Father Frank's eyes. "On the first day of the conference, Thursday, I asked Mr. Granet if I could talk to him about my novel. He said yes, but he was booked up most of the day. He wanted me to meet him at his cabin at nine that evening."

Chapter 10

FATHER FRANK'S EYEBROWS arched up, but he said nothing.

Holly glanced down at the floor for a second, then returned her focus to the priest. "I thought that was unusual, but if a best-selling author would look at my work, I would be there. I asked him if I should bring my manuscript and he said, 'Sure. Bring it with you.' Thinking back on it, I now realize that was just a throw-away line. But at the moment, wow. A *USA Today* bestselling author was going to look at my manuscript."

The left heel picked up the beat again. "I arrived at his cabin, over near the lake, precisely at nine. When he opened the door, I took a step back. I didn't think about it. My body just reacted. He was in a..." She paused for a moment. "I guess you'd call it a dressing gown, monogrammed. He stepped aside and invited me in. When I hesitated, he promised not to bite. So, I did, but when he closed the door, I swear it sounded to me like it clicked a lock closed." A slight smile tried to materialize but didn't quite make it. "You might say I was nervous. The lights were dim, but I don't know. Maybe the cabins don't have good lighting. He handed me a drink, offered me a seat on the couch and then he sat down on the couch also."

She shook her head. "I'm not very ... experienced. And I don't drink much. It looked like a Coke to me, so I took a big gulp. Maybe it would help my nerves. But wow. It was so strong I thought I might choke. I began coughing. He slid over and put his arm around me like he was trying to help me stop coughing. And he pulled me close and told me to just relax and take another drink but slowly. All I could think of was, maybe it was a date-rape drug in there. By now, he had both arms around me and was whispering in my ear." She looked down and took in a large breath. "I wiggled out of his arms and just bolted."

Father Frank picked up the box of tissues and offered it to Holly. She grabbed one and pressed it to her eyes. After a bit, he said, "But you got out unscathed. Thank your guardian angel that she did not let the aura of a successful author lead you into trouble."

"But then, Billy John showed up."

"Billy John's your fiancé?"

Holly nodded.

"So he's attending the conference also?"

She shook her head. "No. He snuck in to see me."

The priest's lips pressed together and his brow knitted together. "I understood the police had a video of the only entrance into Lakota Retreat, and nobody came in Thursday evening."

"Billy John knows a way to sneak in on his motor bike. It's pretty quiet so nobody would have heard him either."

"And you're worried about him because?"

"He could see I was really upset. So I told him I'd left my manuscript in cabin 2. But Billy John really knows me. He knew there was something else and kept asking questions. Finally I told him what happened. Like I told you. He almost blew his top. He said he'd go get my manuscript and teach that old ... guy ... a lesson. Before I could stop him, he took off."

"What time was that?"

"It was after ten by then. Maybe ten-thirty."

"Is your fiancé very aggressive? Is he likely to pick a fight?"

Holly took a moment to answer. "I don't think of Billy John as aggressive. But he wouldn't back down from anybody. He was the best linebacker on our high school team. Almost got a college scholarship to play football. He's big and really strong. Looks like he could really hurt somebody. But, he's not that way at all. He's ..."

"But still, you're worried he might have ... hurt Rod Granet?"

"Yes. I mean no. I'm sure he wouldn't hurt him. But he was really, *really* mad after I told him what happened. The police might look at him and decide ... he did it."

"Did he get your manuscript?"

"Yes. And I asked him if there was any trouble. He laughed. Said Rod took one look at him and went over and got the papers and gave them to him without saying a word."

"So, Granet was alive at ten-thirty." The priest rested his chin on his hands and closed his eyes. After a few seconds, he looked at Holly. "Did Billy John see anybody when he was going to Granet's cabin or when he was coming back to your room? Or could anybody have seen him?"

"I don't know. He didn't say anything about it. I can ask him."

"That would be a good idea. So, if I understand, you're not worried Billy John might have killed Granet. You're worried the police might think he did."

"Yeah."

"He was pretty angry over what Granet did."

Holly was shaking her head. "I know, but Billy John would never kill anybody. He might have punched his lights out, but he wouldn't take it further."

"Does Billy John carry a knife?"

"Sometimes."

"Did you tell Billy John you thought the drink might have had a date-rape drug in it?"

Her eyes closed. When they reopened, she was studying the floor. "Yes." She looked up, a frown on her face and she was shaking her head. "No. He wouldn't kill anybody. I think he punched him in the face, probably broke his nose. But he wouldn't —."

"Holly, I'm not going to the police with any of what you've told me." She let out a breath she had been holding. "But you need to ..."

The priest stared off into middle space. *What does she need to do? Tell the police? Confront Billy John and ask him what he did? Say nothing?* Each option carried a risk. Father Frank knew he needed to give this young woman some advice. But what? *Dear God, don't let me tell her the wrong thing.*

"First, I suggest you pray about this. Ask God for guidance." She nodded. "Second, you do not believe Billy John killed Granet and you have no actual evidence to give the police. So I believe you are under no obligation to tell them about any of this. At least not at this point. Should your knowledge change, then you might be obliged to talk to the authorities."

She looked relieved, and Father Frank hated to continue—but he knew he had to. "There's another way to look at this, though. If the police knew about this visit from Billy John, they would question him. So why not come clean now? If he has nothing to hide, then the questioning would do no harm and you'd have that out of the way."

Holly was shaking her head. "Sometimes innocent people get convicted."

Father Frank nodded. "That does happen. But it is very rare. Our justice system works amazingly well. Still, I can see your dilemma. If he were unjustly convicted, you would carry a heavy burden of guilt."

"I already have enough of that. As I ran away from Granet, my mind was screaming, 'I hope he dies.' When I heard he had been killed, I almost choked." She reached for a tissue and wiped at her eyes. "I'm so sorry. I didn't really mean that."

The priest waited until she had composed herself. Then, "Did you say that to Billy John?"

Her mouth gaped open. "No. No, I'm sure. I didn't say that to him."

"Okay. That brings me to number three. You call Billy John your fiancé. If he is deeply in love with you, he might do something to protect you, something he would not normally do. Try to look at things more critically than usual. Is he exactly the same as always, as before this week? Has there been any change in him, how he reacts to things?"

"You're asking me to not trust him?"

Father Frank reached over and took one of her hands in his. "No. Not at all. But observe. And what you see may just make you love him more. The more you know about a person, the better the marriage will work."

He released her hand and stood up. "And here's an important bit of advice. Drop the guilt. Granet tried to take advantage of you. This made you angry and you reacted. You didn't mean what you said. When we're angry, we often say things we don't mean, and then wished we hadn't said them. But please, do not carry any guilt for something that popped out of your mouth at a time when you had been severely traumatized. My advice, as a priest, is — forget it."

Chapter 11

AS MAY HAD predicted, Sean O'Reilly was waiting outside when Father Frank emerged. He was an imposing man. O'Reilly looked to be about six two and probably tipped the scales at about two hundred pounds. And he had a full head of striking reddish-orange hair.

The priest stuck out his hand. "Hi, I'm Father Frank. And you must be Sean O'Reilly."

Sean's hand completely engulfed Father Frank's, but the grip was measured, not meant to intimidate. "Thank you for taking the time to talk with me. Rod Granet's death presents a problem for me."

Father Frank nodded several times. "Let's talk about your problem. But, if you don't mind, let's walk over to the drink machine. I need a Dr Pepper. My throat feels like the French Foreign Legion has marched down my throat."

* * *

Five minutes later, the two men sat in the interview room. Father Frank downed half the can of soda, set the can on the table and looked at Sean. "Okay, how has Granet's death caused you a problem?"

"Let me start by saying I didn't like the man. He was pompous, overly impressed with himself, and cutting down a struggling writer came very easy for him. Before his latest book, *he* was one of the struggling writers. I doubt if any of his previous books sold over a thousand copies. Maybe not all of them added together. Then he came up with this great plot. And I've been told the organization, the pacing, the movement of it is absolutely top notch. I haven't read it myself, and don't intend to."

Father Frank gave a small laugh. "I can tell you didn't exactly care for the man. What do you write, Mr. O'Reilly?"

"Call me Sean. And I don't write. Don't intend to."

Father Frank's eyebrows knitted together and he cocked his head slightly. "But you registered for this conference. And you scheduled a meeting with Rod Granet."

"Let me go back three years. To the conference then. Granet was a speaker at that conference also. My beautiful daughter, her name is Shannon, writes books. I think she calls them fantasy, whatever that means. She was just starting and signed up for the conference to help her with world building, whatever that means. But that's what she said. Anyway, she came to the conference and I guess she met Granet."

Sean took a deep breath and let it out slowly. "When I got home Saturday - I'm in construction in Dallas, high rise stuff. We were settin' girders that day. When I got home, I found a note from Shannon. She said she was goin' to New York with Granet. It'd be good for her career."

When Sean said nothing more, Father Frank asked, "That's all that was in the note?"

Sean nodded slightly. "And I haven't heard from her since."

"And the purpose of your meeting with Granet?" Father Frank asked gently.

The man looked right through Father Frank. It seemed tears long pent-up might break free. But they didn't. "I wanted to ask him about Shannon. Where she was. How she was doing. How could I get in touch with her?"

"Has anyone in the family heard anything? Maybe her mother?"

"Cancer took Kalin six years ago."

Father Frank made the sign of the cross and for a minute he closed his eyes and said a silent prayer for Sean's dead wife.

"Kalin's departure was very hard for us. But we knew it was coming. When Shannon disappeared, it was a sudden spike in my heart."

"What did you think you might learn If you'd talked with Granet? "

"How to get in touch with her? How she was doing?"

"But you never got the chance to confront him."

"No."

"I'm curious. Why did you make reservations to stay here at the center, instead of just talking to Granet and leave?"

"I live in Dallas. And I wanted to be here all the time, to make sure I got to talk with Granet, get some answers. When I heard he was dead, I tried to leave, but the Sheriff wouldn't let anybody leave."

"So, Granet's death left you with no answers. And now, no one to ask."

Sean nodded. "Yeah. And I think the Sheriff has me down as a suspect."

"Do you know why?"

"Oh yeah. That Texas Ranger, Richards, I think, questioned me. And when I said I didn't write books, he began to pound me with questions. I told him what I told you. He thinks maybe I went to see Granet Thursday night and didn't like what I heard."

"But you had an appointment with him Friday afternoon."

"Yeah. I told him that. Know what he said? Clever. I was clever to set that up as an alibi."

Father Frank let that sink in. Finally, he asked, "What can I do for you?"

"I don't know anything about east Texas. If this Sheriff keeps me, I need a lawyer. Can you find one for me who can keep me out of jail? One I can afford?"

"Maybe it won't come to that. But if it does, I'll find you a lawyer. In the meantime, ask some of the women, or men, here if they knew Shannon. Maybe some of them, as fellow writers, might have kept in contact with her. It's worth a try."

For the first time since they began talking, Sean smiled, just a little. "That's a good idea. I'll ask around. I've got nothing else to do until this Sheriff let's me go. If he does."

They walked out of the room, said goodbye, and headed in opposite directions.

As Father Frank headed for his car, his mind was racing. Normally he thought the Texas Rangers were very sharp. Could this one have been on the mark? Certainly Sean had motive, particularly if Granet had given him bad news. And he had opportunity. He was staying onsite. And a knife wouldn't have been difficult to bring in. As for the killing itself, he was certainly big and strong enough to overpower Granet. And if he put in girders on skyscrapers, he had the focus, the cool nerves, and the guts to kill a man who might have swept his daughter away.

* * *

Before he reached his car, Holly Waterton came rushing up. "Father Frank, Father Frank."

"Hi, Holly. What's up?"

"Are we still on the confessional deal? You know, you won't tell anybody."

He suppressed the laugh that tried to surface. "Same as before."

"I was talking with some of the women over at the residence hall. Rod Granet died from having his throat cut."

"Yes. We knew that."

"But he also had a broken nose."

Father Frank pursed his lips, but said nothing. *So the police knew there was some sort of a fight before Granet was killed.*

"Don't you see? That's something Billy John might do. It says he was there. Before Granet died. So, he could have killed him."

"Do the police know Billy John went to see Granet?"

" I don't think so. Not yet. I don't know. But if they come to question me, what am I going to do?"

"You are going to stay calm and answer their questions truthfully. Do not lie. And do not make up a story. Don't say what you *think* might or might not have happened. Simply answer their questions truthfully. And if you do not know the answer, say you don't know." He took one of her hands between his. "You are imagining the worst. They are going to question everybody who stayed in the residence halls. They're not going to ask you about Billy John. They will want to know what you did, or saw. Tell the truth."

Her breathing began to slow down and she nodded. " Okay. I'll try to stay calm. I'll answer their questions with the truth. No adding things I don't know."

"I think you'll be okay."

Father Frank watched her walk away. Billy John sounded like he was mad enough to kill somebody. And he clearly had opportunity. The question now was whether he had a knife. Holly said he sometimes carried one. Was Thursday one of those times?

Chapter 12

FATHER FRANK HAD finished Sunday Mass and had just put two eggs in a frying pan when his cell phone rang. He walked into his office fumbled around and finally found his phone in his shirt pocket. "Prince of Peace. This is Father Frank. How can I help you?"

"Come get me out of jail. And bring a lawyer."

"Hold on, Maggie." Father Frank walked back into the kitchen and turned the burner off. "What jail are you in? And why?"

"Because this dumb Sheriff doesn't like me. I'm in the Timber County jail. Can you come get me?"

"I can come see you. And I'll try to get you out. Do you think we need a lawyer to get them to release you? Have you actually been arrested?"

"I don't know."

"What happened?"

"Old Dog Bark — "

"It won't help your case if you call him names."

She almost spit it out. "His name is Bark."

"Sheriff Bark."

"Okay. This morning Sheriff Bark-Bark wanted me to answer more of his questions. I said no. I'd already answered everything. Then he said I could come down to the station and answer them again there. I said no, and I said it politely. I didn't yell, or say anything else but no. He pulled out a pair of handcuffs and said he had probable cause and he could take me to the station either in handcuffs or I could go peacefully." She growled. "I went peacefully. I asked him, politely, what the probable cause was and he said he was not required to tell me. I didn't say another word to him on the trip to the county jail."

Father Frank looked at his watch. 11:40. He could be at the Timber County Sheriff's office by 12:30. If they needed a lawyer, he could probably get Norm Winters over even on Sunday, if he was home. Norm had helped him before.

"Have you called Jeff?"

"No. And don't you call him. He'd probably have a heart attack. I'll tell him later - when we know more."

"All right. Hang tight. I'll be there within the hour."

Chapter 13

INSIDE THE TIMBER County Sheriff's office, the priest addressed the woman sitting at a desk behind a glass wall. She did not have on a deputy's uniform. "Hi. I'm Father Frank DeLuca. I'm the brother of Margaret DeLuca. I believe she's in custody here. I'd like to see her."

The woman picked up her phone, turned away from Father Frank and spoke very quietly. After a moment she hung up and turned back to face the priest. "Please have a seat over there. The Sheriff will be out in just a minute or two."

Father Frank sat and studied the area. It wasn't high security here. The glass wall looked tempered, not bullet proof. Other than the clerk's desk and chair, the area had two file cabinets, half a dozen plastic folding chairs, and two doors. There was an American flag on one side of the woman's area and a Texas flag on the other side.

After about five minutes, Sheriff Bark marched through one of the doors. Father Frank held out his hand, but the Sheriff ignored it.

"I want to remind you of what I said at the retreat center. Do not get involved in my case. If you interfere, I won't hesitate to arrest you, minister or not. Is that clear?"

"Yes. But I want to remind you of what I said. If my sister is implicated, I *will* be engaged. I will not obstruct your investigation. But I will be engaged." For nearly a minute, the two men stared at each other. Finally, Father Frank asked, "Can I see my sister now? And do you want to tell me what the probable cause was to bring her in?"

"She threatened the victim. In public. At least a dozen people will testify they heard it." He had a smug look on his face. "You can see the pris —ah, your sister now." He turned to leave.

"If she answers your questions, will she be free to go?"

Bark half turned. "If I like her answers."

"I'd like to sit in on the questioning."

"Are you her lawyer?"

"No."

"Lawyers are allowed to sit in, not brothers. Or ministers."

Father Frank just shook his head. "Okay. If that's the way you want to play it, I can have a lawyer here in thirty minutes." He pulled out his phone and punched in a number

The Sheriff's eyes narrowed and he aimed an icy glare at the priest. "Fine. Let's just get on with it. If she agrees to answer all my questions, then you can sit in. But you will not be allowed to speak."

"That will work."

A few minutes later, a deputy came out and ushered Father Frank into the back area and to a small room. Maggie sat at a table. Father Frank thanked the deputy, hoping that would send him away. It didn't.

"I see your mouth has gotten you into trouble again, big sister."

"Have you talked them into releasing me?"

Father Frank turned his head and noted the deputy had disappeared. He shook his head and smiled. "No, but the Sheriff indicated you could leave if you answered his questions. Oh, he did add, if he liked your answers."

"I don't have to answer his questions unless he's ready to arrest me," said Maggie.

"That may be true, but he has probable cause, so he can hold you. It might be in your best interests to answer a few."

"What probable cause?"

"A dozen people testified you threatened the victim the afternoon before he was killed."

"Ah, come on. I never said I was going to kill him. I said he'd have to pay for stealing my novel. I didn't say anything about murdering the man, though he surely deserved it."

"That kind of talk will not get you out of jail," Father Frank scolded her. "Look, the sheriff said I could sit in on the questioning, if you agreed to answer his questions. If you don't agree to that, then I need to call Norm immediately and get him over here."

Maggie shrugged. "Okay. Let's get this circus on the road."

Father Frank stuck his head out the door. The deputy was standing down the hall opposite an open door, apparently talking to someone in another office. The priest called to him. "Officer. Would you tell Sheriff Bark that Ms. DeLuca is ready to answer his questions?"

The deputy nodded and disappeared around a corner.

Father Frank turned back to Maggie. "Please do not antagonize the man. Think before you answer any question. Of course, if you don't know the answer, just say that - no opinion of what you think about the question. If I think he gets to a point that you should have a lawyer, I'll step in and stop things. Of course, you should do the same. No wise cracks. Just say you are not going to answer that question or any others until you have your lawyer beside you."

"Yes, sir." She gave a mock salute.

"Did you like your accommodations here?"

"A nice private cell that smelled of urine. The jailer said I'd probably have a cell mate before long. She made it sound like that would be a scary thing, so don't worry. I'll be a good girl."

The Sheriff walked in and sat in the chair opposite Maggie. A deputy followed him in and stood in a corner of the room facing Maggie. Father Frank took the other corner. The Sheriff placed a tape recorder on the table and pressed the record button. "This is an interview with Margaret DeLuca, thirty-six year old female from Dallas, Texas,. It's being held in the Timber County Sheriff's headquarters. It is Sunday, November 1, 2019 and is starting at..." He looked at his watch. "Thirteen twenty. Attending is Deputy Manford, and the suspect's brother Frank DeLuca." He looked up at Maggie. "Ms. DeLuca, are you agreeing to this interview?"

"Yes."

"And you are aware that it is being recorded and can be used against you?"

"Yes, either against me or for me."

Bark's head jerked up and he glared at Maggie. Father Frank shook his head and frowned at her.

"At the Piney Woods Writers Conference on October 30, you appeared to be very angry with the victim, Rod Granet. Is that true?"

"Yes."

"And why were you angry with the victim?"

Maggie gave a brief description of how Granet had appropriated her novel, and how he had access to the entire manuscript.

"So you felt cheated."

"I *was* cheated."

"He had a national bestseller and you had nothing. So you were angry."

Maggie nodded once. "Damn straight."

The Sheriff raised his eyebrows. "Please refrain from using any ... unpolite words."

Father Frank saw Maggie's hand come up and he immediately shook his head no. He was certain she was about to salute. She glanced at her brother and eased her hand over and rubbed her eye, as if a gnat might have gotten into it. She said simply, "Impolite."

The sheriff scowled at her correction but continued. "So, you threatened him, publicly."

"I didn't threaten to kill him. I said he'd have to pay for stealing my book."

"Pay?" The Sheriff cocked his head to one side. "And how did you intend for him to pay?"

Maggie threw a hand up. "I don't know. Try to get his publisher to see my manuscript, dated before his, and realize he had to have copied mine."

"He could have written his before you wrote yours. Just didn't get it published that early."

"Mr. Bark, a mystery novel is a complex thing. For two people to take the exact same idea and each write a book and have every scene, every chapter, every character be the same is virtually impossible."

The Sheriff's head came up when she called him Mr. Bark, but he said nothing.

When he didn't respond, she continued. "Add to that the fact he had a copy of my manuscript three years ago, and it just about makes it certain he simply copied my book. Oh, and he did write me and suggest I put it aside, forget it, and just start another book entirely." She tilted her head to the side and opened her eyes wide. "Doesn't that sound like he didn't want me to get my book in an editor's hands? It might really confuse things with two books, virtually the same, coming from two different authors."

Sam Bark set his jaw very tight. "You said he had your manuscript three years ago. If that was the case, why wasn't it out before this year? Explain that to me."

Maggie almost smiled. "Be happy to. The publishing business is very slow. At least it is with the big publishers. So it might take him half a year to find the right agent, and then that agent to find the right publisher. Next, it can take six months to go through all the committees to finally get staff to work on it. Getting the various editors — developmental editors, copy editors, and proofreaders — to sign off on it is another six months. And then it has to be scheduled for publishing. That could be a number of months right there. And it came out nearly a year ago. So, it means as soon as he read my manuscript, he made a copy and sent it to his agent."

For nearly a minute, the room was quiet. Finally, the Sheriff asked, "What exactly did you mean when you said he deserved to die?"

Maggie just stared at the Sheriff. Father Frank could tell she was weighing how to answer. *Be careful, Maggie. One wrong word and he'll lock you up.*

"I meant he was not a nice person."

"So people you think are not nice deserve to die?" The Sheriff's laser focus zeroed in on her.

"He was a thief."

"So all not nice thieves deserve to die?"

"No. That's not what I said."

"Just this one."

She let out a slow breath. "People often say something like I did when they're angry. They don't mean it literally."

"And I'd ignore it ... if Rod Granet wasn't murdered. Ms. DeLuca, you had opportunity. You had means. And clearly, you had motive. You admit you were angry with the man." He paused and looked at Father Frank, then back at Maggie. "You are a good suspect. I am arresting you on suspicion of murder. Deputy Manford will read you your rights on the way to your cell."

Father Frank spoke for the first time. "You said you'd release her if she answered all your questions."

"No, sir. I did not. I said if she answered all my questions and I liked her answers. I do not like all of her answers. She has the anger and motive to commit the crime. Even you cannot disagree that she is a good suspect."

"I think she's a *convenient* suspect. She is not a *good* suspect." The priest looked at his watch. "I'll have her lawyer here first thing in the morning."

"This concludes the interview with Margaret DeLuca." Bark turned off the recorder. "I will not oppose bail. But until sufficient bail is posted for a capital murder suspect, she stays in my jail. And as such, she must be handcuffed when not in her cell. Deputy, have Deputy Rensler settle her in for the night. "

The deputy put handcuffs on Maggie and when she turned to face her brother her eyes widened and the pupils appeared dilated. Her breathing had accelerated. Father Frank thought that perhaps for the first time in her life, she looked scared.

"Maggie, I'm sorry. I'll be here with Norm first thing in the morning."

The Sheriff turned to go.

"Okay," Father Frank addressed the Sheriff. "You played me for the fool and got me to encourage my sister to let you question her without a lawyer present. My mistake. How early in the morning can the lawyer come to request bail?"

"We're open twenty-four hours a day. But we won't bother the judge with a bail hearing request before ten o'clock."

Chapter 14

MAGGIE, ACCOMPANIED BY her attorney Norm Winters, and the Assistant District Attorney sat in the Timber County courtroom. A bailiff stood behind Maggie. Norm had suggested Father Frank not come. It would make his job easier if he didn't have to referee the brother-sister bickering. "And I'll be able to control Maggie better," he said with a small laugh.

While the courtroom was small and the dais only about eight inches high, the setting was imposing. Highly polished mahogany enclosed the judge's desk (called the bench), the witness box on the left and the court clerk's desk on the right. Both the witness box and the court clerk's desk were lower than the bench. Dominating the high-ceiling room was an impressive panel fifteen feet tall, as wide as the bench, and containing the great seal of the State of Texas. Intended to impress all with the authority of the court, it succeeded.

Judge Jimmy Hamm looked at the Assistant DA and tilted his head slightly to one side. "You say she is your main suspect in a capital murder case. Do you have a suggestion for the amount of bail, if bail is granted?" Hamm sat hunched over his bench as if he could see the prosecutor better. He measured a slender five feet ten inches tall. He had thinning brown hair, cut short, and pale blue eyes. He looked like he'd be more comfortable sitting a horse than a judge's bench.

"I do not believe she is a flight risk and she poses no threat to any other person. So $5,000 should do. "

"So, lemme get this straight." The judge raised his eyebrows skeptically. "No flight risk. No imminent threat. But you still locked her up."

The ADA shifted uncomfortably. "Yes, sir. It is a murder case. And we only locked her up overnight. "

The Judge shook his head. Then turned toward Maggie. "It says here you threatened the victim in public."

Norm Winters whispered something in Maggie's ear. She nodded and rose. "Your honor, I did not threaten to kill him. I said he'd have to pay. He stole my story and published it under his name. I thought he should pay some restitution."

The Judge lowered his eyes and appeared to ponder her answer. He looked up. "And if you are released on bail, the district attorney's office would insist you stay in this jurisdiction. It says you're from Dallas. Where would you stay out here?"

"I'd stay with my brother, Your Honor."

"And who is he?"

"Father Frank DeLuca, pastor of Prince of Peace Church in Pine Tree."

The Judge's eyebrows shot up. His head leaned back and he looked down his nose at her. Very slowly, he said, "*The* Father Frank who helped convict a state judge of bribery?"

Maggie just nodded, but a frown covered her face.

"You think he might come after me if I don't allow you bail?"

"Judge McFatage had tried to poison my brother."

The Judge laughed. "I promise I won't try to poison anybody in your family." He turned serious. "Unless there is a strong objection from the ADA, I'm inclined to release Ms. DeLuca on her own recognizance. Any objections?"

The ADA's mouth fell open. "R.O.R., your honor?"

"That's what I said."

The young man took a deep breath. "We would want her to wear an ankle monitor to ensure she stays in this jurisdiction, you Honor."

"Granted. Bailiff, please take Ms. DeLuca to my office to sign the necessary papers for ROR. Also fetch a new ankle bracelet for the lady. Try to find a nice looking one. And not too heavy. I doubt she'll try to cut it off." He rapped his gavel. "This Court is adjourned."

* * *

After the formalities with the justice system, Norm drove Maggie to the Lakota Retreat Center to get her car.

An hour later, Maggie, Norm and Father Frank sat in the living room of the small rectory at Prince of Peace Church. Maggie and Norm each had an ice-cold can of Coors beer, while Father Frank opted for his favorite drink: Dr Pepper.

"I'm surprised they didn't ask for a cash bail." said Father Frank.

Maggie nodded. "I was too. I was all ready to call my little brother and say, 'Come bail me out.'"

"Me? I don't have any money."

"Yeah. But with that trust the church got, you could swing it."

"But, I couldn't use that money for my personal affairs."

Her eyebrows came down and she frowned. "If it was a member of your parish, I'll bet you'd bail 'em out."

Father Frank took a long drink of his soda. "Ah, that would be different. I would be using parish money for a parish member."

"What about a family member?"

"Not a member of my family. The Bishop wasn't happy about my accepting the money in the first place."

Norm raised his hand. "Okay, you two. Enough of the sibling squabbling. My thought is, Bark knew he didn't have much of a case. I think he got irritated that your answers made sense, so he thought he'd punish you with a night in jail. But before a judge, he wanted to sound reasonable. I think Judge Hamm saw right through it. And Father, you would have been surprised at how polite and lady-like your sister was in court."

Maggie frowned and looked crestfallen. "I can act like a lady - when the situation demands it."

They all laughed. "I do love her and she is my favorite sister."

"Thank you, Frank." She turned to Norm. "Of course, I'm his only sister. That helps." Now she sat up and bounced just a little and put her hands in her lap. "Okay, now what's our strategy? With the conference over, it will be harder to question people. Any suggestions?"

"Stay out of it. That's my professional opinion," said Winters.

"As he is the only professional in the room," said Father Frank, "I suggest we follow Norm's suggestion."

"Well, think again. I don't think ..." Maggie paused and looked at her brother. "The Sheriff couldn't solve a Hardy Boys Mystery." Now she turned toward Norm. "As Frank said to the Sheriff last night, I was just a *convenient* suspect."

Norm looked at the priest. "How did the Sheriff react when you said that?"

Father Frank looked down and pursed his lips. "I don't remember he reacted at all. Just concluded the interview, shut off the tape and told the deputy to escort her to a cell."

"Actually, in fairness to old Bark-Bark, that deputy handed me off to a female deputy. All very proper."

"Good."

"Okay. But how do we get started." Maggie looked at the lawyer. "Sorry, Norm. But I've got to find other suspects. If I'm the only suspect, Bark is going to keep looking for something, anything, to give him some kind of a case against me."

Norm shook his head. "He'd have to have some evidence."

"I've got to disagree. Since I write mysteries and suspense books, I read a lot about court cases and trials. And I can tell you right now, innocent people *do* get convicted. I think the police reasoning is that if you eliminate all other suspects, whoever is left, no matter how innocent they might look, must be guilty. And right now, I'm his only suspect. I'm the one that's left."

Norm nodded slowly. "All right. Think about suspects. But please, do not get involved. He will find out if you do. You've got the location monitor on you. He'll know where you go. So, stay here. Think about other suspects, motives, but leave the investigating to —"

"My dear brother." Maggie focused a radiant smile on Father Frank.

"You heard what he said to me," Father Frank protested. "Or maybe you didn't. The Sheriff told me not to interfere with his investigating. He said he'd charge me with obstruction." He turned to the lawyer. "Can he do that? And how bad is it if he does?"

"Yes, he can. And it can be serious. But usually, it means tampering with a witness, or a juror. Or it could be furnishing false information, or destroying evidence. You must not impede an investigation."

"And the penalty?" asked Maggie.

"Depends on the severity of the obstruction. Actually, Texas doesn't list obstruction of justice as a crime. So the courts may treat it as a misdemeanor, or as a felony. Could be a fine. Could be jail time."

Father Frank's hands gripped one another. "Neither of those sound too good to me. How about community service?" He tried a little smile but it didn't come across well. "The sheriff sounded like he'd be happy to lock me up."

Norm leaned his head to the side and looked down at the floor. "I suppose community service could be an option. It'd be up to the judge." He looked up at his friend. "I wouldn't count on it. The prosecutor would say that's what you do all the time. Wouldn't be a punishment." Now he looked at Maggie. "Get a private investigator to look at any suspects you can come up with."

"First, though," said Father Frank, "you've got to come up with some suspects." He stood and looked at Norm. "Sorry to end this discussion, though we weren't getting anywhere. But I've got to make an appearance at the Women's Bible Study Group over in the parish hall. They're taking the lead on the Thanksgiving food drive this year. We'll keep you in the loop, Norm."

"Please do. Keep in mind, this could get a lot more..." He looked from Father Frank to Maggie. "Complicated."

Chapter 15

FATHER FRANK HAD returned from the women's bible study and now sat on a stool in the kitchen watching Maggie cook. "So, have you come up with any suspects?"

"Suspects. No. But one of the men at the conference saw the police retrieve a knife from under a bush, somewhere between Granet's cabin and the cafeteria. The guy said it looked like it was hidden there." Maggie's eyes sparkled and her whole body was in motion. "And he described the deputy putting it into an evidence bag. So, maybe with luck, they'll get finger prints off it and Bark-Bark will have the killer."

"Probably not the murder weapon," said Father Frank.

Maggie's head jerked back. "Why not?"

"If the guy —"

"Or gal," added Maggie.

Her brother nodded. "Or gal, slit Rod's throat, he.... or she, would have thrown the knife in the lake. Rod's cabin isn't twenty feet from the water. Why leave it where the police can find it?"

"Hadn't planned it all the way through, probably."

"This wasn't a spur of the moment thing. Whoever did it planned ahead. If that knife was the murder weapon, the murderer had decided at least early enough to steal the knife from dinner. There wouldn't be any fingerprints on it. But why throw it under a bush? I'd say the murder weapon's in the lake."

Maggie's body deflated a little. "Yeah. I'm sure you're right. Would have been nice, though, to find the murder weapon with some finger prints on it. Save me a lot of trouble."

"Where would be the challenge there?" Father Frank teased.

She gave her brother a little punch on the shoulder. "Yeah. I might not even get to wear my new ankle bracelet. But you can bet this experience will end up in my next book."

* * *

Maggie had prepared an interesting dinner for the two of them.

"So, what am I about to eat?" he asked.

"These are zucchini boats," Maggie said.

"And what all is in this boat?"

"Lots of good stuff. Zucchini, of course, eggs, cherry tomatoes, pinenuts, lemon zest, parmesan and various spices. I guarantee you'll like it."

They had agreed to take a break from discussing the case until they finished eating. Better for the digestion, Father Frank assured his sister.

Now, they sat in the living room, Father Frank in his favorite La-Z-Boy and Maggie lounging on the couch.

Father Frank started. "Before we get into suspects and motives, have you called Jeff?"

Maggie ran her hand through her hair, a sign her brother knew meant she was searching for a way to avoid answering. "Yes. I called him today."

"And what did he have to say about the situation here and your night in jail?"

She crossed her arms over her chest. "Not much."

Father Frank tilted his head to the side and frowned. "You didn't tell him, did you? How could you not tell him? You're still under house arrest, so to speak."

Now, Maggie straightened up and thrust her chin out. "You know how Jeff is. He'd go to pieces. This is best for ... for both of us. He's just picked up a big client for his bookkeeping business and he's a little nervous about it. If he falls apart, then I'll have more problems. And I'll feel even worse than I do now."

Father Frank started to say something, but Maggie went right on talking. "Besides, the little PR work I do doesn't bring in much money. We need Jeff's business to do well."

"So when are you going to tell him?"

She waggled her head back and forth. "I don't know. Maybe when I feel like Bark-Bark starts considering other suspects."

For several minutes, neither said anything. Finally, Maggie looked at her brother. "Okay, I'll call him."

"And tell him what?"

"Frank, I can't tell him I'm under house arrest. I just can't."

"Because he can't take that?"

"Yeah, well and something more. I didn't want to tell you this way -- but I'm pregnant."

"Wow! That's great. Congratulations." He jumped up and gave his sister a brief hug, then sat back down in his La-Z-Boy.

"Jeff finally agreed to that. And thank you. Your suggestions —," She smiled a little. "Your *counseling* made a difference. We talked and listened to one another, and it worked out." She shook her head. "I don't know how this might affect him." She let out a breath that came out as a sigh. "I don't know yet how it's going to affect *me*. And I'm the stable one. If Bark-Bark finds another suspect and leaves me alone, then there's no need to tell Jeff anything, at least until it is all over."

"And if the Sheriff doesn't cut you loose?"

"Then I've got all sorts of problems. And I will have to deal with all of them."

"Maggie, give Jeff a little credit. You've told me he loves you, and you love him. You owe it to him to let him know when things are going great for you. And you owe it to him to tell him when they aren't going well. He's a husband, and also a helpmate. What do you think, that he'll ask for a divorce because you're in trouble with the law?"

She jerked her head down. "No. But he'll worry and get crazy. And I don't know how quickly this will be over."

Again, the two sat silently staring at each other.

Maggie waved a hand, as if shooing away a fly. "Okay. I'll call him tomorrow and tell him what happened at the conference and why I've got to stay here a few more days."

"Tomorrow? You think you're Scarlett O'Hara? Today would be better." He looked at his sister's expression and relented. "Okay. Tomorrow. On to suspects. Do you have anybody in mind?"

"I haven't come up with much yet. To be truthful, I've spent most of the time feeling sorry for myself. You know me. I'd like to be out there looking for the bad guy. That's my nature. And instead, I'm stuck and can't do anything."

"Not true. Your mind is not restricted to this house. And my phone and internet are at your disposal. So, suspects. Imagine you are not restricted in your movements. Who is a suspect you'd want to be checking out?"

She sat forward on her chair. "There was a guy who said Granet stole his title."

"Mmmm. A good place to look. What's his name? Where's he from?"

Maggie mashed her lips together. "I don't know. I wasn't paying attention. I can sort of picture him: six feet tall, dark hair, maybe with some grey in it. Maybe mostly grey. I don't know. I wasn't accused, then, so I wasn't looking at people closely."

Father Franks mouth curved up just a little. "He said Granet stole his title and you think he might be a suspect. And you said Granet should pay for his theft of your novel. But you don't think you should be a suspect."

"Of course not. I *know* I didn't do it."

"But the Sheriff doesn't know you didn't do it."

"I told him I didn't do it."

The priest gave a small smirk. "That certainly should have done the trick."

"Okay. I see what you're saying. But Bark - all right - Sheriff Bark doesn't seem to be looking for anybody else. If he doesn't look, he's not going to find anybody else. And if he doesn't find anybody else, he's going after me."

"He could just leave it an open case. But I see where you're coming from. So, let's find some other suspects for him to look at. Can you find out who said his title was stolen?"

Maggie took a deep breath and let it out. "I can try to find out more about him." She shook her head. "No. Not try. I will find out who he was and what the title was."

"That's a start. And it'll give you something to do. Now, who else?"

"There was a rumor going around that Val Monroe had a brief fling with Rod three years ago. She was in charge of inviting the faculty for this year's conference. Some said she had a thing for Granet and that's why she invited him. I'm not sure I buy that. He's hit the *USA Today* bestseller list now. For this conference, that makes him the premier draw. I'd have invited him too if it were up to me."

"And why would that make her a suspect?"

"This is all rumor. I don't know whether any of it is true or not. But apparently she made a move to reignite that fling and got rudely turned down. Actually, one woman said he laughed at her and told her to buzz off."

"Hmmm. Hardly sounds like much of a motive for murder."

"Depends on how rude he was. Remember, hell hath no fury like a woman scorned."

Father Frank laughed. "I've heard that. But I have no firsthand knowledge of it."

"Oh?"

Father Frank sat back a little and glared at his sister. "Oh? What do you mean by that?"

"Well, I heard you left a young college coed, who really was interested in you, when you entered the seminary. I heard she was very disappointed."

The priest put up both hands, palms facing Maggie. "We had a nice, quiet conversation. I explained the strong pull I had to the seminary. She smiled and said I should go to the cemetery, ah, seminary."

"Was that a Freudian slip of the tongue?" She raised her eyebrows. "Or maybe, the truth?"

By now, Father Frank's face was red and the color was creeping down his neck. "Not the truth. She understood how strongly I felt about the call to the priesthood. At the time, my ego thought she was probably disappointed. Most likely, she was relieved. 'Wheee. I finally got rid of that boring guy.'"

"I heard she was gorgeous."

"I certainly thought so at the time, but –. It's all in the past. She's happily married now, and I'm happily a priest. So, it worked out best for all parties."

Maggie continued to smile. "But, before you told her, I'm wondering —"

"Stop right there. I'm not saying another word about that long-past part of my life. And if you want my help on the Granet case, you'll put that out of your mind."

"Just pulling your leg, little brother."

"Back to the case," Father Frank said firmly. "A stolen title is not as serious as a stolen plot, I'm guessing. So, we need some other suspects. Val may be a possibility. Who else?"

"I just don't know who they are. I heard someone, I don't remember who, say someone, a boyfriend maybe, slipped in a back way that night, so he didn't appear on the monitor of the entrance."

Father Frank clenched his teeth together, trying not to show he already knew this. "Ah, that's interesting. Can you find out anything else about that?"

"I don't know. I can't remember who said it."

"Well, it won't do us any good unless you can come up with a name and the particulars."

"I'll make some calls."

"Good plan. That will give you something to do tomorrow." He looked at his watch. "I've got a counseling session in fifteen minutes. You and your constant new friend can —"

"New friend?"

"You and your beautiful new ankle bracelet can stay out of sight in the bedroom. I'll take the couch in my office tonight. See you at Mass in the morning."

Chapter 16

"WHAT DO YOU mean you want me to come in for more questions?" Maggie's voice rose an octave.

"Do you have transportation, or do I need to send a police cruiser over to bring you in?" The Sheriff's voice was firm, and cold.

"I have transportation."

She dropped the phone back in the cradle and slumped back on the bed. She felt like crying, but decided by force of will she would not let this ... this Bark-Bark make her cry. She knew she was innocent and justice would win out. It usually did. It was the occasional mistake that worried her now.

* * *

It was after one o'clock by the time she got to the Sheriff's office. She was tired and angry and consciously worked to keep her voice neutral. Instead of a comfortable chair in his office, she was in an interrogation room on a hard, metal chair that was about as uncomfortable as possible. *Probably made it that way on purpose.*

The Sheriff asked her the same questions he had yesterday. In fact, many of them were the same questions he had asked her at the Lakota Retreat Center on Friday. She was getting tired of it. When he asked her the same question he had just twenty minutes ago–what did she do after dinner Thursday night– she couldn't stop herself.

"You asked me that on Friday. You asked me that question on Sunday. And you have asked me that same question twice today. What's the matter? Can't you remember what I said?"

As soon as she said it, she realized he had made her lose her temper - and her composure. He was wearing her down. And that could lead to mistakes. She wasn't guilty, but she might say something that would give him more reason to hold her. Now she was sorry she didn't have Norm with her.

"Okay. I'll give you the same answer I have each time before. The truth. You want the truth and that's what I am giving you. To answer your question, again, I went back to my room and climbed into bed, feeling sorry for myself that my book was a *USA Today* Bestseller, but it had Granet's name on the cover. He was getting the royalties. No, I didn't see anybody once I went into my room."

"Yesterday you said you stopped at the cafeteria to get a soda. This time, you skipped the cafeteria." The Sheriff fixed her with a half smirk, satisfied he had elicited a slight change in her story. "Where else did you go? Maybe to Rod Granet's cabin?"

Maggie opened her mouth to let him have a blast of her anger. But she caught herself. Took a deep breath and actually smiled at the man. "Yes. I did get a soda at the cafeteria and carried it back to my room. I didn't know you wanted all the minor details."

He kept the smirk on his face. "I do. As they say, the devil is in the details."

"Once in my room, I took two drinks from the Dr Pepper can. I put it down. I took off my blouse and pants and put them on the chair. I went into the bathroom, pushed my panties down." She stopped and gave him a questioning look. "Just how detailed do you want?"

"Don't get smart with me, young lady."

She wanted to leap on that, tell him she didn't think he'd recognize smart. But she literally bit her tongue. *Don't give him any excuse. You don't want to go back into that cell.* "Okay. How about this. I did not leave my room again until 8:15 the next morning."

The Sheriff slammed his notebook closed. An angry scowl covered his face, but he said simply, "You can go now."

* * *

That evening, she called Jeff. They talked about the baby, and what Maggie was doing. Finally, she told him about her house arrest and that the sheriff kept calling her back in, trying to find something incriminating he could use. Maggie was amazed at Jeff's reaction. He asked a few questions, but calmly. She had expected he might go into a frenzy. Quickly, she returned the conversation to the baby, and their visit ended on a happy note.

Chapter 17

WEDNESDAY MORNING, FATHER Frank was having cereal, much to the disgust of his sister who thought all breakfasts had to start with eggs. "And what did Jeff say about it all?" he asked in between spooning Cheerios into his mouth.

"Not much. I could tell he was upset, but I don't know if that was because I spent the night in jail, or because I didn't call him sooner. In fact, he was unusually quiet. He asked me a few questions. How long would I be in Pine Tree? Was there anything I needed?"

"That's it?"

"Well, of course he asked how I was doing. Was I feeling the baby yet? Stuff like that." She pulled a bagel out of the toaster oven and spread cream cheese on it. "Do you eat that stuff for breakfast often? Or is this just to annoy me?"

"I never do anything *just* to annoy you. Well, not since I was thirteen and you were seventeen. Besides, you're having a bagel and cream cheese."

"I'll get to the eggs in a little bit."

"So he asked about the baby. Sounds like you've really won him over to the idea of having a child."

"I'd say so. Once we agreed to try and get me pregnant. Actually, that's not right. I think he still wasn't sure. Then at about nine weeks, I had a scheduled doctor's appointment, and he decided to go with me. The doctor used a fetal doppler to check the baby's heartbeat. Then Jeff–and I was really surprised by this –Jeff asked the doctor if he could listen. She said sure and handed him the stethoscope. I watched him. He closed his eyes and I could tell he was really concentrating. I was hoping he would hear something. Then, he looked up at me. 'Sounds like a team of horses galloping.' Then he frowned and asked the doctor if it should be that fast. She said it was just right. I've never seen Jeff more excited."

Maggie burst into the biggest grin Father Frank had seen from her in years. "He was absolutely captivated. Never missed a doctor's appointment after that. Always asks how the baby is doing. I'll swear, Jeff's more excited than I am."

"Fantastic. I'm happy for both of you. Is he coming out?"

"I think he was ready to drive out, but I convinced him not to do it. He's got that new client. And what can he do out here anyway? I don't expect we'll see him unless I'm here for a month."

"I'd like to see Jeff, but I hope you're not here for a month."

"Getting tired of company already?" Maggie had a devilish grin.

"No. No. Of course not. But I hope this Granet investigation doesn't drag on that long."

* * *

At 10:30, Jeff walked into the Timber County Sheriff's Office. "I'd like to see the Sheriff, please."

"What is your name and what do you need to see the Sheriff about?" asked the deputy sitting behind the glass wall.

"My name if Jeff Armstrong, and I am Maggie DeLuca's husband."

"She's not in our custody now."

"I know that. Can I see the Sheriff?"

Without answering, the deputy picked up a phone, punched in a number and waited. "A Jeff Armstrong, who says he's DeLuca's husband would like to speak with you." He waited a few seconds. "I'll bring him back."

Two minutes later, Jeff entered the Sheriff's office. Bark did not get up from his chair or offer Jeff a seat, but continued to read some papers on his desk.

After half a minute, Jeff sat down in the chair in front of the Sheriff. It was another two minutes before Bark put the papers down and looked at Jeff, a sneer forming on his lips. "Armstrong? You didn't take her name?"

"No. Is Bark your wife's name?"

The Sheriff's head jerked up and his eyes turned hard. "Don't get smart with me, boy. My wife took my name."

"Apparently Maggie is more independent than your wife. But I didn't come here to jaw about names. I came here to suggest you stop harassing my wife. Now."

"She's a murder suspect. I'll harass her if I want. And put her butt back in a jail cell if I feel like it."

"You don't have the evidence to hold her. Oh yeah. I know. She said in public he stole her book and he should pay for that. That sure is a strong case."

"She had motive, means and opportunity. I shouldn't have let her out on bail."

"As I understand it, you didn't let her out on bail. A judge did. And on her own recognizance." Jeff smiled just a little. "Sounds like the Judge didn't think you had much of a case. I want you to quit harassing her."

Sam Bark narrowed his eyes and leaned a little forward. "I think you and I are through here. I'll keep asking her questions as often as I like. And if I don't like her answers, I slap her back in a cell." Bark stood up. "We're through here. Get out."

Jeff stayed in his chair. "If you continue to harass her, I'll be back. And I'll be bringing a lawyer who just loves to take down power hungry people. And who just happens to be very good at it. Unless you come up with some other evidence, don't bother my wife. Get out and find the murderer."

"Are you threatening me? Are you threatening a member of law enforcement?" Bark was almost shouting.

"No, sir. I am not threatening you. I would never threaten you or any other peace officer. I was just offering some advice." Jeff stood. "Thank you for your time."

Bark was fuming, trying to think of something else to say, as Jeff walked out of the office.

Chapter 18

FATHER FRANK OPENED the door to find Jeff standing outside. "Well, hello. This is certainly a surprise. Does Maggie know you're coming?"

Jeff stuck his hand out and the two men shook hands. "No. We talked a long time last night. But I didn't decide to make the trip here until - well pretty late."

"Come on in. I'll tell her you're here." The priest turned and called, "Hey, Maggie. Come on in here. I've got a surprise for you."

"I love surprises," she said as she came out of the kitchen, wiping her hands on a dish towel. She stopped as if hitting a wall. "Jeff." With that, she rushed over and wrapped her arms around her husband and gave him a welcome kiss. "What are you doing here?"

"Oh, I just thought I'd drop in and see how you and the baby are doing?"

She pulled him close and kissed him again. "Well, I'm certainly glad to see you, but surprised. You didn't say anything last night about coming."

"I didn't know I was coming until about one o'clock this morning. I couldn't go to sleep. I just kept thinking about you and how the sheriff was bothering you. Finally I decided I had to come down and talk to the man."

Maggie pulled back a little, holding Jeff at arm's length. "Talk to Bark-Bark? I don't think that's a good idea. He's already threatening to toss me back into the slammer."

"I told him to quit harassing you or I'd take legal action."

Her mouth dropped open. "You did what?"

Father Frank's mouth dropped open and his eyebrows shot up. "You've been to see him?"

"I have. And Maggie's right. He's not a nice guy. He tried to intimidate me. Then accused me of threatening him."

"It's a wonder he didn't throw you in jail." Maggie pulled her husband over to the couch and pushed him down, then sank beside him, her head resting on his shoulder.

"You two visit. I'll go finish preparing lunch. Is there enough for three?"

Maggie laughed. "You know me. I always cook a lot more than we can eat."

As Father Frank hustled into the kitchen he heard Maggie say, "Jeff, you're not ... What I mean is you don't usually ..."

"My wife isn't usually in trouble with the law."

Father Frank might have eavesdropped a bit more, but he looked up and saw the potatoes boiling over.

* * *

That evening, Georgia Peitz, a parishioner of Prince of Peace and close friend of Father Frank, and Georgia's fiancé Detective Mike Oakley of the Pine Tree Police Department, dropped in to see Maggie and meet her husband. After a few minutes of introductions, Father Frank said, "Maggie made some fantastic brownies. Plus, I bought Blue Bell ice cream. What say we help ourselves to a little dessert? And we can lay out some of the details to our resident detective."

Georgia grabbed Mike's hand and started for the kitchen. "Well, I'm going to make some tea, so let's all just sit around the kitchen table and solve this mystery."

Quickly bowls and spoons were on the table. Father Frank got the ice cream and a scoop. Maggie brought out the brownies.

"Tea's fine for Georgia," said Mike. "But if we're going to struggle over suspects, I suggest we put on a pot of coffee."

The five sat around the table in the kitchen and for several minutes, the conversation was on the brownies, ice cream, and the particular tea blend Georgia pulled out of her purse. "This is Peach Cobbler Guayusa."

"Never heard of it," said Maggie.

"You should try it. Here, have a sip." Georgia passed the cup to Maggie. "I know Father wouldn't like it. He's stuck on Dr

Pepper. But this is a rare tea native to the rainforest of Ecuador. Of course, you can get the basic Guayusa tea, or get it infused with different flavors. My favorite is Peach Cobbler. But the chocolate is pretty good too."

"This is amazingly good, Georgia. And I'm not usually a tea drinker."

"I'll bring you some, if you won't waste it on your brother," Georgia said with a laugh.

"I won't."

"Works for me," said the priest.

By the time much of the dessert had been consumed, the coffee was ready.

Jeff leaned forward in the chair and looked at his wife. "Okay, Dear. I know you must have a handful of suspects. What's the plan?"

Maggie glanced at her brother, and then her husband. "Besides me, the only one I've identified - and even here I don't have his name - is a man who said Rod Granet stole his title."

"And this is serious?" asked Georgia.

"Not really. You can't copyright a title. And lots of books have the same title. But it's irritating enough to make someone angry," said Maggie.

"Angry enough to kill?" asked Jeff.

"I know it seems a stretch." Maggie folded her bottom lip in. "I guess it depends on the person."

Mike nodded. "Some people can get pretty ticked off at someone beating them to a parking spot. Depends on the person's anger threshold and how the day been going."

Jeff shook his head. "Okay. But you need to come up with more than that, I'm afraid."

Maggie snapped her fingers. "I did hear about one man - again, no name - who came to the conference, but wasn't a writer. Apparently his daughter was at the conference three years ago when Granet was here. Afterwards, she left a note saying she was going to New York with Granet. The father wanted to talk with Granet and see if he could get some contact information from him."

"Sean O'Reilly," said Father Frank.

Everybody turned to look at the priest.

"He came to me and asked if I could find him a lawyer if the Sheriff held him. Apparently he told the Sheriff his reason for coming to the conference and he was afraid the Sheriff might slap him in jail as a suspect. His wife is dead and his only child is gone. He said he might need a little help."

Maggie snorted.

Father Frank ignored Maggie. "I said I would help if he needed it. But I guess he didn't need a lawyer."

"Of course not. Old Bark-Bark's got me. Why look for anyone else?"

Father Frank looked around the group. "O'Reilly lives and works in the Dallas area. In construction. Jeff, do you think you could - ah, check him out a bit?"

"Like, check into what, exactly?"

"General personality. What is his nature? Is he prone to violence? Were he and his daughter close? Does he have a record, or been arrested for violence?"

"I can take care of that last one," said Mike. "If he has any priors, I can find out. But, Jeff, be very careful what you do when 'checking him out'. You are doing this because he *might* have killed a man. So, at this point, we consider it a possibility that his anger can result in deadly violence. Do not put yourself in his crosshairs. If you can't do this in a way that he never knows you exist, then do not do it. Comprende?"

"Got it."

"Good advice, Mike. This might -" The priest shrugged. "Or might not - shed any light on Sean. So don't take any risks, Jeff."

Georgia raised her shoulders and pursed her lips. "Doesn't sound like a great prospect, or suspect anyway."

"I rarely disagree with Georgia," said Mike. "But in this case, I have to. Loss of a family member is a great motivator. In this case, with his wife deceased, this was the last of his family. And his only child. Granted, she wasn't a real young child, but he could look at it as kidnapping almost."

Father Frank nodded. "It seemed very important to Sean. Remember, he came to a writers' conference, wasn't a writer, and stayed in the conference housing, just to make certain he got to talk with Granet. I asked Sean what he would do if he got an address. Without hesitation, he said he'd get in touch with her, see how she was doing, fly up to New York to see her – if she was agreeable."

Mike raised a finger. "Strong motive."

"Here's a question, though," Father Frank said. "If Sean killed Granet near midnight, why wouldn't he have left right then? Made sure he wasn't around when the body was found?"

"Leaving in the middle of the night would make him look guilty to me," said Mike.

"Besides," Maggie offered, "The entrance is covered by surveillance cameras. The police would look at the tapes, see him leave right after the murder, and be after him in a second. Smarter to just stay, blend in, give Frank a heart-wrenching story."

Jeff had gotten up to refresh his coffee. "All right. I'll look into O'Reilly. Who else have we got?"

Maggie looked down for a second, and then up at the group. "I don't know whether this is worth much."

"We need to look at everything, or everybody, who has even the slightest possibility of being the murderer," said Father Frank.

"Okay. Three years ago, Rod Granet was a speaker here at the conference. The story is that he and Val Monroe had - ah - a fling. Some believe that's why he was invited back. But with his/my bestseller, it made sense to have him at the conference again." Maggie paused just long enough to take a sip of her coffee. "The story going around the conference, well, at least among the women, is that she went to visit him at his cabin and got rejected. In fact, one woman said she was walking nearby and heard Granet tell her he wasn't interested in a fat pig."

"Wow," Georgia gasped. "That had to hurt. And hell hath no fury like a woman scorned."

Father Frank laughed. "That's exactly what Maggie said. But I didn't hear Sheriff Bark say it."

"Of course not. He has me."

"But you're here," Jeff said.

"Yeah. With an ankle monitor on."

Father Frank looked at the group. "Okay guys, we've got a couple of people to look at. Sean, Val Monroe, and the guy who had his cover stolen."

"Not cover. Title," corrected Maggie.

"Anyone else?" Father Frank looked around the group.

Jeff looked disappointed. Georgia was frowning. Mike showed no emotion. And Maggie just shook her head and looked down at the table.

Father Frank tried to sound upbeat. "Don't look so glum, guys. That's three reasonable suspects."

"Actually, four," said Jeff. Everybody turned to look at him. "Including Maggie, I mean."

"Ha ha. Not very funny. And I'm the *only* one Bark thinks is a good suspect."

There was an uncomfortable silence. Georgia stood up. "More tea anyone?"

Chapter 19

THE NAME BILLY John popped into Father Frank's mind. But he had told Holly he wouldn't give Billy John up to the police. Could he at least get the police to consider the possibility that someone came into the center they don't know about?

An hour later, Father Frank stood in Sheriff Bark's office.

"What do you want?" Sheriff Bark's eyes bore into Father Frank.

The priest tried a small smile. "Is Ms. DeLuca still your main suspect?"

"I'm not going to discuss this case with you. I told you to stay out of it."

"Sheriff, since you have my sister as perhaps your *only* suspect, I can't be uninvolved. You'd be involved if it were your sister." Father Frank was aware of someone coming in the door just behind him.

"I don't have a sister. And you can be interested. But keep your distance, don't start poking around. I told you before, if you get in my way, I'll have you up on obstruction of an investigation. Is that clear?"

"Ms. DeLuca's brother?" the man behind Father Frank asked. "Then you must be Father Frank."

Father Frank turned to see the man who had just come in. His appearance, besides the alligator boots, string tie and cowboy hat, was rather plain. But his manner and carriage suggested confident authority. "Yes, I am. And I see by your badge you're a Texas Ranger."

"I am. Dick Richards." He extended a hand and the two men shook hands. "So, how are you interfering with Sheriff Bark's investigation?" His voice was neutral.

"I'm not interfering, Mr. Richards." Father Frank knitted his eyebrows. "What is a proper way to address a Texas Ranger?"

"Well, if you knew my rank, you could call me Lieutenant Richards. But, since you don't, Ranger Richards would work."

"And you're stationed where?"

"Tyler. Now I get to ask a question. Tell me how the Sheriff thinks you're interfering."

Sam Bark stood, his angry mood ratcheting up a notch. "He's trying to tell me how to run my investigation. His sister had motive, means, and opportunity. I'd say she's a good suspect."

"Well, Sam has a point. Motive, means and opportunity make for a good starting place. But, I'd still like to know why the Sheriff thinks you're interfering."

Father Frank nodded a couple of times. "He told me he had cameras on the entrance, so he knew who came and went from nine the night of the murder until six the next morning. I just wanted to know if there were any other ways to get into the Lakota Retreat Center."

The Ranger raised his eyebrows and looked at the Sheriff. "Sounds like a reasonable question."

"There are no other roads into the center. There's no other way a car could get in. Plain and simple. *Nobody* came or went during that time period."

Now Dick Richards looked at the priest. "Anything else?"

Father Frank shrugged. "I did ask him if he had any other suspects. He told me, respectfully, that was none of my business. I said if my sister was a suspect, it *was* my business."

The Ranger walked over and sat in a straight backed chair. After a moment, he addressed Father Frank. "I understand your interest and concern in this case. But the Sheriff is perfectly within his rights not to release information on the investigation. And because you're the brother of a suspect, he certainly should not be imparting details on the investigation to you."

Sheriff Bark looked at the priest, a sneer curling his lips.

"But since I am assisting the Sheriff on this case, I'll tell you as much as *I think* is reasonable, without in any way jeopardizing our investigation."

"I appreciate that, Lieutenant. Thank you."

* * *

Half an hour later, Father Frank sat in Mike Oakley's office in the Pine Tree Police Department. "So what do you make of it all?" Father Frank asked.

"First, Sam Bark is the Sheriff of Timber County. Has been for about three years. And he does not like me. Or anyone in the Pine Tree police department, for that matter. I'm not aware of any reason for this, but any time there's an interaction between us and his office, it appears to be true. So don't expect me to be a go-between. Won't work."

"And Lieutenant Richards?"

Mike smiled. "He's a Texas Ranger. That means he's good. And I'm not aware he has any ax to grind with Pine Tree."

"But will Bark listen to him?"

"Oh yes. The Texas Rangers are considered one of the most elite law enforcement agencies in the world."

Father Frank's eyes opened wide and his mouth formed an O. "Wow. I didn't know that. I mean, I've always thought highly of them, but ... well that surprises me."

Now Mike broke into a laugh. "And, a ranger outranks any other lawman in Texas. Rangers are at the top of the police pecking order. Bark will absolutely listen and if he's smart, follow it up with 'Yes, Sir.'"

"And you say the Rangers are the best. So, I guess I should take some comfort in that. He did say he would tell me whatever he could."

"I'd say that's a plus. I can guarantee you Richards will be looking for other suspects. For whatever reason, sounds like Bark has put you on his shi ... ah, list. Maybe because you're from Pine Tree and he just doesn't like anything associated with Pine Tree. I thought it was just the police department. But who knows? Maybe it's the entire town. Of course, it could be because you solved two cases here, one of which tossed a state judge out of his office."

Chapter 20

FATHER FRANK MADE his way down the center aisle and out the front door of Prince of Peace Church. He had just finished morning Mass and was headed for the rectory to have breakfast. He came to an abrupt halt. In front of him stood a man wearing a large white Stetson. The sun reflecting off the felt almost made it glow.

"Hello, Lieutenant Richards. I didn't know you were a Catholic."

The Texas Ranger gave a half smile. "Actually, I'm not. But I wanted to catch you and talk this morning. I was about to knock on the door of your house when a woman in the parking lot said you were still in church."

Father Frank nodded a couple of times. "Okay. Let's go over to the rectory and have some coffee while we talk."

"I don't expect it will take us very long. We'll be finished before you'd get the water hot. Why don't we just sit on that bench there?"

The two men walked forty feet over to the bench and sat down under a towering southern pine.

Father Frank looked at the Texas Ranger. "Okay. What do you have to tell me?"

Richards chuckled. "Actually, today I'm hoping you will tell me something."

"If I can."

"You asked the Sheriff about another way into the center. Did you have something particular in mind?"

Father Frank looked down at the ground. *How do I handle this? I don't want to be the cause of Holly's fiancé getting unjustly accused.* But, he did want him checked out. He remembered something Maggie said last night. "Maggie said there was some talk about a man who slipped in to visit his girlfriend Thursday night. No name, just some gossip. If there was someone else in the center, I would certainly want the Sheriff and his men to question him."

For several long seconds, the Ranger studied the priest. "I have checked the property. And you were right - there is another way in, which I believe you knew about and were trying to get the Sheriff to investigate." Again, he stared at Father Frank. "But for some reason you didn't want to tell us directly."

When Father Frank said nothing, Richards continued. "I found where a motorcycle could come in. And in fact, one did come in before midnight Thursday, and left after midnight. I can even tell you a good bit about the cycle." Again, the Ranger stopped and just stared at Father Frank.

"I'm impressed. How could you tell when the person came in and left?"

A smile broke the rigid look on the Ranger's face and he fingered the opal stone on the clasp of his string tie. "Just lucky. But I'm happy to have luck on my side anytime. The bike came in on dry dirt. Around midnight, we began to have a light rain. The bike left after the trail was wet. And yes, since I've heard you are sharp on investigation, we did get a cast of the tires. Semi-knobbed tread, but with some cuts and nicks. Pretty distinctive." Richards was now back to dead serious. "Now, who do you suppose came in on a bike?"

"I don't really know." *I could tell you what I suspect, who it might have been.*

"But, you have some ideas on the matter, right?"

Father Frank looked down, his eyes closed. What to say? He did not want to reveal what Holly had told him. And he didn't know if the tracks Richards found had anything to do with Billy John. "I'd rather not say."

Richards leaned forward and fixed the priest with a laser focus. "Did your information come in the confessional?"

"No."

"Then you can tell me whatever you know."

Father Frank pursed his lips and let out a breath. "It was told to me in confidence. I said I would not reveal what was said."

The Ranger sat back and studied the man in front of him. "It never fails to amaze me how good, honest people can often delay or disrupt an investigation." *Or just make my job harder.* He shook his head. "Okay. here's the deal. I'll give my men 'til the end of today to find out who rode in. But if they can't come up with a name, or at least a good lead, then I'm coming back for some answers." Once more, he just stared at the priest for several moments. "And to show you I play fair, I'll give you a little bit of information on the investigation. Right now, your sister is not Bark's best suspect." He paused to let that sink in. "She's his *only* suspect. So you might want to give us some help in finding someone else."

With that, the Ranger marched across the parking lot, got in a Chevy Tahoe and left.

Father Frank watched him go. What to do? He had promised Holly to keep her information in confidence.

Unless.

There had been a caveat—unless it might save a life. *Would keeping Maggie from a life sentence in jail be considered saving a life?* He refused even to let a death penalty enter his mind.

The chances of the Rangers finding Billy John today seemed very unlikely. Could Father Frank find him? He knew his first name and his fiancée's name. Even with that, it would be a difficult task, particularly limited to one day.

He shook his head. If he started asking questions, looking around, undoubtedly Richards's men would find out. *They'll probably be watching me, now that he's put the pressure of a short deadline on me.*

What can I do? Leave it alone appeared in his brain, as bright as a neon sign. *No. I can't. Maggie is Bark's only suspect. And it doesn't sound like he's looking for any more. I can't sit this one out.*

He got up and started toward the rectory. Some coffee might get his mind working. It was a beautiful day. He looked up at the deep blue sky. No rain expected. Maybe he would shoot some baskets after breakfast. That usually cleared his mind, helped him think more clearly.

With that thought, he picked up his pace. He made it to the house just as Jeff was leaving. "Heading back to Dallas already? Might as well stay for breakfast."

"I grabbed a cup of coffee and Maggie fixed me an egg sandwich." He held up a clear baggie with a sandwich inside. "I need to get back to the office. But, I'll be back."

Inside, Father Frank had just poured a cup of coffee when the telephone rang.

"Prince of Peace. How can I help you?"

"Hi Father. It's George Turner. Just checking if the finance committee meeting is still on for Saturday?"

The smile on Father Frank's face evaporated. "Tomorrow?" He had forgotten about it. But it had been scheduled. "Yes, George. Tomorrow. Here. That's four o'clock."

"Just checking. I'll be there. Thanks." The call ended.

Just what I need. Another deadline. Dear Lord, you know accounting is my nemesis. You could have insisted I take an accounting class in college.

No basketball today.

Chapter 21

MAGGIE HAD CALLED and determined May Ellison was not in the conference office today. Perfect. Father Frank didn't want her in the office.

Even with the conference over, the staff hung around for another week or two to tie up all the loose ends. Today, Val Monroe was the only one working in the office. At nearly six feet tall and in heels, she was an impressive, if somewhat overweight, woman. Only her mouth, a tad too wide with thin lips, kept her from being a beauty. Not a strand of her dish-water blonde hair was out of place as it curved down and stopped just short of her shoulders. It appeared no one else was in the office – exactly what Father Frank wanted..

"Hi. I'm Father Frank. Is May in today?"

"Sorry. She's not coming in today. Can I help you?"

"I'm sorry. I don't think we've met."

"I'm Val Monroe. I was in charge of hiring the faculty for this year's conference."

"Congratulations. I've been told this was the best faculty the PWWC has ever had."

That brought a smile to Val's face. "I was pretty proud of it. And the attendees all seemed impressed."

"Even when your star attraction died?"

"Well, that was... sudden. He did have the big name this year. But to be honest, many of the other faculty members gave better talks and workshops."

"Still, I'm sure many people registered to hear Granet talk."

"A few, perhaps."

"I'll bet there were a bunch who came just to meet the man. Get to shake his hand."

Val snorted. "Ignorant young writers."

"Ignorant? What do you mean?"

"They didn't recognize him for what he was."

"You mean as a person, not as a writer?"

"Right. He was rude. He didn't care whose feelings he hurt. He could be cruel, even to people he knew."

Father Frank looked completely puzzled. "Rod Granet? I thought he was a nice guy, here to help aspiring writers."

"Not on your life." Val had been working on some papers. But she pushed them aside and gave the priest her full attention. "He was here for the money. And the publicity."

"But he was here three years ago. And you invited him back."

"He was a different person back then." Her voice grew somber "I guess the fame went to his head. Now, he was above everybody. I'm sorry I invited him back. I thought we'd —." She stopped and a look of alarm came over her face. "What I mean is, I thought *he'd* be the same... nice guy he was back then. He wasn't. He didn't care who he hurt."

"Still, you had to be devastated to lose a prominent faculty member."

Val's eyes had turned dark and a muscle in her jaw twitched. "Not one bit." She almost spit out the words. "We were better off without him. I'm sorry I invited him. I'm glad he got his just rewards."

Father Frank's eyes opened wide and he looked at the woman with disbelief.

Val focused on the top of the desk. Her teeth remained clamped together and the muscles in her neck were so tight her veins stood out. For a minute neither said a word, then she looked up at the priest. "I need to get back to work. I'll tell May you were here to see her."

* * *

Father Frank was back in the rectory half an hour later. "Okay, big sister. Time for you to get to work."

Maggie was looking through the pantry, trying to decide what to fix for lunch. She straightened up and shut the cabinet door. "Good. I'm getting a little bored. I love to cook, but that doesn't take me all day. What can I do? And how did your visit with Val Monroe go?"

"Those go hand in hand. I asked Val a few questions about Granet, and how losing him affected the conference. Bang! She took off. His untimely departure was a blessing — from her point of view. But the kicker was, she said and I quote, ' I'm glad he got his just rewards.'"

Maggie's eyes shot wide open. "Wow. She actually said that? What did you say back?"

"Nothing. I was too stunned. By the time I got over the shock, she'd pulled herself together and dismissed me."

"Guess she realized she had let her mouth get ahead of her brain. Sounds guilty to me."

"Certainly doesn't sound like she shed any tears over his death." The priest leaned his head back and stared up toward the ceiling. "Wasn't a good thing to say. But while uncharitable, it does not mean she acted on it. We don't want to let that bit of poor judgment convict her in our minds."

"You're right. It was my popping off that got me into this mess." She snapped her fingers. "Did you know she stayed in the residence hall?"

"No. But so did you. So that doesn't make her look guilty."

"I don't live ten minutes away."

Father Frank nodded a couple of times. "So why would she stay there?"

"Actually, I asked her Thursday - before all this happened. She said she wanted to be there and see how everything went. She was in charge of selecting the faculty, but she wanted to make certain all went well for those staying on site." Maggie smirked. "More likely she wanted to be there for a late night rendezvous. One that didn't pan out."

"So she was there at the time of the murder."

"Just like 80 or 90 other people." For a minute, neither said anything, letting this bit of information sink in. Finally, Maggie said, "Okay. So what do you want me to do, that I can do from here? I don't want to get Bark on my case."

"See if you can find the woman who said she heard Rod call Val a fat pig. It would be interesting to see if she remembered anything else."

"That's a tough assignment."

"C'mon Maggie. You write mystery novels. Think like a detective."

Chapter 22

SATURDAY, AS FATHER Frank left the church after morning Mass, he saw Richards sitting on the bench they had shared yesterday. Immediately the smile faded from his face. *He's going to demand to know about Billy John. What do I say?*

"Hi, Ranger. You know, you can come inside during the morning service." He tried to sound casual, friendly. "It might give you some inspiration."

"I'll keep that in mind," said the Texas Ranger, returning Father Frank's smile. "Have you gotten inspired to give us a little help on this case? The one that doesn't look good for your sister?"

Father Frank sat down beside Richards. "I'm not really worried about Maggie. She's innocent and I trust our legal system."

"But sometimes, it does fail. Innocent people do get convicted."

"They do. But I've been told the Texas Rangers are the elite of investigative groups in the world. You'll get it right. I have faith."

"So, are you ready to help us out?"

"You didn't give your men very much time to locate the rider."

Richards nodded. "Maybe not. But it was enough. As you pointed out, we are the best of the best."

"I am impressed. Can you tell me how?"

"Now why would I want to do that?" His smile didn't fade, but his voice hardened slightly. "You don't want to share any information with me."

"It's not that I don't want to. It's that I gave my word I wouldn't."

"Okay. Then I propose a trade. I'll tell you how we located him and you tell me who he was going to see."

"Uh-oh. I'm falling into a trap."

"No. Here's the deal. We know who the man is. And he will tell us who he went to see, eventually. But, if we know who he went to see when we *start* to interview him, it will put us in a stronger position. Gives us a little extra edge."

"Gotcha. He was going to see Holly." He stopped. Technically, he wasn't breaching his promise. But he was apprehensive he might be putting Holly in a difficult position. "I *am* falling into a trap. I tell you who he was going to see and that helps you find who he was."

Richards laughed. "Good. Very good. You decide to leave the priesthood, you come see me. We might recruit you for the Rangers. But no, this was not a trap. The rider was Billy John Bartok. And he rides a dual sport bike, a Suzuki DR650. Not a particularly jazzy bike, but good on the road and in the dirt. We were able to get some nice casts of the tires of his bike. As I said yesterday, they were pretty distinctive. It took a bit of legwork, but we located his bike and now we know who he is. We'll interview him this morning, but I was hoping for a little extra help from ... the clergy."

"Holly Waterton. Very nice young woman." He frowned, still not feeling comfortable with supplying her name. "Are you going to interview her also?"

"Yes. We'll need to see how their stories line up. But I won't tell her you gave us anything. Of course, you really didn't. We would have gotten her name from Bartok. Or Facebook or Instagram. Romanic relationships often show up there."

Father Frank got up, ready to leave.

"That said," Richards stopped him. "There might be other information you have that will help us." He gave the priest a quizzical look.

Certainly a different approach than the Sheriff took. After a moment he looked back at Richards. "Nothing right now. But let me think about it. Why don't you stop by after Mass tomorrow?"

* * *

Father Frank had invited any teenagers who wanted to play a little basketball to join him on the Prince of Peace basketball court. It was only a basketball hoop with the circle and a free throw line painted on one side of the parking lot. But it worked. The high school team could only handle ten boys. A lot of other teens liked to play. So, Father Frank had organized some half court games to let them play and perhaps keep them from any less-savory activities.

He had played basketball two years in college. He believed he was a good coach and helped the boys improve their shooting and defense strategies. One of the boys from the summer league Father Frank had organized was now a starter for the high school varsity. More importantly, he believed he gave them a love of the game, perhaps even helped their outlook on life.

Besides, it gave him a good excuse to get out on the court, shoot baskets, and keep from getting too sedentary. Today was a perfect day for it. Perfect temperature, bright, blue sky with an occasional wispy cloud, and not enough wind to deflect a perfect shot from swishing through the net. Eight boys had showed up today. Last week, two girls had joined. But they didn't show up today. Father Frank hoped they felt welcome and the boys hadn't scared them off.

"Don't keep your elbows tucked into your side. Spread them out." He demonstrated how to do it.

"I thought we should keep them close. Give us more control," said a small, towheaded kid.

"That's true when you are small and don't have much arm strength. But now, with your elbows out, you are protecting the ball. It's much harder for someone to reach around and slap the ball away without fouling you. And you have more flexibility over what you can do with the ball quickly. Try it for awhile and see how it works for you."

The boys played a little half-court for another forty minutes until Father Frank said, "That's it for me today. You guys keep playing if you want. Just put the ball over in the locker when you finish."

With that, the priest turned and walked into the rectory. He needed to go over some accounts one last time before the financial committee meeting in a few hours.

Chapter 23

"TELL ME HOW the financial committee meeting went," asked Maggie. "But first, say a quick prayer over dinner. It's an experiment."

"Uh-oh. What are we having?"

"Talerine." It sounded like "TAL-er-ray-nee."

"Never heard of it."

"I remember our grandmother talking about it. I thought I'd just give it a try."

"What's in it? Or dare I ask?"

"You might be better off not knowing. Basically, whatever I could find. But the basics are ground beef, egg noodles, tomatoes, cheese, mushrooms. Stuff. Give it a try. Grandmother liked it." She looked at her brother with a slight grin. "Of course, she's dead now."

Father Frank laughed, said a brief prayer thanking God for all He provided, and then preempted the discussion. "Have you talked with Jeff today?"

"Yeah. He mostly just wanted to know how the baby was doing. I said, 'Hey. How about the mother?' He apologized and said he was sure I was in very good hands with you. He hasn't found out anything on that Sean guy yet. Now, the committee meeting yesterday."

"It all went very smoothly. No complaints on my shabby books. But they did want to know what was happening with the trust the church received from Syd Cranzler. We've received several suggestions from parishioners. Truth is, things have been so busy around here lately, Norm and I haven't had a chance to review them." He scooped out a large slice of the steaming dish Maggie had prepared. "Tell me again, what are we eating?"

"Just eat some of it and see how you like it."

For several minutes they both concentrated on eating Maggie's dish.

"Actually, this is very good," Father Frank said.

Maggie jerked her head up, her fork suspended halfway between her plate and her mouth. She puffed up and said, "What's that 'actually' bit? It's like you didn't expect my cooking to be any good." Maggie faked a hurt look, her lower lip quivering a little.

"No, no. I think you are a great cook, but you did say this was an experiment. And you said I needed to pray over it."

"I'm just yanking your chain, little brother. That's what big sisters do."

"Thanks, big sister. What have you found out about the woman who heard Granet talking to Val?"

"Amazingly enough, I have made a little progress. I have a lead on a person who may know who heard it. But I haven't managed to make contact with her yet. I'll keep trying this evening."

"Try to move it along. Lieutenant Richards will be here tomorrow after Mass. He's really pushing for more information. And I think he'll follow through if we can give him a place to start. From what he's said, the Sheriff isn't looking at all. He's got his candidate. So the Ranger is our best hope of finding the right person."

"And you're going to help him?"

"I am. The sheriff doesn't want me to do any investigating. So I'll give Richards leads and let him do the leg work. I think this Ranger is good. And I'm hoping fair."

"Let's hope so. Bark-Bark would like nothing better than to lock me up."

"Richards gives me the impression he doesn't think you're the murderer. I mean, he hasn't said anything like that. But I sense that's the way he's leaning."

"But I'm still under house arrest."

"Good. Gives you more time to get on the phone and find that person."

"And what are you going to be doing?"

"Right now, I'm going to work on my Sunday homily. I still have a day job, you know."

"Okay. I'll give you an hour, and I'll make my calls. Then we'll have dessert."

Father Frank and Maggie had finished some pumpkin pecan squares and were talking in the living room.

"So you've made some progress on finding the woman —
"

"Who heard Granet call Val a fat pig. I finally got a woman who heard her say that. I got her name and number. I haven't talked to her yet. Must be her house phone. So far, she hasn't answered. I'll keep on it."

"Good work. I think Richards will follow through on any leads we give him. That gives him more suspects."

"I'm for that. This is one mystery I do not want to have the starring role in."

"Keep calling her. I don't want to give Richards a name and then that person denies having said anything about Granet and Val."

"Gotcha. I'll keep at it."

"Now, I don't want you to jump down my throat. But I'm going to make a suggestion you may not like."

"Won't be your first."

"Thanks. You said you bought a copy of Rod's book."

"Yep."

"And you read it enough to know the scenes and chapters were the same as yours."

"Right again."

"I think you need to take a few scenes, maybe more than a few, and read them carefully. Yes, they cover the same stuff your corresponding scene did. But, did he rewrite it and make it better?" Maggie started to object, but Father Frank held up his hand. "Now, don't get all out of whack. It has made the bestseller list. Can you learn anything from it? Did he add any value to what you had written? Did he say it better? Were his descriptions better? If you find it is exactly or very close to your wording, that should give your ego a boost. Your wording, your sentences are bestseller quality."

"My plot," Maggie interjected. "You do know he won the Austin Benedict Award. Very prestigious. But do you know what that award means? What they base it on?"

"No idea."

"It's for the best plot of the year. For *my* plot."

"Congratulations. But my advice still stands. See if you find he changed anything in the plot, enhanced some of it, and if so, how did he do it? A different twist? Was his dialog sharper, more descriptive of the character, truer to life than yours? And is it really better, or just different? "

He looked at his sister. She seemed to be considering what he said. "Either way, you learn something. And you've got nothing to lose."

Maggie pursed her lips, then let a tiny grin creep across her mouth. "Sometimes you really do make sense. Hard to believe little brother Frankie can open my eyes to opportunities." She reached over and patted his arm. "I'll do that tomorrow. Tonight, I'm still trying to track down the elusive listener of Rod's rude remarks." She snapped her fingers. "I like that. Rod's Rude Remarks. It goes in my next book."

* * *

An hour later, Father Frank was satisfied with his homily for tomorrow. He was just shutting down his computer when Maggie knocked on his office door.

"Okay, little brother. Here it is. I've even written down her name and phone number so you won't forget, or get it wrong. Eleanor Jones."

"Fantastic. I'll give it to Richards tomorrow. Let him do the leg work."

"Sounds like exercise. I just let my fingers do the walking."

"Good. You'll be well rested. Tomorrow, see what you can find on the man who said Granet stole his title."

Maggie snapped a salute. "Yes, sir. I'll take care of it."

Chapter 24

WHEN FATHER FRANK came out of the church Sunday morning, Richards was sitting on the bench under the southern pine waiting for him. But the priest had to visit with parishioners. They came first. Ten minutes later, he strolled over to the bench.

"I notice the service was a bit more well-attended today over yesterday," the ranger commented.

"Well, it's Sunday. That tends to bring in more people. But I'm here every day no matter what, for whomever can make it, three hundred sixty-five days a year, rain or shine."

"Good to know there is something you can count on. Did you find out anything that might help our investigation?"

"Maybe." Father Frank reached in his pocket, pulled out a piece of paper, then sat down beside Richards. "First of all, this is all hearsay. As they say, not admissible in court."

"Noted. We'll check it out and see what will be admissible. Go ahead."

Father Frank told him the rumors about the Granet and Monroe affair three years ago. "Monroe was in charge of selecting and securing the faculty for this year's conference. Some think she invited Granet back to rekindle that affair. The conference had never had a repeat speaker before. Of course, he was more successful now, so it made some sense. At any rate, the story is she went to his cabin and got rebuffed. The woman whose name I'm about to give you, was walking near his cabin Thursday night and heard them talking. She says she heard Rod tell Monroe he wasn't interested in a fat pig."

Richards nodded slightly. "That would hurt."

"Or make one very angry." Father Frank handed Richards the paper with the woman's name and telephone number.

The Ranger looked at it. "Eleanor Jones. Sounds pretty serious to me. Does she go by Ellie?"

"Beats me. I just got the name. Why do you ask?"

"If she insists on Eleanor, she's probably a no-nonsense person, not prone to embellish the story."

"Interesting. I don't know. I'm just giving you a name. I don't know what she likes to be called. This may or may not lead to a suspect."

The Ranger looked down, furrowed his brows and frowned for several seconds. "But I don't think Monroe had opportunity. She wasn't staying at the retreat at night."

Now it was Father Frank's turn to frown. "No. Actually, she was."

Richards cocked his head and looked at the priest. "How do you know?"

"Well, I guess I don't know for sure, but Maggie indicated to me that she was."

"Interesting."

"What?"

Richards took a deep breath and let it out. "The Sheriff asked May Ellison for a list of all those staying at the Center Thursday night. Ellison had Monroe compile the list and Monroe gave the list to Bark." He shook his head once. "Monroe's name wasn't on the list."

"So you didn't question her?"

"Didn't think there was a need."

"I believe Maggie's information is correct. But I'm sure you can find out for certain."

Richards got up. "We'll check it out." He started to leave, then turned back. "Just curious. Have you talked with Ms. Monroe?"

"I have."

"And?"

Father Frank rubbed his chin. "I don't want to prejudice your visit to her."

"You won't. But I believe you are a good judge of character. And I strongly believe — rather — I *know* people will tell you things, or say things to you, that they won't to me."

Father Frank opened his mouth and ran his tongue over his upper lip. "Let's just say, I gave her the opportunity ... and she was not very complimentary."

Richards nodded. "We'll talk --" He glanced at the paper. "Eleanor Jones first. And then we'll talk with Monroe."

"One other thing," Father Frank added. "It might not mean anything, but Monroe only lives about ten minutes from the conference center. But, she was staying in the retreat residence rooms the night of the murder."

Richards smiled a little. "I really wouldn't mind having you on my team." He stuck the piece of paper in his coat pocket, turned and headed for his Tahoe.

* * *

Father Frank finally made it back to the rectory to find Georgia and Maggie visiting in the kitchen. Father Frank wasted no time in pouring himself some coffee and then sank down on a kitchen chair.

"You look beat," said Maggie. "You're only thirty-three. Are you getting old before your time?"

"I find having a Sunday Mass with a sermon and then visiting with the parishioners afterward as tiring as a basketball game."

Georgia had no sympathy. "Maybe if you gave a shorter sermon, you wouldn't be so tired, and the congregation wouldn't be either."

"Thanks, Georgia. I needed that."

Both Georgia and Maggie laughed. "Just teasing, Father," said Georgia. "Actually, I loved your sermon today. Make the most of the talent the Lord gives us."

"I did too, little brother. God gives each of us a talent. And it's up to us to develop it, let it blossom." She shrugged. "I'm still looking for mine. But when I find it, I'll try to make the most of it."

Father Frank sat his cup down and looked at his sister. "What are you talking about? You have several talents. And one is writing. From what you are claiming, you've written a bestselling mystery."

"Fat lot of good it's doing me."

"What, just because it didn't make you rich and famous, it doesn't count? You got a raw deal. I'm not arguing that. But that's no reason to down play your talent. Remember how I ended the sermon. 'For unto whomsoever much is given, much is required'. Luke 12:48."

Georgia nodded. "Much as I hate to feed your brother's ego, Maggie, I've got to agree. You've got the talent. I had a young girl, maybe four or five years ago, in my English class. Boy, could she write. The year she graduated, she won that writing contest the Piney Woods Writers hold each year. Got some kind of a plaque or something, but a nice size check. She was *good*. But, I haven't heard a thing about her writing since."

Maggie's expression showed surprise. "I bet I've met her. She was at the PWWC three years ago. She got the award." She lowered her head and closed her eyes for some seconds. "Grace. I think that was her name. Grace something. Absolutely stunning beauty. Athletic. I think she had a scholarship in swimming. T.C.U., maybe. But her writing was what got my attention." Maggie laughed. "At first I was piqued. I'd entered the contest and this ... *kid* beat me out. They had copies of the winning entry available. So I got a copy. It was outstanding."

"I never heard of her," said Father Frank.

"That was three years ago - just before you got here," said Georgia. "In fact, she and her dad used to come to Prince of Peace. At least they did when she was in my class. Now that I think of it, I haven't seen them in several years." She snapped her fingers. "Sullivan. Grace Sullivan. Dad's name was Bud Sullivan. Kind of rough. Her writing talent must have come from her mother."

"But you don't know what became of her, or them?" the priest asked.

"No. Lived across the lake, if I remember correctly."

Maggie thought about Grace. She couldn't have been over eighteen at the time. But the way she put words together was amazing. She made the reader experience the emotions. When Maggie had read the winning piece, it brought tears to her eyes, and joy to her heart. There was talent. Where is she now, and is she still writing?

Chapter 25

MONDAY MORNING AFTER Mass, Father Frank came out of the church and looked over at the bench under the pine tree. He laughed a little, a bit surprised to find himself disappointed not to see Ranger Richards sitting there.

A light drizzle had begun to increase, showing signs a full-fledged rain was in the offing. They needed it. Contrary to the belief of many non-Texans, this part of Texas was not dry and dusty. Pine Tree received a sizable amount of annual rainfall. But right now, the area struggled in a drought. Rain would be welcome.

Maggie fixed breakfast for them: eggs and toast for herself and a waffle with sliced bananas for her brother. As Maggie took a sip of the French roast coffee she'd made for both of them she remarked, "I wonder whatever happened to Grace Sullivan. I'd forgotten all about her until Georgia mentioned her yesterday. Do you think she moved away? She really had a gift with words. I might have expected to see her back at the conference."

"Their names are still on the church rolls. No note that they moved, or anything. But the last mention of them, their monthly donation to Prince of Peace, happened just before I arrived here. I'm sure I never met them. Although, in that first month I shook so many hands I just might have forgotten."

"You'd have remembered Grace. She was a knock out."

"I'm a priest. I don't register women by their looks."

"You're a man. You'd have noticed her. I guarantee it. Anyway, you ought to check. See if she's still writing. That talent shouldn't go to waste."

"Check what?"

"I don't know. Are they still there? Is she going to college?"

"Actually, I tried to call them. The number in the church records is disconnected, and information couldn't provide a number for them."

"Was there an address?"

"The one in the church records is, like Georgia said, across Lakota Lake. But who knows if they're still there or not?"

"Well, the next time you're over there, I think you should check out the address. See if they still live there. What happened that they stopped coming to Prince of Peace? Maybe they didn't like the last priest. They'd love you, I'm sure."

"You're prejudiced."

"Yeah. Maybe." Maggie got up and started stacking the breakfast dishes. "Mostly, I want to know if Grace is still writing. Now there was a person with talent."

"As luck would have it, I'm going over in that direction today. If I have a few minutes to spare, I'll drive down Lakeside Lane. See if their name is still on the mailbox."

"A lot of people don't put their names on the mailbox."

"Then I'll keep driving. I'm not going to knock on the door unless I know who they are."

"Coward."

"No. I just have a plan B." Father Frank grabbed his cup off of Maggie's stack of dishes, and poured himself another cup of coffee. "One of my parishioners happens to be a mailman. And I think he delivers mail in that area. I'll ask him."

Maggie shook her finger at her brother."That's cheating."

"That's using the resources you have."

Chapter 26

FATHER FRANK HAD visited an elderly man whose health was failing. He had made it to eighty without experiencing any health issues. So now, he didn't know how to deal with an extended illness that had kept him bedridden for the last month.

The priest had suggested he spend more time thinking about all the good times in his life and thinking about this illness only when necessary to follow the doctor's orders to take some medicine. Father Frank had asked the man to describe some of the special times in his life. When the man got into the stories, his face brightened and his voice got stronger. Several of the stories led to smiles, and even a few laughs.

When Father Frank stood ready to leave, the man invited him to visit again. This had been the highlight of his month. The priest agreed to come back next week, and reminded the man this was an excellent time to thank God for all the great things God had given him.

Father Frank made a brief stop at a nearby 7-11 for a Dr Pepper. The drizzle had stopped and the sun was valiantly trying to break through the lingering clouds. He pulled out his cell phone. Maggie had shown him how to get a map of the area and he quickly saw that the Lakeside Lane address where the Sullivans lived was only a few blocks away — if they hadn't moved.

Five minutes later, he parked at the curb opposite a mail box with the name Bud Sullivan neatly stenciled on the side. *What do I say? Why haven't I seen you at Prince of Peace? And he'll say, "Who are you?" Not my favorite part of the job.*

Swallowing his reluctance, he followed a flagstone walk, bordered by an array of fall flowers, up to a neat brick house. The doorbell set off a Westminster Chime inside the house, but he didn't hear anyone coming to the door. After a minute or so, he pressed the button again. After two minutes, he shrugged, turned and headed back down the walk.

While the house was unremarkable, the view was outstanding. Across the road was perhaps twenty-five feet of grass and then the lake. There were a few boat ties, but otherwise, the houses on this block had an uninterrupted view of the blue waters of Lakota Lake. Directly across the lake, he could see the Lakota Retreat Center, where he could pick out the small cabins the faculty used during the conference. He wondered which had been Granet's

Halfway to the car, he heard the door of the house open. He turned and looked back at the house. Standing in the half-open door was a young woman. She stood hunched over, head down, but watching with upturned eyes. He started up the walk slowly, watching to see her reaction. She took a step back and for a moment, Father Frank thought she was going to close the door. She didn't retreat any further, nor did she raise her head any. He was glad he had worn his Roman collar. Perhaps it would help ease whatever was worrying her.

"Hello. I'm Father Frank from Prince of Peace Church over in Pine Tree."

She nodded once, but said nothing.

"Is this the Sullivan house? Are you Grace?"

Again, a single nod.

"I understand you and your father used to come to Prince of Peace. I believe I started at the church just after you stopped coming, so I have to apologize that I haven't been by earlier. But I wanted you to know that we'd love to have you back. You're always welcome."

For a minute, Father Frank thought she would not utter a word. This time, there wasn't even a nod. But then, in a slow, almost childlike voice, she said, "I don't go anywhere."

The priest was struck by the contradiction. She was a beautiful young woman. More than one person had told him she was a gifted writer. But all Father Frank saw was someone who looked unhappy and scared.

"Do you still write?"

Her head jerked up, almost as if she'd been slapped. Then, she bowed her head again and said nothing.

"Perhaps this is not a good day for me to visit. Maybe I could stop in tomorrow instead—maybe about two o'clock? "

She backed up another step, nodded twice. Then she closed the door.

* * *

In his car, Father Frank sat for a moment before starting the engine. The encounter had been brief, yet he felt exhausted. Grace seemed almost in a trance. Fearful? Perhaps on drugs. *And yet, she did say yes, or at least agreed, when I asked if I could come visit her again.* He turned the key and started the engine.

He started the car, drove one block and turned left to cross the half-mile long bridge that stretched across Lakota lake.

* * *

Maggie was waiting at the door when Father Frank arrived. "Did you find them?".

"Yes. I found their house and when I knocked on the door, Grace answered." He paused. "Well, that's not quite right. She opened the door, but she didn't say anything. I introduced myself, asked a couple of questions. All I got was an occasional nod. In fact, the only thing she said while I was there was she didn't go anywhere. Literally, four words. 'I don't go anywhere.' Strange."

"That is strange. Was she sick? Maybe on medication of some kind?"

"I wondered that, too. Certainly a possibility. I'm not a good judge on that. But there was something. I can't put my finger on it. I'm planning to go back tomorrow, and see how she is then."

"Good." Maggie paused only a second. "Now I have news for you. I found the name of the man who said Granet stole his title. Of course, I don't think you can really steal a title. But Kace Ruffer thinks you can and Granet did."

"Kace Ruffer? That's really his name? Or a pen name?"

"That's really his name. He was in the residences at the conference, so he had opportunity."

"And stealing a title could be motive enough? What was the title?"

Maggie shrugged. " *A Garden Variety Murder.* I didn't think the title was *that* good. I like it, but I wouldn't kill somebody for it."

Father Frank laughed. "I'm glad to hear that."

"I looked up Ruffer to see if he had published anything. Surprisingly, there were a number of authors named Ruffer." She held up her finger. "But no Kace Ruffer."

"Maybe he just needs a good title."

Chapter 27

"THIS IS ALMOST becoming a habit." Father Frank was addressing the Texas Ranger sitting on a bench outside the Prince of Peace church. The temperature was a pleasant 68 degrees, just about right for an early November day in Texas. Overhead, a few fluffy white clouds emphasized the deep cobalt sky.

"It is. But, we still haven't wrapped up this case. I just wanted to make sure I wasn't missing anything."

"Like what?"

"We've talked with Billy John and Holly. And we still have his bike."

Father Frank couldn't suppress a grin. "Is it talking?"

"Don't be too smug. This is completely off the record. Translated, you are not to tell anybody, not even your sister. If you do, I'll find out and I will not be happy."

"Okay. I don't pass it on — not even to Maggie."

"I don't usually tell anybody outside other lawmen anything about a case. But I trust you. I respect your opinion, and I believe you respect a confidence."

"I'm listening."

"We found blood on the bike handles. Which is not all that unusual on a dirt bike. What is unusual is, it's Granet's blood."

Father Frank could tell Richards was watching him closely. "I'm not surprised."

"Why not?"

"Since you're questioning both of them, I think I can tell you. I'm sure you've gotten this out of them. There's been no mention of injuries to Granet, except his throat. But as I'm sure Holly has told you, she believed Billy John smacked Granet in the face. She said he probably broke Granet's nose."

"That did happen. They both confirmed it. Granet had a broken nose and consequently a lot of blood on his face. So, did the blood samples on the bike come from Granet's nose? Or from his throat? Tough to tell."

"So what do you want from me?"

Richards hesitated for a moment, then said, "You seem to have a good feel for people, and when they are telling the truth, or not. Could Holly be leading us astray?"

Father Frank looked away, studied the parking lot, the blue sky and shinning clouds. Then he focused on his shoes before looking at Richards. "Billy John is her fiancé. She would want to protect him. But my honest feeling is, she's telling the truth. And I believe if she tried to lie to you, you would know immediately. She's not a devious person, in my opinion."

"Thank you. I appreciate your comments. And I agree with them. But Mr. Bartok is not as ... forthcoming, not as open, and not afraid to bend the truth. Except for one fact, I'd have him arrested right now."

"And what is that?"

Richards smiled. "Sorry. I can't tell you that." He stood, ready to go. "Thanks, Father. I enjoy these conversations." He turned and started to leave.

"Wait. There's one other thing I wanted to run by you. Have you heard about the man who claimed Granet stole his title?"

"I have, but have been unable to find anything but that rumor. Do you know more about it?"

"Only the name of the man."

"That's a great start."

"Maggie has been on the phone constantly, trying to track it down." The priest gave a small laugh. "She's highly motivated to find other suspects. His name is Kace Ruffer."

Richards frowned. "Are you pulling my leg? Kace Ruffer?"

"That's his name. A number of people heard him complaining about Granet stealing his title. I know it's not like Maggie saying Granet stole her *book*. But some thought Ruffer was pretty angry."

"Thank you. And we will follow it up." He sighed. "I've seen people get killed over a parking space. So this doesn't seem any more stupid."

Chapter 28

AFTER LUNCH, FATHER Frank drove over to Lakeside Lane to visit Grace. Perhaps she would be in a better talking mood today. Grace answered the door, after first looking out the side glass to see who was there.

"Hello, Grace. Is your father here? I'd like to talk with him."

Just as yesterday, she was hunched over, never making eye contact with the priest. Ever so slightly, she shook her head.

Father Frank asked a few more questions. Did she know when her father would be back? Where did he work? For each, a shake of her head indicated she did not know. Was she going to school now? Another head shake. Was she doing any writing?

This time, she raised her head a little. "I'm trying to start."

Just hearing her actually answer a question with a sentence made Father Frank happy. "That's great. I have been told you are a talented writer."

He could almost believe she smiled, ever so slightly. "I hope you will continue to write. My sister thinks you are very good with words."

But this time, her head stayed down and she did not even nod.

Father Frank told her he would come again and he would try to contact her father and visit with him a little. When she made no evidence she even heard, he said goodbye and started back to his car. But after two steps, he stopped. He reached into his pocket and pulled out one of his cards. Grace was still in the doorway. He stepped back and put his card out. "Here is my telephone number. If you ever want to talk, at any time, please call me and I will come as quickly as possible." For a few moments she just stared at the card. Then, slowly, she reached out and took the card. She closed her hand over it, but did not look up at the priest, nor utter a sound. He took a deep breath. "Anytime. Just call." When she gave no sign of even hearing him, he turned and walked to his car. As he opened the car door, he looked back at the house. The door was closed.

As he got in the car, a dark brown car slowed as it passed him. Father Frank could see the driver looking at him, almost studying him. Then the car sped up, turned at the corner and disappeared from Father Frank's view. *Strange. I don't think I know him. Maybe he thought he knew me, then decided he didn't.*

He glanced at the houses in this block. He hadn't paid attention before, but now he noticed none had a driveway and no garages were visible. He decided they must have access from the back, through an alley. The garages had to be situated on the back of the houses.

Father Frank considered visiting another parishioner on this side of the lake. He pulled out his phone and punched in the number. He didn't want to show up without making an appointment. After ten rings, he decided they were out. For a few minutes, he studied his calendar. Nothing pressing today. He returned the phone to the clip on his belt. He started the car, buckled his seatbelt, checked the street behind him and slowly drove toward the end of the block. A left turn put him on the half-mile long bridge that crossed Lakota Lake. With no appointments demanding his attention, he poked along, admiring the gorgeous day.

He was looking out over the beautiful blue lake, when the driver's side window exploded in his ear, sending glass flying through the car.

Chapter 29

INSTINCT AND SHOCK caused Father Frank to duck and turn away from the shattered glass. *What on earth happened?* When he looked ahead, he was racing for the opposite side of the bridge, toward a low railing that would not keep him from plunging into the lake.

He jerked the steering wheel just as his front fender hit the railing. But the tires grabbed the pavement and he didn't go over the edge of the bridge. He released the breath he was holding. Suddenly a loud air horn yanked his attention ahead. A gigantic eighteen wheeler was racing directly at him.

He wrenched the wheel to the right. He could see the semi-trailer trying to slow down, but it was too close. He smashed down on the gas. The tires screeched and the Ford jerked forward, barely clearing the lane as the big rig barreled past, less than a foot from the left rear fender of the Taurus. The wash of air from the truck pulled the Ford in to a fishtail. But as he had cut the wheel sharply to the right, now he struggled to keep from plunging over the right side of the bridge. He pulled the wheel to the left and smashed his foot hard on the brake. With tires screaming, he came to a stop, the car rocking slightly on its springs, the right front fender scraping up and down on the concrete barrier some fifteen feet above the water.

Even as he tried to get his breathing under control, he uttered a brief prayer. *Thank you Lord for saving me.* He glanced in the mirror. The tractor-trailer was just turning off the bridge. *And thank you Lord that I did not cause that truck to have an accident.*

He was amazed that with all the glass crashing into him, he was not cut. He inspected some of the pieces on his shirt and pants. They were small pieces, and smooth. Lucky. He started to get out and see what damage his car had sustained. But as he opened the door, a horn blared and a car raced past him, the driver yelling something at him.

Good grief. Pay attention. You're on a two lane bridge, blocking one lane, and almost stepped out in front of a car. He settled back in his seat and took several deep breaths. As his heart rate slowed and his breathing returned to normal, he turned the key. The engine started and he decided checking the damage had best be done off the bridge in a safe location. He looked behind him before starting to straighten the car. What he saw were flashing red and blue lights.

A minute later, Sheriff Bark stood staring in at the priest. "Would you turn off the engine and step out of the car." It was not a question.

"Should I try to get off the bridge first?" Father Frank asked.

"Just turn off the motor and step out of the car."

Father Frank switched off the engine and got out of the car. "Something happened and—"

"Have you been drinking?"

"No. The window—"

"Will you take a breathalyzer test?"

Father Frank's head jerked a little and he blinked as his brain tried to process what he had just been asked. "Why would you want a breathalyzer test?"

The Sheriff smiled just a little. "What a funny question. To see if you've been drinking. Are you willing to take the test?"

The priest shook his head. What was going on? And then he remembered. He had, as usual, taken a small amount of wine at the morning Mass. Probably two ounces. Would that show up on the test? And if it did, what happened next?

Bark shifted his weight from one foot to the other. "We can do that here, or we can take you into the county office and administer it there."

Father Frank shook his head as if to clear his mind. "Okay. Let's do it here."

The Sheriff turned and yelled at his deputy. "Bring the drunk kit."

"I'm not drunk," said Father Frank testily.

"So you say. Let's see what the machine says."

The deputy brought the small hand-held machine, which looked like a small hair dryer, and handed it to the Sheriff. "You put a new mouthpiece on it?" The deputy nodded. Bark turned it on, watched a small LED on the device for several seconds, then held it out toward Father Frank. "Take a deep breath and blow into this tube for at least six seconds. A steady blow. You can stop if the beeper stops."

Father Frank placed his mouth over the plastic tube and blew.

As soon as the beeping sound stopped, the Sheriff held out his hand to take the device. then he watched a small display. After a few seconds, Bark cursed under his breath, tapped a button and waited.

"How'd I do?" asked Father Frank.

"Didn't get a good reading. We'll do it again." After about a minute, he held the device to the priest again. "Blow more and longer."

Father Frank complied and when the noise stopped, handed the device to the Sheriff. After a minute, Bark turned to the deputy and handed him the machine. When he faced the priest, he said, "Driver's license, registration and insurance papers." The priest got into the car, opened the glove box and retrieved insurance and registration papers. He pulled his wallet out of his pocket, retrieved his license and handed the papers to the Sheriff.

After studying them, the Sheriff began writing out a ticket.

"What's the ticket for?"

"Reckless driving, failure to maintain a lane, crossing into the opposite lane, weaving." He handed the ticket over and asked for Father Frank's signature.

"Something shattered my window. And in fact, you can see something also put a hole in the windshield. I was not driving recklessly."

"Just sign the ticket. You can take it up with the judge."

Father Frank signed the ticket and handed it back to the officer, who tore off a copy and handed it back to the priest.

"Aren't you even going to inspect the window and windshield? See if you can tell what caused it?"

A smug grin appeared on the officer's face. "I imagine banging into the concrete side of the bridge could do it. Not many drivers can manage to hit both sides." He turned and walked towards his cruiser. Over his shoulder he said, "And we'll be watching. Do not drive recklessly, or violate any laws or we'll take you into the office right now."

Father Frank replaced his paperwork in the glove box and inserted his license into his wallet. After fastening his seatbelt, he started the engine, clicked his turn indicator and slowly straightened into the lane and proceeded across the bridge. Once off the bridge, he pulled to the side of the road, ready to check out his car.

The Sheriff pulled up beside him. "Can't park there. Move it on before I give you another ticket."

Slowly, Father Frank moved back into the driving lane and drove slowly, to a 7-11 convenience store. He needed a Dr Pepper anyway. The whole experience of the shattered window, the near plunge off the bridge, the eighteen-wheeler nearly crushing his car, and his near crash into the other side of the bridge had made him a little shaky. Then the police arrived. Father Frank had noted the Sheriff's cruiser did not have "To Help and Protect" painted on the side as the police cars in Pine Tree did. But then, the Sheriff was neither helping nor protecting him.

"Wow," the boy in the 7-11 said, looking out at Father Frank's Ford. "Don't see a lot of cars with both front fenders smashed. But, hey, the center of the grill looks good."

"And it seems to drive okay," Father Frank said as he paid for his soda. He got back into his car and called his insurance agent. At least he was helpful, giving Father Frank clear instructions on what to do.

He took his time finishing his Dr Pepper, keeping an eye on the sheriff's car in the mirror. After Bark had finally given up and turned off, Father Frank headed back to Pine Tree.

Chapter 30

"LONG TIME, NO see."

Dick Richards sat relaxed on the bench, a smile on his face. "I've been pretty busy lately."

"I hope that means you are making some headway on the Granet case."

"That might be too optimistic a term. But we are working on it. I've located Ruffer in Fort Worth and sent a man over to interview him. More forensic data coming in. Progress."

Father Frank sat down on the bench and studied the white Stetson sitting on the bench beside Richards. "You know, I don't wear hats. But if I did, I'd want to have one like yours."

"If you join the Rangers, you'll have to get one."

"Oh?"

"Absolutely. Western hat, western boots, western belt - all part of the Ranger dress code."

"A white Stetson? I'm having trouble seeing myself in a white hat. Priests usually wear black robes, and hats."

"Doesn't have to be white. Some rangers wear brown or beige, or even black. But I grew up thinking the good guys wore white hats. So I chose white."

"Good looking boots, too. But, no spurs."

"Only if we're riding horses. I do have spurs. Beautiful, sterling silver. My wife gave them to me."

Father Frank laughed. "String tie, too?"

"You must wear a tie, but the style is up to you." He paused for a moment, then asked, "Got any new information for me today?"

The priest laughed again. "No. 'Fraid not."

Richards stood. "Well, then I guess I'll go work on what you've already given me. By the way, did you get a raise?"

Father Frank frowned. "Raise? Not that I know about. What makes you ask?"

Richards tilted his head toward the rectory. "Looks like you're driving a new car."

"Oh. It's a rental. I banged up my Ford yesterday." He glanced at the car. "Actually, would you mind taking a look at something? Something happened as I was driving across Lakota Lake yesterday. The driver's side window suddenly shattered. And then there was a hole in the windshield. Caused me to run into the side of the bridge. I need your opinion on what happened."

* * *

Eight minutes later, Richards was inspecting the windshield of the Ford Taurus, with Father Frank watching him. "I'd say that's a bullet hole," Richards concluded a few minutes later. The bullet went through the side window, shattering it, then passed through the windshield. Windshield glass is different - laminated. Has a thin layer of vinyl in the middle, so it didn't shatter. But that hole makes me believe your car was hit by an AK-47 bullet, or maybe an AR-15."

"You mean, some random shot hit my car? But I was on a bridge. No one was near me, unless they were in a boat."

"An AR-15 or an AK-47 could do this damage from half a mile away. Someone on shore could have made the shot."

Father Frank just shook his head. "Wow. From half a mile?"

"Where were you on the bridge?"

"Not too far. Maybe a third of the way across."

"So, someone on shore might not have been 400 yards from your car."

"But through the window *and* the windshield?"

"It's completely possible," Richards confirmed. "Just depends on how much powder was in the bullet. And if it had a Teflon coating, it would go right through. But, you do understand, if it went through the windshield, it could go through your skull."

For a few seconds, the priest just stared at the Ranger. "Are you suggesting what I think you are?"

Richards raised his eyebrows. "Have you made anybody mad lately?"

Father Frank raised his shoulders. "Don't think so." Then he chuckled. "Maybe Sheriff Bark."

Now the Ranger laughed. "Well, I don't think the Sheriff shot at you. But you do seem to rub him the wrong way."

"He might be watching me. He got to my crash pretty quickly."

"I happened to be there when the call came in. A truck driver said there was some crazy driver on the Lakota bridge. Said he nearly hit him. I didn't realize that 'him' was 'you'."

"He missed me by a few inches. A big eighteen wheeler. I was so unnerved by it I hit the other side of the bridge. So, when Sheriff Bark got there, he insisted I take a breathalyzer test."

"Just hassling you. If you'd refused, he could have taken you into the office and administered one. He's getting pretty antsy over this murder case since it's been nearly two weeks and no viable suspect. He's just trying to annoy you."

"He was too late. The bullet put me way beyond annoyed. And the eighteen wheeler."

"I've got to move on. Watch your step. Don't rule out that it was aimed at you."

Father Frank shook his head as Richards left. No. It was a random shot. Dangerous but not deliberate. *Not aimed at me.*

Chapter 31

THURSDAY MORNING, FATHER Frank left the church after morning Mass and saw a Sheriff's car in front of the rectory. By the time he crossed the parking lot, a deputy was escorting a handcuffed Maggie out to his car.

He ran and intercepted them at the deputy's cruiser. "What's going on?"

"Sheriff Bark is arresting Ms. DeLuca." The deputy opened the cruiser's back door and began to push Maggie in."

"Frank, do something," she yelled.

"I'll call Norm. We'll be over there as soon as possible." He turned and headed for the rectory.

"Don't take very long," Maggie called after him. "Who knows what old Bark-Bark will do to me this time."

* * *

Forty-five minutes later, Father Frank and Norm Winters arrived at the Timber County Sheriff's office. Norm demanded to see the Sheriff immediately and he and Father Frank were quickly ushered into Bark's office.

"What going on, Sheriff?"

"I'm re-interviewing Ms. DeLuca." The Sheriff continued shuffling papers on his desk, not looking up.

"You don't seem to be interviewing her. Where is she?" By now, Norm had his hands on the sheriff's desk.

"Step back, Mr. Winters. She's in lock up until I get time to interview her."

"And when might that be?"

"Depends on how much paperwork I have and how many people come in to hassle me."

"Then I want her released now. I'll take responsibility for her and return her when you are able to interview her."

"Nope. I don't know when that will be and I need her close at hand when I get some time."

"The Judge released her on her own recognizance. He did not say she should sit in jail while you shuffled papers." Norm threw up his hands. "Never mind. I'll go talk to the judge myself." He turned and started to leave.

"Now just hold on, Winters. Don't get your drawers in a twist. Just for you, and the Reverend there, I'll get her now."

* * *

Five minutes later, Norm, Father Frank, Maggie, Sam Bark and Deputy Manford crowded into a small concrete block room with two chairs and a small table. Only the Sheriff and Maggie were seated.

The Sheriff placed a recorder in the middle of the table and recited into it the necessary details of the interview. "Now Ms. DeLuca, we've uncovered new evidence. Would you like to rethink your story? Maybe if you confess now, we can offer some leniency."

Maggie just looked at the man as if he might have grown horns. Norm took a step forward. "As Ms. DeLuca's attorney, I'd like to know what new evidence you have."

"I'm not required to tell you that at this time."

"Bark, don't play games with me. Either you tell me what it is, or Ms. DeLuca and I walk out of here." Norm's voice had risen a few decibels.

"No you won't."

"Is she under arrest? Are you prepared to indict her? Because I heard the Judge say she was ROR until the court called her in."

The Sheriff fixed his gaze on Maggie. "You said you were angry because Granet stole your book. Right?"

"Yes," said Maggie.

"But you didn't tell me how much money that book had already made or how much it might make."

Maggie glanced at Norm, who nodded for her to answer the question. She turned back to the Sheriff. "I have no way of knowing that information. That wasn't the point. He took my idea, my plot, and published it as his own."

"Oh, you're so rich that two hundred fifty thousand dollars right now and probably much more in the next year wouldn't make any difference to you?"

Maggie's head shot up. "Where'd you get that number?"

"Simple math, Ms. DeLuca. I checked. He's sold about ten thousand books. I priced one at the book store. Twenty-five dollars. You can multiply that out, can't you?" The Sheriff was sneering now. "That's quite a motive for murder, don't you think?"

Maggie almost laughed, but caught herself. "Bark, do you know anything about the publishing industry? Anything at all? If he sells that twenty-five dollar book, he gets about two dollars and fifty cents, not the twenty-five dollars. And most of his ten thousand books sold were digital books. On those, he probably made less than two dollars a book."

"What do you mean he only gets two-fifty. It's his book. Although I admit he won't get the whole twenty-five. The store gets some."

"Bark, —"

"It's Sheriff Bark, young lady." His glare might have melted ice off a glacier, but it didn't bother Maggie.

"Okay, Sheriff Bark. And it's Ms. DeLuca, not young lady. The store gets at least half. The publisher gets about forty percent. That leaves the author with ten percent. That's two dollars and fifty cents on the twenty-five dollar book."

Bark swallowed and tried to stretch up to look more imposing. "The digital books wouldn't need a book store taking half of it."

"No, that's right. And the author probably gets thirty-five percent on those. But the digital book sells for four dollars and ninety-nine cents. So, again, the author gets maybe a dollar seventy-five." She shook her head. "He's not getting rich."

After a few false starts, the Sheriff said, "That's still maybe twenty to twenty-five thousand. Plenty to cause a jealous person to resort to murder."

Norm stepped in closer. "Sheriff, that's enough. Your new evidence is worthless. Yes, people may kill someone for ten bucks. But this is not really any new evidence. Unless you have something else, let's quit this nonsense and all go home."

Bark drew his lips in a thin straight line. His eyes crowded together. "I'm going to check her numbers. If I find she's lying, I'll yank her butt back in for giving false testimony."

"We're not in a court, Sam. And she isn't under oath. She's outlining a few basics you obviously don't understand. But check away. You know where we are." Norm turned to Maggie. "Let's go."

Maggie looked at Norm, then back at the Sheriff. He didn't look at her, but waved her away with his hand.

Chapter 32

WHEN FATHER FRANK and Maggie arrived back at the rectory, they were both in a much better mood than when they left. At they opened the screen door, Maggie reached down and picked up an envelope that had been dropped off just inside the screen door. "Fan mail, Frank."

"Maybe someone really liked my sermon last Sunday."

"More likely they're asking you to make it shorter this week."

She handed the letter to the priest, who quickly ripped open the envelop. He pulled out a folded sheet and opened it. "Not about a sermon." He passed it over to his sister.

She stopped just inside the door and read it aloud. "Keep your nose out of the case or it might get smashed in dirt." She handed the note back to Father Frank. "Not too good grammatically. But, it does get the idea across. Think we ought to give this to Bark-Bark?"

Father Frank shook his head. "No. But probably should turn it over to someone. I'd pick Lieutenant Richards. He seems like a straight shooter."

"I agree. I just don't want to be in his sights."

The priest laughed. "He'll probably show up tomorrow after morning Mass."

"Don't wait. I'm getting tired of this house arrest bit. And so is Jeff. He'd like me home."

"You're going to tell him about today, right?" Father Frank looked at his sister for a moment. "You're not planning to, are you?"

"There's not much to tell. It will only upset him."

"If there's not much to it, it'll be easy to tell him. Otherwise when he hears about it - and he will - it'll be a problem for you. Secrets are not good in a marriage. Tell him. Once you explain that the Sheriff had no idea what he was talking about, Jeff won't get too upset."

"Yeah. Easy peasy for you."

"Have some faith, Maggie."

She pursed her lips. Finally, she said, "Okay. I'll call him. And you call the Ranger."

* * *

An hour later, Father Frank answered the door to find Dick Richards standing there. "You're fast. Come in, Come in." He opened the door and ushered the Ranger into the living room. "Here is the note I was telling you about." After a moment, he added, "Both Maggie and I handled it. I guess that will mess up any fingerprints."

The Ranger looked up. "No. That won't be a problem. But I doubt we'll find any other prints. Whoever did this cut words out of a newspaper. They were being careful. So I imagine they wiped it clean of their prints. You said you found it after visiting the Sheriff's office. So you're saying today, late morning or early afternoon, right?"

"Yes. I'd say about between 12:45 and 1:00."

The Ranger pulled a small plastic bag from his inside coat pocket and carefully placed the note in it, sealed it, and returned the bag to his pocket. "I'll have the tech guys look at it. Sometimes they find prints even when people think they've wiped it clean. We'll see what we can find."

"Did you ever talk to Val Monroe?"

"We did. Talked to Eleanor Jones first, and then to Monroe."

"And? Did that lead to anything?"

The Ranger raised his eyebrows and cocked his head to one side. "She had means, motive, and opportunity. Other than that, not much."

Father Frank's eyebrows pinched together. "That sounds like a lot. I mean, aren't those the things you want for a suspect?"

"Certainly a good start. But we have those for Maggie as well. The only difference is, there's one thing that makes Maggie a better suspect than Monroe."

Having heard over a thousand confessions, Father Frank knew how to avoid showing surprise at something a person said. But experience deserted him at this moment. His hands tightened around each other. "And what is that one thing?"

Richards laughed slightly. "Well, of course, I can't tell you that, Father. You and I may be friends. And you've been a big help to me. But your sister is still a suspect." Father Frank just stared at the Ranger. "I'm not saying Monroe is off the list. What I'm saying is, there are many other things we take into consideration. And one of those lessens the case against Monroe. Doesn't eliminate it. Just doesn't help us. With Maggie, we don't have that same item. Sorry."

"What about Billy John?"

"A similar situation. I think I told you earlier there's a good case against him, except for one item." He smiled. "And no, I can't tell you what that item is. However, we still have his bike and we're seeing he can get pretty angry. He's admitted punching Granet in the face. But he claims he did not kill him and that he was alive and cursing when he left him."

A sharp knock at the front door jarred the two men out of their conversation.

Father Frank suddenly looked up. "Good grief. I forgot I've got a counseling session right about now. Sorry, but I've got to call this quits and work on my day job."

Richards laughed and got up, "I've got to go anyway. I'll let you know if we find anything out with this note. Don't dismiss it. Be careful."

Father Frank let the Ranger out and ushered in a middle-aged man and woman. "Let's go into my office. It will be more private there."

Chapter 33

THE COUNSELING SESSION had gone well, better than he expected. It seemed to Father Frank that both parties wanted it to work. It was just that neither wanted to give in. That would make them feel weak. But when an outside person, in this case a priest, suggested a path to take, each opted in immediately. He felt certain the two would work it out now.

As Maggie cooked dinner, Father Frank went through the mail. Nothing much there. He glanced at the Lakota Community Current, a small local paper devoted to news around the lake. *Wonder if they have anything on my accident on the bridge.* He certainly hoped not. Priests shouldn't be having auto accidents. Or being given breathalyzer tests. He flipped through the few pages. *Good. nothing about the crazily driving priest.*

But on the back page, an article caught his attention. A man named Ryan Potter was calling for the board of directors of the Lakota Lake Association to issue strict rules for all those using the lake, particularly regarding night time boating. Apparently, he had been out around midnight ten days ago in his motor boat. Although his boat had running lights he'd hit another boat which had no lights. He'd circled around and found a canoe, now badly damaged. There was no sign of anyone in the water, leading him to ask why was an empty canoe floating in the lake? "The board should draw up strict rules regarding the proper care of water vessels, and also the use of the lake after dark. Anyone whose boat drifts into the lake unattended should be fined, and prohibited from using the lake until the fine is paid." The article ended by asking anyone who had suggestions for lake rules to contact Mr. Potter and listed his telephone number.

Ten days ago. That could put the accident after the conference had ended. But, when was the article written? Father

Frank went into his office, picked up the phone and dialed the number listed in the article. The woman who answered said Ryan would not be home for several hours. "Can I help?" she asked pleasantly. "I'm his wife. Is this about the rules for using the lake?"

"Indirectly," Father Frank said. "I was wondering when exactly Mr. Potter had the accident on the lake?"

There was a moment of silence and Father Frank wondered if she was deciding whether to answer or trying to remember the date. "I'm pretty sure it was October 29, his poker night. He has moaned and complained about it every day since then. But, it has given him and others the impetus to get some water rules for this community. Right now, anything goes. I'm all in favor of more rules. Maybe it will keep Ryan from driving me crazy."

"Was the canoe out in the middle of the lake?"

"No. It wasn't too far out from the shore. Ryan thinks it probably just drifted out when someone didn't tie it up when they beached it. Just careless. Of course, he thinks several of the people here on Lakeside are careless with their boats."

Father Frank thanked her, hung up the phone and sank into the chair. A canoe on the lake, after midnight. The night of the murder. *I'm betting Lakota Retreat Center doesn't have any security cameras pointed at the lake.*

Chapter 34

"WHOSE CANOE WAS it?" Maggie asked.

Father Frank shrugged. "Don't know." He and Maggie were sitting at the kitchen table having some of the warm apple pie Maggie had baked. The heavenly aroma of cinnamon and apple pie filled the room. But their thoughts were on a more sinister topic.

"Did you ask?"

"No. Didn't get to talk to Ryan, just his wife."

"And she wouldn't know if Ryan did?" She gave him an incredulous look.

"Okay. You're right. I should have asked. But it sounded like they didn't know." He frowned. "She said he called and searched, but didn't find anyone. So maybe it did just drift out."

"And maybe whoever was in the canoe didn't want to be found. Didn't want anyone to know they'd been there. On the lake. At midnight. When someone had just been murdered."

Father Frank put his elbows on the table and cradled his face in his hands. "A canoe is very quiet. One might tie up at shore, get out, visit one of the cabins, get back in the canoe and paddle away without ever being detected."

"But do any of our suspects live over in that direction?"

"Don't have any idea." He looked up. "But, I can find out. Probably. Who are our suspects?"

"Well, there's me. But I don't live over there." She waggled her head. "Val Monroe and that guy, Ruffer - I think he was from Fort Worth, maybe. I'm told Val only lives ten minutes from the Conference center or retreat center, whatever it's called. So she could be over there."

"Any idea where Billy John lives?"

"No. But why don't you ask Georgia? She seems to know everybody."

Father Frank nodded. "Okay. I'll work on Billy John's address. You track down where Monroe lives. We know O'Reilly lives in Dallas. By the way, what did Jeff find out about O'Reilly?"

"Don't know. I tried to call him last night, but he didn't pick up. I'll try him now."

"Good. Let me know what he found out, if anything."

* * *

Thirty minutes later, Father Frank found Maggie in the kitchen. "Well, I've put Georgia on the case. If I know her, she'll find something."

"Good. I had a nice talk with Jeff. He did find O'Reilly."

"I hope he didn't engage him."

"Well, the Jeff I knew - prior to my getting jailed - wouldn't have gotten close to him. But, now, I have a new Jeff."

Father Frank looked puzzled. "I'm not following."

"He's changed. I could never have imagined he would stand up to old Bark-Bark. But he did. And to my surprise, he – shall we say – engaged O'Reilly."

Father Frank grabbed a Dr Pepper out of the refrigerator and sat down at the table. "So how did that go?"

"Amazing, is the word that comes to mind. First, he did some research, contacted several people to get their take on O'Reilly. Then, he found O'Reilly often went to a bar after work. So, Jeff - meek, introverted Jeff - followed him yesterday. He had a few beers and then got to talking to O'Reilly. After awhile, Jeff starts talking about his daughter."

Father Frank's forehead wrinkled and his hand shot up. "Hold it. Does Jeff have a daughter I don't know about?"

"Of course not. But he starts telling O'Reilly about his 'daughter' - Jeff's daughter - who ran away with a man Jeff had only met once. And he didn't know what to do. O'Reilly doesn't say anything for a long time and Jeff thinks he's not going to. But without looking at Jeff, he starts spilling it all. Says his daughter also ran off with a writer. Went to New York. He didn't know where she was or what she was doing.

"When O'Reilly stops and just looks into his beer bottle, Jeff finally says, 'You don't know where your daughter is. But I know where mine is. But when I call, that guy won't let me talk to her. He won't let me talk to my own daughter. Won't tell me where she is, what she's doing. Nothing.' Jeff said he slammed his beer bottle on the bar to emphasize how angry he was. Ended up splashing beer all over himself." Maggie laughed. "Neat, finicky Jeff doused in beer. Kinda wished I'd seen that. Anyway, O'Reilly finally says, 'I'd go there and knock his head right off his shoulders. I'd cut ...' He stopped abruptly and was quiet for a moment. Then he muttered, 'I'd make him tell me.' Jeff said the guy was so dark, so intense when he said that, it really freaked him out. He didn't even finish his beer, just hightailed it out of there quick as he could. "

Father Frank sat there agape, his eyes open wide and his head tilted to one side. "Sounds like O'Reilly really meant it. We already know he had means and opportunity. Now, I'd say he had a great motive."

Chapter 35

"GOOD MORNING, RANGER Richards. How are you doing this bright sunny fall day?"

Dick Richards was relaxed on his favorite bench. "I'm doing about as fine as new pair of boots - which means things are a little tight. The case is stagnating. Got any help for me today?"

The priest dropped down on the bench and stretched his legs out. "Maybe a little. But what have you got for me? We got interrupted with my counseling session yesterday."

"Nada, Zip, Zilch, Zero. You know everything we know. Well, almost."

"Come on. You have to have learned something new on the case. Anything new on Ms. Monroe? You know she lives probably ten minute away from the conference center. Yet she stayed in one of the center's residence rooms. And by now, I'm sure you know she lives on the other side of the lake."

"Yes, we know where she lives. We've interviewed her again. And we asked why she was staying at the conference center when she lived so close. She said, as the person in charge of the faculty, she wanted to be close at hand all the time. Any problems or questions, she would be right there to take care of it. Sounded reasonable to me."

"I suppose."

"We pushed pretty hard on her. She finally acknowledged she had gone to Granet's cabin the night of the murder. She admitted she foolishly thought they'd get together and take up where they left off. But exactly the opposite happened. She felt worse after her encounter with the man."

"I would imagine so."

"She did *not* admit he called her a fat pig. But she did say he was very rude and made it clear he wasn't interested in rekindling their previous relationship. I asked her how she felt about being rejected like that. She said she went back to her room, cried a little, and went to sleep. I asked her straight out if she killed Granet in a fit of rage and she said with no hesitation she did not, even though he probably deserved it."

Father Frank mouth formed an O. "Wow. She actually said he deserved it?"

"She did."

"You believe she didn't do it?"

The ranger twisted his mouth to the side. "I don't believe anything or anyone except proven evidence."

"I'll take that as a definite 'maybe'." Father Frank switched tracks. "How about Billy John? Anything new on that front?"

"Not really. We've released his bike back to him. I just wished we could tell whether the blood on the bike came from Granet's nose, or his neck."

"So Billy John's off your list?"

Richards pursed his lips and looked away for a moment, then turned back to Father Frank. "Of course you know I can't tell you that. Nor can I really comment on Ms. Monroe's status. But I'm still looking for clues and suspects."

"Any other news?"

"I can tell you we've eliminated Kace Ruffer. He had left the conference in early afternoon and has witnesses he was in Fort Worth at the time of the murder. We've done a bit of checking on Sean O'Reilly, but can't find much to work on there."

"I might be able to help a little there."

Richards turned to fully face the priest. "Oh? What do you know about Sean O'Reilly?"

Father Frank turned to say "Hello" and wave at three women walking toward the church hall. He turned back to the Ranger. "Jeff Armstrong, Maggie's husband, —"

"I know Jeff."

Father Frank repeated much of what Maggie had told him about Jeff's encounter with O'Reilly. When he finished, Richards asked. "He actually said 'He'd cut–' And then stopped short?"

Father Frank raised his eyebrows and dipped his chin. "That's what Maggie claims Jeff told her. Now that shocked me. But he could have been about to say something more graphic, like cutting off his male —"

"I get the picture," Richards interrupted. "But you're telling me Jeff claimed the man appeared very angry, then dark and frightening. And O'Reilly said, 'He'd tell me.' I think we need to interview him again."

Chapter 36

GEORGIA AND MIKE had come to the rectory for dinner at Maggie's invitation. Jeff had also driven out from Dallas. She had made ossobuco alla Milanese, and wanted to show off her culinary prowess, according to her brother. It worked. The Italian dish impressed everyone. Maggie had topped the tender veal shank with a gremolata, a mix of chopped parsley, lemon zest and a little garlic. A saffron risotto, its subtle aroma making everyone take notice, complemented the veal.

After they had finished the meal, Maggie asked Jeff to help prepare the dessert. Georgia turned to Mike. "Why don't you help her, too. I need to talk to Father Frank."

"What? And I can't hear?" questioned Mike.

"That's right. But not to worry. Neither can Maggie or Jeff. So, you help them while Father and I have our private conversation." With that, she grabbed the priest's hand and led him into his office.

"This sounds clandestine. What's up?"

"I have some other information I don't think I want to share with ... well, with anybody. But I need to tell you. As I was visiting with various people, I found out something that perhaps the police need to know. And since I understand you and the Ranger are on daily speaking terms, I'm going to pass it on to you. It's about Grace Sullivan. You said she seemed to be almost in a trance the day you saw her, maybe on strong medicine."

"That's right."

"Apparently she's become a recluse. Doesn't go anywhere, doesn't talk to anyone. And always seems to be in a daze. There's information, pretty reliable, that she was raped and that changed her into this person who's constantly in a stupor."

The priest let out a heavy sigh. "I've heard and read about that happening sometimes when a sensitive young girl is raped. Depending on the degree of violence, it could lead to PTSD. That does make it all add up."

"And what would you think if I told you the rape probably occurred three years ago?" She tilted her head slightly to the side. "At the time of the writers conference."

His eyes narrowed and his head moved back a little. "The previous one Granet was at?"

"That very one. And the reliable source said Granet asked Grace to see him, to talk about the piece which won her the contest that year." Father Frank started to say something, but Georgia kept on talking. "And this source says Grace wasn't seen the next day, or for the remainder of the conference."

For over a minute, neither said anything. Finally, the priest said, "So you think —"

Georgia's hands shot up. "I'm not thinking, or proposing anything. I'm simply delivering information, unverified information. But it comes from what I believe is generally a reliable source. Who also claims there were several allegations of sexual harassment specifically mentioning Granet during that conference. Although no others mentioned rape. And no one ever filed any charges."

"I'm amazed such would occur at a writers conference. I mean, these people were here to talk about writing and publishing books."

"I've never heard of it happening before or after that one conference three years ago. There was even some talk, I understand, about canceling the conferences in the future. But, the board decided to continue and just be more vigilant. And it seems almost no one knew about the rape allegation."

"I'm gathering from your secrecy you're not going to give me the name of your 'reliable source.' Are you willing to share it with the police? Or perhaps a Texas Ranger?"

Georgia lowered her head and closed her eyes. After several seconds she looked up at Father Frank. "There's no real evidence connecting that to this year's murder, so I don't feel required to by law. I am not withholding evidence, as far as I know."

"But it could lead to some evidence."

"Yes it could. And since it might, I will ask if my source is willing for me to tell the police what I've been told. If they say yes, then I will certainly talk to ... I think I'd rather tell it to the Texas Ranger. But if the source says no, then I'm not going to take it to the authorities." She smiled a sweet little smile. "Then, it's up to you to decide what to do with what I've just told you."

"Thanks, Georgia. I love to have these weighty decisions thrust upon me."

A loud rap shook the door to the office. "Are you two coming out or am I going to have to come in and see what you're up to?"

Father Frank opened the door. "I think I was just hearing Georgia's confession. So you know I can't tell you what she said."

"Yeah. I'll bet. But one minute more and Mike, Jeff and I would have started on the crème Brulèe without you two."

Chapter 37

SATURDAY, AFTER MASS and breakfast, Father Frank called
Ryan Potter, introduced himself, and asked if he could make an
appointment to see Mr. Potter mid-morning.

Twenty minutes later, he was in his car, hoping the trip
would be less eventful than the one last week. Father Frank had
noticed last week that opposite the Sullivan's house, and several
around it, there were posts at the water's edge where canoes or
small boats could be tied up. Today, across from the Potter house
a block farther down Lakeside Lane, he saw a dock extending out
fifteen or twenty feet into the lake. Tied up to it was a small, sleek
motor boat. Its overall design suggested speed. The first foot of
the bow was painted a bright, cherry red which then slowly
feathered out to a gleaming white. The white continued until
about four feet from the stern, where the red feathering took
over. The entire boat looked as if it had just been scrubbed and
polished.

Potter's house had some of the same qualities as the boat:
small but sleek. Precise flower beds flanked a neat porch covering
the center third of the house. On one side of the front door was a
colorful talavera pot with an interesting plant Father Frank
couldn't name but looked exotic. The other side of the porch
contained two comfortable looking wicker chairs.

Before Father Frank even knocked, the door opened.
"Hello. I'm Ryan Potter. You must be Father Frank."

"Yes. And thank you for seeing me on such short notice."

Ryan stepped out onto the porch. "It's a beautiful
morning. Let's just sit on the porch."

As they settled into the wicker chairs, Father Frank
judged Potter to be in his fifties. He was clean-shaven, trim and
fit, and sporting what appeared to be a genuine smile.

"My wife said you were interested in my collision with the canoe.

"Right. What can you tell me about it?"

"Well, not much to tell. It was around midnight, maybe a little after. I was over at Potkiller's, down by the neck of the lake. A few of the guys play a little penny ante poker there on Thursday's. We quit around midnight, maybe a little after. The easiest way for me to get there is by boat. So, I cranked up Ginger– that's the name of my little speedster. Anyway, I was headed home and this canoe had no lights at all. I was almost on top of it before I saw it. I swerved. Almost missed it. But caught the bow. Gave it quite a jolt. I actually knocked off a good sized chunk of it."

"How big is a good size?"

"Oh, I'd say I probably knocked six or eight inches off one side of the bow. It was a strong collision. If the person in the canoe didn't see it coming, most likely he would have been knocked out of the canoe. So, I circled back around, looking, calling. I cut the engine, but I couldn't hear anyone splashing around. And no one answered my calls."

"And after midnight, it was probably too dark with only your running lights to see anyone, I'd guess."

"It would. But I keep a powerful flashlight in the boat and I searched around the canoe. Never saw anybody, or any trace. So, I cranked Ginger up and after a few more circles around the canoe, I decided it was adrift. Hadn't been tied up properly. Just drifted out in the lake. Dangerous."

Father Frank put his hands on his knees and leaned forward a little. "I would think so. I'm not into boating, but it sounds dangerous not to have some sort of a light if you're going to be out on the lake at night. Or worse yet, to allow your boat to drift out."

"You're right about that. Dangerous for the person in the canoe *and* the person hitting it. Both could be in the water in pitch black. And if I'd been knocked into the water, Ginger would have kept going for awhile."

"I'm glad you weren't hurt. So you think someone didn't tie the canoe up and it drifted out into the lake."

Potter nodded. "I did think the canoe was a drifter, at first. But later, I wasn't so sure."

Father Frank's head jerked up at that statement. "Why not?"

"Well, two things. First, in replaying it in my mind, I think maybe there *was* someone sitting in the canoe. I'm not sure. Just a feeling there was a shadow there. Second, as I hit the bow, I didn't see any rope. If it had drifted out, the rope would be in the water. If it had been taken out, the rope would be inside the boat. I didn't notice any in the canoe. Mind you, I'm talking about a split second. And in the dark. So, it could have been there. But my mind didn't capture an image of any rope."

The priest looked down for a moment, trying to process what he had just heard. He looked up at Ryan. "So you're not sure you saw somebody and you're not sure you saw where the rope was - in or out of the canoe - right?"

"Right. Both were just impressions. It all happened so quickly and it was dark as hell out there. Oh, excuse me, Father."

Father Frank laughed. "Quite all right. I imagine hell is very dark." He paused a second. "How was your boat? Ginger? Did she sustain any damage?"

"Oh, just a little scratch and some damaged paint. Took me about an hour to get it looking like it did before."

"Anybody claim the canoe?"

"No. And I haven't seen the hull anywhere."

Father Frank leaned back a little. "Could it have just sunk?"

"Not likely. Canoes are pretty buoyant. Even with a bigger hole, it ought to be riding on the surface. I didn't take a look the next day. Should have. But I was in a rush the next morning and just drove off without looking for it."

"Nobody complained about being hit? No one missing a canoe?"

"Not that I've heard. And as you know, since you got my number from that article, I'm pretty visible around here. I've been advocating safety rules for boaters for - maybe two years." Ryan ran his hand over his cheek and looked at the priest. "But I've got a question for you. Why are you interested in my little accident? Do you boat? Or are you planning to on Lake Lakota?"

Father Frank shook his head. "No. Directly across from here is the Lakota Retreat Center. There was a writers conference there a couple of weeks ago. And a man was murdered there, during the conference." He took a deep breath and looked squarely at Ryan. "The murder happened on October 29."

Potter straightened up, a slight frown creasing his face. "The night of my accident." He looked down for a moment, then back at the priest and caution colored his voice. "Are you thinking maybe I motored over and killed the person?"

Father Frank's eyes opened wide. "No, no. Not at all. Someone would have heard your motor. I was wondering about the canoe. Just a slight possibility, something to consider. They don't have a good suspect yet."

For nearly a minute neither spoke. Without looking up, Ryan said, "Of course, I could have shut the engine off out a ways and just coasted quietly into shore." Now he looked at his guest. "And what is your part in this investigation?"

"Nothing official. But my sister is on the suspect list. I know she didn't do it. So, I'm anxious to find any leads that might help the sheriff find the actual killer."

"And why is she a suspect?"

"She believed the victim had basically stolen her book and, unfortunately for her, confronted him the day he was murdered and said he'd have to pay for the theft." He gave a slight laugh. "Maggie, that's my sister, is not bashful, or subtle. She did this in front of fifty people. So, Sheriff Bark considers her a prime suspect."

Ryan nodded a few times. "I don't want to get that Sheriff on my case. He can be pretty rough."

"A number of people, including my sister, stayed in the residence rooms at the center. And there are security cameras monitoring the entrance. So they believe they have a closed group which includes the killer. I just wondered if it was possible for someone to come across the lake, commit the crime, and then paddle back to the other side - sight unseen."

"I see where you're coming from."

"So, no idea whom the canoe belonged to?"

Ryan folded his arms across his chest and lowered his eyes for a moment before looking back at the priest. "I don't know. But I did notice that Bud Sullivan's canoe was missing. He lives about a quarter mile back down Lakeside. He just ties his boat to one of the posts embedded at the edge of the lake. A number of the houses in that area do that. Some with canoes, some with row boats. No motor boats down in that area. You really need a dock if you have a motor boat. Or a sail boat, for that matter."

Father Frank wanted to ask more. Had he talked to Bud Sullivan? What was he like? Did Ryan know about Grace and her transformation after the conference three years ago. But, he felt he had asked enough questions. And while Ryan had been very generous in his information, any more questions would be putting pressure on the man.

"Ryan, I want to thank you for your time and your information on the accident. Needless to say, I'm very concerned for my sister. The Sheriff seems to like her for the murderer. There's no physical evidence. But she had a motive. She was on site. The man had his throat slashed, so anybody with a steak knife could have done it. And she publicly told the victim he would have to pay for stealing her book. I'm more than a little worried."

"I understand. And if I come across anything I think might in any way help, I'll definitely call you."

"I would really appreciate it. And you can also call Texas Ranger Lieutenant Dick Richards. He's working on the case." Father Frank pulled out a card. "Here's my number. Feel free to call at any time."

Ryan looked at the card. "Prince of Peace Catholic Church. We go to the Pine Street Methodist Church."

"Bobby Thomas. I've never heard him preach, but we've worked together on community projects. Good man. Good ideas. Good heart."

"We like him."

* * *

Father Frank was half way back to Prince of Peace when his cell phone rang. Georgia's name was on the readout. He pulled over, stopped the car and answered the phone.

"My reliable source wants to talk to you," she said. "Today."

Chapter 38

FATHER FRANK HAD agreed to meet Georgia's reliable source in the parking lot of the local McDonald's. He drove in, parked and went inside to buy two medium Dr Peppers. As Georgia had promised, when he returned to his car, a woman was sitting in it. She wore a neat but nondescript dress, tennis shoes, and a sunbonnet. The priest tried to remember the last time he saw a woman wearing a sunbonnet. He couldn't tell much about her age, but she might have been in her fifties.

He offered her one of the Dr Peppers. "Hi. I'm Father Frank from Prince of Peace Church."

"Thank ya," she said. "You can call me Jane."

"And thank you for coming and agreeing to talk to me."

"I'm gonna tell you some of what I know and what I believe. Those are not always the same. You can weigh it. If you and I agree on terms today, you can repeat some of it to Texas Ranger Richards. My sources tell me he's a true white hat, a straight shooter. If he thinks it can help, I'll meet him and tell him ever thing I know and some 'a what I believe." She stopped, picked up her Dr Pepper and took a long drink. "Well, what 'cha think?"

"Sounds like a plan I can live with. What are your terms?"

"First, we did not meet today. Iffn we meet in the future, you don't let on we ever met before. Two, most likely I won't answer any questions you have. You can ask. Just know I probly won't answer. Three, iffn the Ranger don't think this'll help his case, you forget all of it. You never talk 'bout it to nobody. And the Ranger don't do nothing with it neither." Jane looked at the priest. "You agree with all that?"

Father Frank nodded several times. Then slowly, "Okay, Jane. I agree to those conditions. But I am not speaking for the

Texas Ranger. I'll tell him your conditions and get his response. If he does not say yes to those, I'll relay that to you and then you can decide where I go from there. Okay?"

Jane nodded. Before she could speak, he added, "Let me ask you a question before we start. Why all this secrecy? I don't even think your name is Jane."

"Well, that's the first question I won't answer. But if you agree to my conditions, I'll start."

He hesitated a moment. Not knowing what she might tell him, he found it uncomfortable agreeing to such terms. But it was clear Jane would tell him nothing if he didn't. "I agree."

"I been round a long time and lots of folks know me and most trust me. I don't have no ax to grind. People 'spect me to give facts, no more. Sometimes, less. I don't talk good - my English ain't always right. But people know I tell facts or what I truly believe is true."

She took a long pull on the Dr Pepper. "I've known Grace Sullivan a long time. Imogene, Bud's wife and Grace's mother's dead, you know. Died more'n a dozen years ago. Imogene and me was real close. So when she died, I became like a grandmama to Grace. And that was real important 'bout three years back. You seen her now. So you can think how tough it was to dig out what happened back then. I might git a nod or a shake of her beautiful head. Iffn I got a word, I was surprised - and happy. Well, maybe not happy. There was no happy then. Or now. She don't know happy no more."

Jane's tone had progressed from melancholy to disconsolate.

"But over many days I found out things. I knowed she won a contest with her writing. And this ... beast ... said he could help her, invited her to his cabin one night. This was at that writers convention thing. She went, all atwitter. She loved to write. She won a contest. She was gettin' ready for college. Life was good and maybe this guy could help her git her writin' career going.

"Well, he had other things on his mind. She was so innocent. He gave her a drink. Said it'd relax her. So she drank it."

Jane stopped and took another long drink. For a moment, Father Frank saw moisture in her eyes. She clamped her jaw shut for a minute and looked out the window.

"Well, she wasn't *that* relaxed. She fought him. He slapped her a few times, tore her clothes, and had his way with her. She got away and ran home. That's near two miles. She was a swimmer, had strong legs. But she was changed. Still is. Bud called me, said I needed to come see her. She needed somethin' and he didn't know what to do. He loved her a whole lot. But he was a man and didn't know what was wrong or how to help her. He just knowed she wouldn't talk, eat, do nothin' but cry and sleep.

"Well, I go see her right away. Purty quick I know what happened. I seen it before. But never like with Grace. I talked to her, held her, listened to her cry. Cried with her. Told her it would be okay, give it time. All sorts of nonsense. Now, three years later, she still don't talk much. For a long time, she never wrote a word. Some say she died a little that night. I say she died a lot. The Grace I knowed was gone."

For a few moments, Jane just stared out the window. Then, without looking at Father Frank, she continued.

"So she reads about the writer thing a few weeks back and gets all agitated. I never seen her like that. She shows me the thing in the paper and rips the picture of one of them speakers in half, then drops it on the floor and stomps on it. I asked her if that was the one who raped her, and she jerks her head up and down so hard I'm worried she might hurt her neck. But she settles down and goes to sleep and I go home."

Both were quiet, Jane staring out the window and Father Frank saying a silent prayer for Grace. Finally he asked, "Does Mr. Sullivan know all this?"

"Well, no. Not all. But he knows a good bit. I had to tell him some of it back then. He was thinkin' she got retarded somehow. I explained the shock she had and she just had to get over it. He pitched a fit, got so angry I thought he might bust a gut. Wanted to kill the bastard. That's his word, not mine. But I couldn't disagree. Last week, I was just hopin' he didn't find the man's picture where Grace had stomped on it."

Jane was silent for a several seconds. "I'm hopin' Bud didn't find the picture. Bud always had a temper." She looked at Father Frank. "Grace's had it bad enough. Don't need her daddy makin' it worse."

Chapter 39

FATHER FRANK WATCHED Jane walk over and sit on a bench near McDonald's. *She's waiting for me to drive off. Doesn't want me to know anything about her. Why?*

Jane is a bit like me. Trusted. People tell her things in confidence. Unless there is something serious, like murder, she doesn't tell other people. He nodded. Unless the Texas Rangers thought this information would help them solve a murder, it couldn't go anywhere. Either way, Jane didn't want a connection with him. She didn't want to lose that trust she'd developed. Smart lady.

He remembered an old saying that seemed to apply here. Two people can keep a secret - if one of them is dead.

He started his rented Nissan and headed for Pine Tree. He had driven less than a mile when he saw red and blue lights flashing behind him. Instinctively he checked the speedometer – a few miles under the speed limit. His seat belt was on. He was not talking on the phone. What could be the problem this time?

He pulled over to the side of the road and turned off the engine.

Sheriff Bark appeared beside the driver's window. "License and registration."

"It's the same as it was on Tuesday."

Bark scowled. "License and registration."

Father Frank dug out his license, then reached over and pulled the registration out of the glove compartment and handed both to the Sheriff.

"What are you doing driving this car?"

"As you know, my Taurus was damaged. It's in the repair shop. This is my rental car while the Taurus is being repaired." *Why am I having to explain what car I'm driving?*

Bark studied the priest's license as if he hadn't seen it a few days before. Then he studied the registration papers, even though he knew it was a rental. He handed them back to the priest. "What are you doing over here in Timber County?"

Father Frank looked puzzled. "Is there some reason I shouldn't be here? Is Timber County restricted?"

"Don't get smart with me. Just answer the question."

"I was visiting someone."

"Who?"

Father Frank set his teeth together to keep from speaking too quickly. Finally he said, "I'm not at liberty to say."

"What does that mean?"

"It means the person ..." He looked down for a moment, then back at the Sheriff. "There was nothing illegal going on. So I don't think that is any of your business. I don't mean to be rude to a police officer, but that question is out of order."

"Were you *investigating* again?" The Sheriff said it like it was a dirty word.

Father Frank's hands gripped one another and his arm and leg muscles tensed. His stomach cramped slightly. He took a deep breath trying to relax. As calmly as he could manage he said, "Do I need to call my lawyer? I respectfully refuse to answer any more questions until I have my lawyer with me."

Bark's face began to turn red. He puffed up as if no air could escape his mouth or nose. His eyes grew smaller, his hands clenched, and for a moment, Father Frank thought he might actually take a swing at him. The priest eased away from the window.

"Are you trying to get smart with me, boy? Have you got something to hide?"

"No sir."

If anything, Bark's face got even redder. "You and your sister think you're so smart. Well, she's going to be in jail soon, and for a long, long time. And if I catch you obstructing my investigation, you'll be in there too, smart boy."

Father Frank said nothing. But one part of his brain worried that the Sheriff might have a heart attack.

Bark put his hands on the edge of the window. "Be very careful. If I see so much as a wiggle out of your lane, or any evidence you're not paying attention to your driving, I'll haul you into jail. Got it?"

"Yes sir. Am I free to go now?"

"Get out of here." Bark jerked around and stomped back to his cruiser, got in, and sprayed gravel as he took off around Father Frank's car.

Chapter 40

AFTER SUNDAY MASS, Father Frank stopped to visit with a number of parishioners. But out of the corner of his eye, there was the now familiar sight of Ranger Richards waiting for him on the bench.

"Good morning Lieutenant Richards. What brings you to our neighborhood this glorious Sunday morning? And do you work every day?

"Sometimes it seems like it. But then, you said you worked every day."

"That I did. So what can I do for you?"

"Well, of course I'm hoping you might give me some good ideas on this stubborn case. But also, I wanted to tell you that my superiors have asked me to look into harassment charges against Sheriff Bark." Richards stopped and just looked at Father Frank.

When the Ranger said nothing further, Father Frank raised his eyebrows. "Don't look at me. I didn't say anything."

"If a citizen feels state or local law enforcement officers have been guilty of harassment, under the Police Misconduct Provisions you can contact the FBI. Apparently a Jeff Armstrong called the FBI and asked that there be an investigation. If a sheriff in Texas needs to be investigated, it falls on the Rangers to do it. So the FBI called the Rangers. I'm out here, so guess who gets to do it?"

"Maggie told Jeff about the Sheriff taking her in last week and questioning her again. He wasn't happy about it. But I'm amazed he went so far as to call the FBI. You do know Jeff visited the Sheriff and told him to quit harassing her."

"Yes. I heard about it."

"And of course you know Sheriff Bark brought Maggie in last week, in handcuffs, to question her about the money Granet was making on the book."

"Yes. And I heard she came in with her lawyer. The Sheriff wasn't happy about that. And I'll tell you, off the record, your sister is still the Sheriff's primary suspect."

"He told me as much yesterday."

"You talked with Sheriff Bark yesterday?"

"I did."

"The ranger shook his head. "Okay. Let's hear the details."

"He pulled me over and asked me why I was in his county. You think maybe he's keeping tabs on me? And he said Maggie would soon be in jail for a long, long time."

Richards again just shook his head. "I don't know what's going on there, but I suggest you stay clear of the man. He could haul you in and, depending on the timing, you could spend a night or two in the county jail."

"I will try to avoid him. But when I'm just driving very carefully on a public road in the adjacent county ... well, let's just say, he makes me feel a bit nervous."

"Got any leads on the case? Or any ideas at all? I shouldn't tell you this, but I don't believe your sister killed Granet. But I can't come up with someone else to propose."

Father Frank studied the asphalt beneath his shoes before looking back up at the Ranger. "I don't know if this has any bearing on the case or not. But on the night of the murder, a man boating on the lake around midnight hit a canoe in the lake. He called and searched, but couldn't find any person in or around the canoe. So his thought was, perhaps the canoe had not been tied up properly and drifted out into the lake. The accident occurred close to the shore along Lakeside Lane."

Father Frank stopped, and after a few seconds, Richards asked, "And I care about this because?"

"It was the night of the murder. From there to the Lakota Retreat Center would be an easy paddle." He raised his eyebrows. "I'm guessing no security cameras point at the lake."

"No. No cameras pointing that direction."

"There's one other thing." Father Frank leaned back and stared at the sky. *How to deliver Jane's information? I don't want it to sound like I'm making an endorsement.* "A person, reported to be a reliable source, says a young woman was at the writers conference three years ago and was raped. It traumatized her and to this day, she doesn't speak much. Acts as if she's in a trance. Her mother is dead and she lives with her father, directly across the lake from the retreat center. And there's a decent chance it was their canoe that was hit in the lake the night of October 29."

The priest stopped, hoping he had given an accurate rendition of what Jane had told him.

"But you implied there was no one in the canoe when it got hit, so that doesn't work."

"Actually, the man who was driving the power boat that hit it said there *might* have been someone in it. But he is not sure."

"And is there any reason to believe that either the woman or her father knew Granet was at this year's conference?"

"There is some reason to believe that."

Richards let out a long breath as he considered what to do with this new information. "Will this reliable source talk to me, answer questions?"

The corners of Father Frank's lips curved up a little, but he suppressed a smile. "She told me she would talk to you *only* if you felt there was a reasonable chance this might lead to something concerning the murder. She also said you could ask questions, but she didn't guarantee to answer them."

"Pretty controlling."

"She claims she knows a lot of things because people trust her not to spread things around unless it's absolutely necessary."

"Who is she?"

"Beats me. I told her I was Father Frank from Prince of Peace and she said she was Jane. I didn't for one minute think her name was Jane. By the way, she seemed to know about you."

"Me?" Richards looked surprised. How would she know about me?

"Don't know, but she said she believed Ranger Richards was a white hat and a straight shooter. Those were her exact words."

Richards laughed. "Well, I'll be sure to wear my Stetson when I interview her. How and when can I see her?"

"I'll tell my contact and she'll make the arrangements."

"Pretty mysterious, huh?"

"Well, I had to go to a McDonald's, buy a Dr Pepper, and when I returned to my car, she was sitting in it."

"Wow. Just like in the movies." He laughed again.

"Jane likes Dr Peppers. And you don't want her throat to run dry."

"Can you set it up for this afternoon?"

"I'll get right on it and let you know as soon as I know."

The Ranger got up and started across the parking lot. "A Dr Pepper. Better than a drink at the bar, I guess."

Chapter 41

TWO HOURS LATER, Father Frank called Richards. "I have good news and bad news."

"Shoot. I can take it."

"Jane can meet with you this afternoon at three o'clock."

"And the bad news?"

"It turns out she's heard about you, but since she doesn't know you, she insists I bring you over."

Richards let out a slow breath. "I can deal with that. Can you?"

"I'll introduce you and then I'll go have a Blizzard while you two talk. Will that work for you?"

"How would it work if we both drove over? Then, you could introduce me and you wouldn't have to stay. And I'd feel better about questioning her if you weren't there."

"Works. Oh, the location has been changed to the Dairy Queen. Come by Prince of Peace about two thirty and we'll go."

* * *

By two fifty, they were in Timber County a mile away from the Dairy Queen. Richards had fallen back a little with two cars in between. A small gap formed just behind Father Frank's car and a sheriff's cruiser pulled in, its red and blue lights flashing. Father Frank pulled to the side of the road.

Sheriff Bark walked up beside the priest's car. Father Frank had already pulled his driver's license out of his pocket and was reaching for his registration papers.

"You're back in my county again. Twice yesterday. Now today. Are you investigating? And you'd better tell the truth."

"I am in no way obstructing your investigation." Father Frank pulled out his phone. "Do you mind if I record this conversation, so we can be sure what I said?"

"Record this? Are you threatening a police officer?"

"No sir. I just want to be able to remember what I said to you."

"You can *not* record anything. But you tell me what you are doing here? Now!" Bark was yelling and he had leaned into the driver's window, getting right in the priest's face.

"He doesn't have to tell you that, Sheriff."

Bark jerked around, bumping his head on the window frame of Father Frank's car. He let out a curse word and turned, prepared to accost the man giving him advice. "Stay out of ..." He found himself looking into the angry face of Ranger Richards.

"Why did you pull him over, Sheriff?" asked Richards.

"He was ... Ah ... " Bark was flustered. He wiped his forehead on his sleeve. "I think he might be obstructing my investigation."

Richards said nothing, but kept his laser focus on the Sheriff.

"He's been over here several times in the last two days," Bark stammered.

"And that's a crime in Timber County?" asked the Ranger.

"Ah, well, no. Ah. But he has no reason to be here."

"So he has to have a reason to enter *your* county?"

"Ah, no. But he's probably obstructing my investigation."

"Which line of your investigation might that be? Please be specific, Sheriff Bark."

The Sheriff looked down at the ground. Sweat dripped from his nose. He pulled off his campaign hat and ran his sleeve across the top of his head. He looked back at the Ranger. "I don't know what he's doing, but I don't like it. And he threatened a police officer."

"How did he threaten you, Sheriff?"

"Ah, well, ah, he wanted to record what I said to him."

"And how was that a threat?"

Father Frank watched as the Sheriff got more nervous, yet the Ranger remained very cool.

"Who knows what he might do with it? Maybe post it on that internet face or something." Bark wiped his brow again. "I don't know what this crazy man might do."

For nearly thirty seconds, Richards said nothing. Then, "We'll talk about this back at your office, Sheriff. I suggest you leave."

"But —"

"Now would be best."

Bark gave Father Frank a severe look, then stomped back to his cruiser, slammed the door and drove off.

Father Frank started to speak, but Richards held up his hand. "We don't want to be late. Lead on."

Three minutes later, they pulled into the parking lot, got out of their cars and walked into the Dairy Queen. Father Frank ordered a large Dr Pepper and a turtle pecan Blizzard.

Richards shook his head. "It's the middle of the afternoon. And you're going to eat all that sugar?"

"Absolutely." He dipped a spoon into the creamy concoction and savored his first bite, then used the spoon to point out the window. "Looks like you have someone in your car. Let's go. And here. He handed the Ranger the Dr Pepper. "If you want her to talk, you have to provide."

The two men approached the passenger side of the car. Father Frank leaned down a little. "Hi, Jane. This is Texas Ranger Lieutenant Dick Richards."

A strange look came over her face as she looked at the Ranger. "Richard Richards? Was ya father into jokes?"

"Actually, he was, ma'am. But not with my name. The Richard came from my mother. She insisted on naming me after Richard Dowling, an officer in the Texas Military Forces who was part of her family tree."

Jane nodded. "Good choice. He was the commander at the second Battle of Sabine Pass."

Father Frank looked puzzled. "When was that?"

"1863," Jane said. "Was the most one-sided Confederate victory in the Civil War."

"I didn't know that," said the priest.

"Should'a paid more attention during Texas history class. The Union staged the largest amphibious assault in the war. Had over five thousand infantry. Dowling had forty-six Irish-Americans. Then eighty confederate guys came up from Beaumont. Now, Dowling's got a whoppin' hundred twenty-five Texans. Well, Richard Dowling's men captured a couple of the Union boats, killed about sixty soldiers and sailors, captured over three hundred Union soldiers. Getting' smart a little late, the rest of them Union forces hightailed it out of there. I'd say your mother picked a purty good man to name ya after."

Richards was grinning. "Once I learned about Dowling, I agreed. And so did my father."

Father Frank licked a little of the Blizzard that was creeping down the side of the cup. "I'm going to leave you two to talk and I'll head on back to Prince of Peace. Ranger, we'll talk later."

Chapter 42

TWO HOURS LATER, Father Frank answered the door to find Richards standing there. "Can you come on out and talk a mite?" His facial expression mirrored his serious voice.

The priest opened the screen. "Come on in. We can talk in the living room."

"No. Let's do it outside, on my favorite bench."

The sky was a deep blue, with only enough clouds to accent it. A cool breeze moderated the 80 degree temperature. No doubt, outside was a great place to be today.

But Father Frank wondered if Richards was worried about eavesdropping or perhaps listening devices in the rectory. Once they were seated under Richard's favorite pine, the priest said, "I have about thirty minutes before I have to get ready for service tonight."

Richards took off his hat. "That will be plenty of time. The Sheriff and I have had a talk. He should not be bothering you anymore."

Father Frank started to speak, but Richards held up his hand. "That's all I'm going to say about the Sheriff. Jane pretty much confirmed what you already told me, but I was glad to have a chance to have her tell it to me directly. I came to talk about the Sullivans. I understand you've been over there. Twice."

"True. But I only saw Grace. As best I could tell, Mr. Sullivan wasn't there either time."

"Did she say anything to you - that you feel you can tell me?"

"Not really. In fact, the first time, she said a total of four words. 'I don't go anywhere.' That was it, other than a nod once or twice. It was very strange and a little disconcerting. The second visit she spoke another four words–' I'm trying to start'– almost child-like."

"Trying to start what?"

"That was in response to my asking her if she was writing now. I'm told she was a very skilled writer before the ... attack. She had a scholarship to T.C.U., had actually enrolled. But she also had a scholarship to the writers' conference and came back for it. All in all, she sounded like a very accomplished young woman. But now, she seems ... I don't know, totally withdrawn."

"But she could probably get along by herself?"

"I would think so. She's twenty-one or twenty-two. She seems physically okay. She doesn't seem to interact with people, but she should be capable of going to the store, shopping for food, that sort of thing."

"I really wanted to get your impression. Should it come to it, that is, come to my arresting Bud Sullivan, can she get along by herself? That's my question. "

Father Frank looked down at his hands for a moment, then back up at Richards. "I think so. But it would be a good idea to get someone she felt comfortable with to ... check up on her, make sure she was doing okay, eating, sleeping."

The priest ran his hands through his hair, then looked directly at Richards. "I did a little reading after my first visit with Grace. I think she may very well have RTS - Rape Trauma Syndrome. She has many of the symptoms."

Richards looked skeptical. "That was three years ago."

"Yes. But what I read indicated these symptoms could last or reoccur for years."

"You don't think her current state could have been any kind of fake, or trickery?"

The priest looked away for nearly a minute as if studying the pine trees that bordered the parking lot. When he looked back at the Ranger, he shook his head slightly. "I don't think so. I felt she was genuine. That was just the way she was - is."

"Thank you. I wanted another opinion. How about Bud Sullivan? Oh, you said you never saw him."

"That's right."

"Well, with me he was not forthcoming. He wouldn't say anything about the canoe. But he became as nervous as a long tailed cat in a room full of rocking chairs. I need to talk to the man driving the power boat and get his story. What did you say his name was?"

"Ryan Potter." Father Frank gave Richards the address.

"After I talk to Potter, then I can go back with more ammunition and pry some information about the canoe out of Sullivan." Richards put his Stetson back on his head, gave it a little tap and got up.

Father Frank stood up also. "Anything ever come out of Jeff's information on Sean O'Reilly's anger?"

"I've had two Rangers interview him. One in our office, pretty intense, and most likely intimidating. The other in a bar, after a couple of beers. Neither gave us anything to go on. " He looked at Father Frank and could see his disappointment. "He has a great motive. In fact, he and Sullivan have more or less the same motive."

"The same?"

"Granet did something bad to the daughter. For O'Reilly, Granet took her away, and now O'Reilly doesn't know anything about her, where she is, what's she doing. O'Reilly has tried to find out whatever he could from Granet. But Granet's agent says Granet wouldn't answer any questions about the daughter, and wouldn't talk to O'Reilly."

"If Granet did rape Grace, then Sullivan has a very strong motive to take revenge." Richards removed his Stetson and ran his fingers around the edge of the pure white felt. "A strong motive is usually necessary for a murder. But there are other factors that must be taken into consideration." He now looked at the priest. "We have not crossed either name off the list. But we're certainly not ready to make an arrest of either one of them - yet."

"Why not?"

"Sorry. Can't give that piece of info out just yet."

"What about Billy John?"

"About the same. Can't eliminate him, but he's not at the top of the list. Depending on his attachment to Holly, which she says is very strong, he has an intense motive. By the way, we did find a partial print on that note you received. Not anything that would stand up in court. But you might be interested to know. It could have been Bartok's."

The priest cocked his head to the right and pulled his brows close together. "What does that mean 'could have been'?"

"It means, what we could pull off matches up with some part of Bartok's print. But there's not enough to make a positive identification. Since Bartok had a reason to send it - you were the one who got us looking for someone on a bike - I'd say there's a very good chance it came from him. The letters and words he cut out of a newspaper to make the note most likely came from the *Timber County Express.* The previous week's paper had those words and in the same fonts as were used in the note."

"Should I worry?"

"If I were you, I wouldn't. I think Bartok tries to sound and act tough. But I don't think he's got the ... the guts to do anything. But just like with the Sheriff, I'd be careful around him."

"Okay. Thanks for the information. Now, who's at the top of the suspect list?"

The Ranger grinned and raised his eyebrows. "Depends on who you ask. For the Sheriff, it's Margaret DeLuca."

Father Frank grimaced. "And who's at the top of the Texas Ranger's list?"

"Hang in there. We'll talk again." Once more, he gave a slight grin. "*Before* we arrest anyone."

Chapter 43

THE RAIN THAT seemed promising a week ago, had finally arrived. Not many were complaining. A week or so late was fine. The problem arose when the rain was months late. East Texas, with its forests of pine, hickory, oak and sweet gum needed a good bit of rain. This year was going to be considerably below average. Texas Ranger Dick Richards slipped a plastic rain cover over his Stetson, got out of the car and headed up to the Sullivans' house.

Ryan Potter had been very helpful, both in information about canoes in general and about the Sullivans' canoe in particular. He felt this meeting with Sullivan would be more productive than the first one. He rang the doorbell and waited.

"Oh. You're back. What do you want?" Bud Sullivan stood in the door, not inviting the Ranger in.

"We need to talk some more. It might be more comfortable if we weren't standing in the rain."

Bud moved back a step. "Okay. Come on in. But I don't have much time. I've got some things to do."

Richards waited until he and Bud were seated in the living room. "It will go quicker if this time you give me truthful and complete answers to my questions."

Sullivan straightened up and took a deep breath, ready to object. But Richards went right on. "I'd still like to know what happened to the canoe you owned and had tied up across the road at the water's edge. Yesterday you told me you didn't know what had happened to your canoe. Have you remembered anything else?"

"I told you, I guess it sank somewhere out in the lake. Somebody must of untied it and it drifted out and then somebody hit it, knocked a hole in it and it sank. I don't know where. And I'm not going to look for it."

"Look Sullivan, you and I both know that canoe didn't sink, unless you put rocks in it."

"Somebody plowed into it."

"That part is true. And in fact, I've talked with the person who hit it. But you and I know canoes are very buoyant. It did not sink. So where is it?"

Sullivan didn't respond. Richards eyes were laser beams boring into Sullivan. Bud's focus flitted around the room, never settling on any one spot. Finally, he looked around at the entrance to the dining room and then the opening to a hall, as if checking to be sure no one was listening.

"Okay. I didn't want to bring this up. Grace has left it untied before. I've cautioned her about that, telling her someone could get hurt with a derelict boat on the lake. When it happened this time, and since it had a hole in it anyway, I just pulled it in and took it to the dump. I didn't want her to know I did that. I just let her think she left it untied and she lost it. Sank, drifted away. It was gone. Maybe it would teach her a lesson."

"Where is Grace? I haven't met her."

Sullivan's mouth almost opened, but he clamped it shut. His voice changed from supplicant to aggressor. "Just leave Grace out of this." He stopped and softened his voice. "I told her it was a mistake to leave the boat untied. Sos now, she doesn't have a canoe." He quickly added. "You don't need to bother her. She doesn't do well with strangers."

Richards just stared at Sullivan. Clearly he was in the habit of protecting his troubled daughter. The Ranger shifted his position in the chair and returned to the discussion of the missing canoe. "And to which dump did you take the canoe?"

"Ah, the big one outside Tyler."

"Tyler. Why not one closer? Timber County has a dump. It's a lot closer. And living here, you wouldn't have to pay a dump fee."

For a moment, Bud just looked distressed. Then, he brightened. "I was, ah, going down that way anyway. So, ah, I just took it. Wasn't hardly out a my way at all."

"You're sure it was the Tyler dump."

"Oh yeah."

"Because my men will go there and find it."

For an instant, Bud's brows came down almost closing his eyes. His hands gripped the sides of his chair. "It's probably gone by now. You know how those big machines grind up stuff at the dump."

"Then my men will find the pieces. We'll be able to put it all together again, if we want to."

Bud's eyes closed and his breathing accelerated noticeably. He shook his head. "It ain't there. I was just about to push it off at the dump when a man came up to me and said he'd buy it from me. I pointed out the hole in it, but he said he'd fix that up in no time. Offered me thirty bucks. So I took it and he took the boat."

"He took it. On what? He just happened to have a trailer there?"

"No. No. He had a big ass dually and he just loaded it in there and took off."

"How convenient."

"I was lucky. Boat weren't no good now anyway and I got thirty bucks."

"And you didn't know him, or anything about him."

"Nah. Nothin'."

"What did he look like?"

Sullivan frowned. "I don't know. Big. Buzz cut hair, kinda grey. Bigger'n me."

"What about his truck? What color? Describe this big ass dually."

"Red. Ford, I think."

"Keep going."

"Kinda fancy hubs." Richards didn't say anything, and Sullivan's eyes again jerked from side to side, his gaze never lingering on anything. The seconds ticked off.

Finally, Sullivan added, "Oh, had Arkansas plates. Don't know what he was doin' 'round Tyler."

"What else?"

Bud ground his teeth, as if that might help him think of something else. "Big mirrors, that really stuck out, like he might be pulling a wide trailer or something." After a moment, "That's all. I swear I don't know nothing else about that guy or his truck."

"Where's the paddle?"

"Sold it with the canoe. Don't need it no more."

"You've lied to me several times about the canoe. Are you sure this latest story is true? Because if it isn't, you're going to be in serious trouble."

"It's the truth." Bud was shaking his head. "That's really what happened to the canoe."

Richards picked up his hat and stood. "We'll find it, Bud. And you better be telling me the truth." He walked to the door. "I will be back."

Chapter 44

FATHER FRANK PUT the phone back in its cradle and leaned back in his chair, eyes closed. *What now? It seems every time he calls and asks me to come down, it's trouble.* He remembered a year ago when Monsignor Decker raked him over the coals because Sid left money to the church. Decker thought the priest was behind it all. In truth, Father Frank had been as surprised as the rest of them when Norm read the will with all the family present.

Now Decker has probably heard I was talking with a Texas Ranger and got worried I might be in trouble. Father Frank could speculate all he wanted, but there was no point in it. He'd find out this afternoon. Right now, he had to turn his attention to his day job. The couple he'd counseled last week, the Gofortines, were coming back for a follow up. Father Frank hoped they'd made some progress.

* * *

An hour later, he ushered a smiling couple out the front door. Mr. Gofortine shook the priest's hand. "If something gets out of kilter, we'll call you. But," he smiled at his wife and she smiled back. "I think we're on the right track. Thanks for the help."

"God helped you. I was just the moderator. I'm so pleased that you two are …" He smiled and cocked his head to the side. "Happy."

Father Frank closed the door and let out a long breath, glad he'd rightly predicted the couple would work through their troubles. *Counseling is tough. I have enough trouble keeping myself moving in the right direction.* Right now, he decided he'd better head down to Tyler. Keeping Monsignor Decker waiting wouldn't make things easier.

* * *

At one o'clock, Father Frank rang the bell. *I'll know in the first five seconds how this will go.*

The Monsignor opened the door. "Come in Father Frank."

Not good. No "Top of the morning, Frank." No "Are ya keepin' well, Frank?"

The Monsignor led the way into the living room. With heavy exposed-wood furniture, wood paneling, cocoa colored carpet, and western art, the room reflected Monsignor Decker's early years growing up on a ranch.

As soon as they were seated, the Monsignor got right to the point. "A year ago, more or less, your sister came to visit you and stayed with you for awhile." Father Frank started to speak, but the Monsignor held up his hand. "Yes, yes. We discussed that and all was fine. However, it has come to my attention that she is back."

Father Frank nodded.

"But now, she is a suspect in a murder investigation. That changes things. We cannot have people, relatives or not, accused of murder. I know she's not convicted, but I'm concerned about the optics—an accused murderer staying at the rectory?"

Father Frank's voice came out a little louder than he intended, but he did not soften it. "Remember, Monsignor, in the U.S., a person is innocent until proven guilty. The Church has a long history of providing a sanctuary for those unjustly accused. And my sister did not kill that man."

"And yet, the sheriff believes she did. He has witnesses who heard her threaten the man, in public, no less. And after he was killed, the Sheriff's deputies heard her say, 'He deserved it.' As I understand it, she is his prime suspect."

"The Texas Rangers are looking for other suspects."

"And how do you know what the Texas Rangers are pursuing on this case?"

"The lead Ranger on this case has talked to me several times. He tells me they are actively looking at other suspects." *Should I say he has said Maggie is not the Rangers' top suspect? Maybe not. If he asks why Richards feels that way, I don't really know.*

"Why would the Rangers tell you anything about this case?"

Tricky question. And I cannot lie. "Frankly, I don't know why he has told me some of the things he's said." That was the truth. "The conference director had asked me to speak with a few of the participants who were having trouble dealing with a murder, and possibly a murderer amongst them. The ranger then asked me what I thought of one of those. I think he figured I might have gotten something out of them that he couldn't, along the theory that people would be more open with a priest than with an officer of the law."

The Monsignor steepled his fingers and considered what Father Frank had said. "I still don't like it. I don't like having murder suspects at the rectory. And from what I understand, your sister is still the Sheriff's prime suspect, regardless of what the Rangers think."

"Monsignor Decker, she is my sister. And she's innocent. Sheriff Bark wants her to stay in his jurisdiction. What do you want me to do? Put her out on the street? She cannot afford to stay in a hotel until..." He almost said "this incompetent, biased sheriff is exposed," but decided against it. "... until they get this case solved. It's bad enough Maggie is separated from her husband. I'm not going to toss her out." He paused only a second. "That would be most un-Christian."

Decker considered Frank's statement. "All right," he conceded. "I don't like it. But for the moment, I'll ignore it. But I will keep posted on how the investigation proceeds. If they indict her, then we must put some space between her and the Church."

"Does that mean if she's indicted, she can't come to daily Mass? Receive the sacraments?" It came out a bit louder and more aggressively than he intended.

The Monsignor's head came up and his eyes opened wide. He opened his mouth, but didn't speak for a few seconds. "Do not be impudent, Frank. I'm thinking about the reputation of your church, of Prince of Peace."

"And I'm thinking about my family. And how I treat *them* also impacts my reputation."

"And Prince of Peace and the Church are also your family."

For a minute, neither said anything. Father Frank broke the silence. "Monsignor, I will do whatever I can to maintain good relations with all parts of my family. Prince of Peace is very important to me. I will never do anything I believe will damage it. Nor will I abandon my sister. But I think I can handle both sides of this and cause no pain, no disappointment, no disillusionment to either."

The Monsignor nodded several times. "Thank you. That reassures me. Frank, you know I only want to protect the reputation of the Church." He got up, signaling an end to this meeting.

At the door, he laid a hand on Father Frank's shoulder. "Pray for help to walk a very thin line."

Chapter 45

THE SEARCH WAS in its third day. The Rangers had visited dozens of boat shops– any place that sold, repaired, or rented canoes. Mid-morning on the third day one of the Rangers, named Lewis, finally got a hit. A shop owner confirmed a customer who fit their description, had the right truck, and had been in buying a little HDPE to patch a hole in a canoe.

"What's HDPE?" Lewis asked.

"That's high density polyethylene. Many canoes are made of it. I told the guy he could probably just use an old plastic milk carton, but he said he wanted it to look good."

The store copy of the sales receipt had the man's name and address.

Outside, Lewis called his partner who was visiting other boat shops. "Meet me at this address fast as you can get there. I think we've found it."

Twenty minutes later, both Rangers were looking at a red dually Ford 350. It looked like Bud Sullivan had been truthful on that front. The truck's owner, Curt Nogalis, almost as big as the truck, confirmed buying the canoe. "Sure, it had a hole in it, but I figured I could patch that easy. I offered him thirty bucks. He took it. I'd a gone to forty if he'd held out. But he was happy to unload it and I was happy to get it."

Lewis pulled out his wallet and handed the man thirty dollars. "Sorry, Mr. Nogalis. But we have to take the canoe back to Texas. It's part of an investigation."

"What kind of investigation? Somebody claiming he caught the world's biggest catfish?" Nogalis laughed and took the money.

"Could be. But I'm not at liberty to divulge that. Where's the paddle? I need that also."

"Wasn't a paddle with it. I didn't care. Still a good deal for me."

"Are you sure there wasn't a paddle with it?"

"Absolutely." Nogalis pulled out his wallet and stuffed the thirty dollars into it. "How 'bout a sawbuck for me hauling it all the way up here?"

Lewis laughed. "Nah. Now, I've got to haul it all the way back to Texas." He turned to move his pickup up in position to load the canoe. "Say, Mr. Nogalis. Was there anything else in the canoe? Anything at all?"

"Lemme think." His hand came up with his index finger pointed to the sky. "Actually there was. Found a pair a' old cotton gloves."

The Ranger jerked around, his attention on full alert. "A pair of gloves? Can I see 'em. Might be worth more 'an a sawbuck." He held his breath, anticipation trying to burst through his face.

"Darn. I should'a saved 'em. But they was dirty. Had some old grease or something on 'em. So, I just tossed them in the burn barrel over there."

Lewis started toward the old fifty gallon barrel, once brown, now a mixture of rust and burn marks.

"No use looking. I've already burned a lot of stuff in there since the gloves went in."

"Mind if I take a look anyway?"

"Go ahead. But it'll just get your nice, clean jeans and shirt dirty."

Both Texas Rangers went over and looked in. Not much chance of finding anything, but they had to look. They turned the barrel over and dumped out the ashes. Then, on their knees, they poked through all the ashes. *Just need a small fragment. Come on. Just a finger. Anything.* Twice, he thought he had something. *Anything. Just a clump that might have some blood on it.*

After ten minutes, Lewis got up, dusted off his pants, and said to his partner, "That's it. We aren't going to find anything here. Even if we found a piece of a glove, there wouldn't be a finger print, unless we got the end of a finger. But a trace of blood? Now that would have made Richards happy." He turned to Nogalis. "Should have listened to you. Got a shovel? I'll clean up the ashes and get 'em back in the barrel."

"Don't pay no mind to it. I'll take care of it."

"Well, thanks Mr. Nogalis. Sorry about taking your canoe, but it will be a big help to the Texas Rangers."

* * *

Once the two rangers, each in a Ford 150, crossed back into Texas, they stopped for fuel. Lewis called Lieutenant Richards. "We've got the canoe. Guy said there wasn't a paddle, though."

He listened for a minute. "We're in Texarkana and should be at the lab in Dallas in about three hours." He listened another minute. "Yes, sir. There appears to be blood near the stern, but it's hard to tell if there're any finger prints in it. I can't see any, but the technicians might find some. The bad news is, there had been a pair of cotton gloves in the canoe when Mr. Nogalis got it. But he burned them. Said they had some grease or something on 'em."

He listened for a few seconds. "Yes, sir. We searched through all the ashes. There wasn't anything we could put together. He'd burned a bunch of paper, wood, who knows what else, and just tossed the gloves in on top." He listened for a few seconds. "Yes, Sir. We'll take it straight to the lab."

* * *

Richards ended the call feeling hopeful for the first time in days. The Texas Rangers tried to stay on top of all the newest technology. The latest was RapidHIT, a method that greatly increased the speed in which DNA could be extracted from a blood sample. Using this new ID system, they might have an answer to the crime as soon as this afternoon.

Chapter 46

THE SUN SAT on the edge of the lake, sending a golden stripe across the sapphire water and out of sight to the east. Grass covering the space from the road to the very edge of the lake was as vibrant a green as the water was blue.

Richards sat in his car in front of the Sullivan's house trying to drink in the beauty and peace, before he had to go talk to the man about murder. He had considered bringing Sheriff Bark with him. But Bark would probably cause even more trouble. Besides, Sullivan was not a threat to him. Sullivan had a very strong motive to kill Granet. Granet had raped Bud's daughter. Richards stopped that train of thought. *Allegedly raped her.* But Jane's information seemed very credible to Richards. Now, three years later, Grace was still traumatized, no longer the ambitious young woman who had won a writing contest and was looking forward to college. It seemed likely Granet should have been tried for rape and the truth discovered. But no charges were filed. Still, that failure did not give anybody the right to murder Granet, not even Bud Sullivan. And unfortunately for Sullivan, RapidHIT had proved it was Granet's blood on Sullivan's canoe.

* * *

"What do ya want this time?" Bud Sullivan stood with his arms crossed over his chest. He was only about five feet seven inches tall, but he had a broad body. His stance covered the doorway and his eyes looked defiant.

"How about starting with some straight answers?" Richards matched the belligerent tone. "There's a lot you're not telling me. Frankly, I'm getting pretty tired of the run around." The Texas Ranger had his hands on his hips, almost as if they were resting on a pair of six shooters. All he needed was his white stallion, Silver, waiting for him to jump on and ride away.

"I told ya what happened and gave ya as much stuff on the guy who bought the canoe as I could remember. Now you're here buggin' me again."

"Yes. You did give us some good information. And Bud." He paused and drilled the man with a piercing look. "We found the man who bought it. We have the canoe."

Sullivan's mouth dropped open and it took him several seconds to speak. "Well, ah, well that's, ah, good work. Where'd ya find it?"

"In Arkansas. The man confirmed he got the canoe at the Tyler dump and that he paid you thirty dollars. Sound familiar?"

Bud's confidence seemed to slip away. His rigid stance slumped a bit. Richards said nothing, but let his gaze bore into the man. Sullivan looked right, then left, then right again. He seemed unfocused, not seeing the sun as it slowly sank into the far side of the lake, or the car that zoomed down the street, clearly breaking the speed limit. Finally, he said, "Okay. Ya got the canoe. I gave you good information. Sos, why are ya here?"

"First, I wanted to bring you a picture of the boat." With that, Richards flipped a picture printed on card stock towards Sullivan.

Bud reached out and grabbed the picture with his left hand, and turned it over to look at the picture. "Looks like he cleaned it up a bit."

Richards nodded a few times. "He did." The Ranger let that sink in a moment. "Fortunately for us, he couldn't clean all of the blood off the canoe."

Bud's tongue ran around his lips even as his focus bounced from one side of the Ranger to the other, never stopping on him. Obviously, Bud had thought the Rangers would never find the boat, and if they did, any blood traces would be gone. Wrong on both counts. "Blood?" It was apparent to Richards that Bud was trying to sound totally confused by the word. But Richards felt sure Bud knew full well what the Ranger was talking about.

Sullivan carefully untwisted his hands and laid one on each leg, trying to keep them steady. He looked up, acting as if he had just remembered something. "Oh, right. The canoe had been in an accident. Right. There was a hole in the bow where some hotrod power boat ran smack dab into it. Ought'a arrested the reckless driver of the power boat. Wish they'd outlaw 'em on the lake."

The Ranger remained silent, staring intently at Sullivan.

Now Bud tried to look concerned. "I hope no one was seriously injured."

"If there's blood, it usually means someone was injured." Richards was quiet for a moment. "I'm not much into boating. But suppose I went out to paddle a canoe by myself, no one else in the canoe. Where should I sit?"

The question seemed to catch Bud by surprise. "Ah, well personally, I'd kneel against the bow seat, facing the stern."

"This canoe seems to get a lot of paddling with someone sitting on the back seat, facing forward, toward the bow."

"That's 'cause —." Sullivan stopped suddenly. He looked down for a moment, then back up. "Somebody borrowed my boat and took it for a joy ride. Happens 'round here. All the time."

"Anybody in particular?"

Bud shifted his weight from one foot to the other. "Naw. I don't pay no attention to it. Always bring it back."

"Are you a good swimmer, Bud?"

"I'm purty good. Not as good as –" For several seconds Bud looked like he had bitten into a lemon. He swallowed. "As many guys. Anyways, I ain't likely to drown around here."

"The man who hit your boat motored around a few times, looking to see if anyone was in the water. He didn't see anyone."

Sullivan looked down at his shoes. Richards waited.

"Like I tole you the other day, somebody untied it and let it drift out in the lake. Or took it fur a joy ride and left it untied. That speed boat hit it, but there weren't nobody in it."

"So where did the blood come from if there was no one in it?"

Bud shrugged. "How'd I know?"

"Where's the paddle?"

"Like I tole ya, I sold it with the canoe. No boat, don't need no paddle."

"The man who bought it said there was no paddle with the canoe. He could have used it, but you just sold him the canoe. No paddle."

"Ah, well, ah." His eyes flitted around, as if he were looking for a paddle on the front lawn. "Ah, I guess it got knocked out when that crazy motor boat guy hit it. Probly at the bottom of the lake."

"What was the paddle made of: wood or plastic?"

"Wood."

"So it's not at the bottom of the lake."

"Must a blown out on the way to Tyler."

"Where were you on the night of October 29 this year? Specifically between ten p.m. and midnight?"

Bud jerked up, as if someone had yanked up on his collar. Why'd ya wana know?"

"A person was murdered about that time. Right across the lake from your house. And your canoe was in the water around midnight."

"Now, wait a danged minute. I tole you what happened. Someone took my canoe, then jus let it drift. I don't know nothing about no murder."

Richards nodded a couple of times. "And yet, your canoe had blood on it."

"Got hit by a guy speedin' on the lake."

"Bud, the blood on the canoe was that of the person murdered." Richards let that sink in. What he did not share was that although the DNA from the blood was a perfect match to Granet, they had not been able to recover a single fingerprint in it.

Sullivan's face grew pale and his breathing sped up. His hands once more were locked together. And he was shaking his head. "What ya' thinkin'?" Richards didn't reply. "I didn't kill nobody. You think I killed that guy?"

"I didn't say it was a guy."

His breathing grew even faster, and despite the cool day, drops of sweat formed on his brow. "It was, ah, in the paper. The paper said it was a guy."

"Do you know who he was? "

"No." It came out too quickly.

Richards said nothing. *Let him sweat. Let him decide how to answer this.* "You didn't answer my question."

"What question?"

"Where were you between ten p.m. and midnight on October 29 this year?"

"Ah, I was out hunting."

"Hunting what?"

 "Deer."

"That's too early for deer hunting in Texas."

"Nah. We was huntin' Axis deer." Now he managed to untangle his hands and his breathing actually slowed a little.

"At night?"

"'It's on private land. So it's okay."

"Can anyone verify that?"

Bud's forehead wrinkled. "That's the law. Guess we could look it up."

"No, I mean can anybody verify you were hunting that night?"

Bud dropped his gaze for a second then looked back up at the Ranger. "Yeah. I was huntin' with Sheriff Dudly, up in Greer county."

Now it was Richards who looked surprised. He blinked a few times, then said, "And what time was that?"

Sullivan almost smiled. "I drove up there 'bout nine or so. Met Dub, that's what I call him, met him 'bout maybe ten. We went out in his four by four. He got a buck. I got nothin'. We didn't git back to his house until maybe seven in the morning. I didn't get home til nearly nine. You call Dub. That's what I call him. Get it? I'm B. U. D. and he's D. U. B." Now he did smile. "Ask him. He'll tell ya."

Richards just stood there looking at his prime suspect. *Hunting with a sheriff?* "You can be sure I will."

He turned on one heel and marched to his Tahoe.

Chapter 47

FATHER FRANK FELT a bit logy. It wasn't the murder case or even his visit with Monsignor Decker. He chuckled. Probably all the good food Maggie had been preparing. Maybe a little basketball would get his blood flowing. He put on his tennis shoes, grabbed a basketball and headed outside.

Fifteen minutes later, he was feeling better. *Clearly, I'm getting old and slovenly. Not that I was ever great, but at least I could dunk when I was playing in college. Today, forget it.*

He stepped to the free throw line and dropped in another shot, his seventh in a row. At least that skill hadn't deserted him.

Richards pulled his Tahoe into the church parking lot and waited a moment, watching Father Frank shoot free throws. It only took a couple of minutes before the priest saw him. Father Frank waved and jogged over to meet Richards. They walked over and sat on the lawman's favorite bench.

"What brings you here on a Thursday Lieutenant Richards? Business or pleasure?"

"Always business. Looks like you can still shoot pretty well. I never played basketball. I was a second string tailback, thought I could run over people. Found out I couldn't. Made the baseball team in college." He shrugged. "In truth, I wasn't all that good at either."

"My passion was always basketball. I played a little in college before I entered the seminary."

"What I heard was you were a standout at UT Arlington. In fact, one of the guys I knew there said you singlehandedly beat S.M.U. your sophomore year. He said —"

"Don't believe everything you hear. I was *part* of that win over S.M.U. but it was a team effort."

Richards laughed. "He also said you'd say that." Now he turned serious. "But, I wanted to talk about the Sullivans. And also RTS."

"I don't know if I can help at all, but what do you want to know? Please remember, I have no personal experience. Thank the Lord, I have never had to counsel a rape victim.

"Well, fill me in on what you do know."

Father Frank paused, trying to remember what he'd read. "It seems Rape Trauma Syndrome is quite similar to PTSD in general. The criteria for PTSD—the same emotional reactions and changed behaviors—can be found in victims of rape. In fact, many articles call it just another example of PTSD. But after reading a number of articles by professionals who deal with rape victims, I've concluded rape is a crime few understand."

Richards focused on some distant space and said nothing.

"Why are you asking?"

"Just trying to understand the dynamics of the Sullivans. What it might mean. "

For a few minutes the two men studied the cumulus clouds that dotted an azure sky.

The priest turned and looked at the Ranger. "Anything come of the canoe that got hit the night of the murder?"

"Yes, actually."

"And?"

Richards shook his head. "I'm not ready to talk about it just yet."

"But you're considering Sullivan as a suspect?"

"A person of interest."

"Like Maggie?"

"Not exactly."

"How long can the Sheriff keep her here, away from her home, away from her husband?"

"As long as he chooses to. Has she ever tried to take the locator off her ankle?"

"Not that I know of."

"She could petition the judge who ordered it and ask if she could return home as long as she kept the locator on."

Father Frank raised his eyebrows. "Would he do that?"

"I don't know. But he could. As I understand, he was willing to release her on her own recognizance. So, there's a chance, especially since she hasn't tried to cause any trouble."

"That's a great idea. I'll speak to her lawyer today."

Richards stood up, placed his Stetson on top of his head and gave it a tap. "Thanks for helping me sort out things, although I still don't know which way to go."

"Any time."

Richards got up, then sat back down.

"I know you're not a psychologist or a psychiatrist. But you've been reading on RTS. I know that someone suffering from PTSD might take some very aggressive action years after suffering the trauma. Could that be possible in the case of RTS?"

Father Frank eyes widened and he leaned back from Richard a little. "Oh my." He tried to swallow the lump forming in his throat. "I don't know. And I don't want to speculate on that. You need to talk to a professional psychologist."

"I guess I'm asking if that is a reasonable thing to talk to a psychologist about. I'm totally unknowledgeable about RTS. Would he think I was crazy to suggest, no, to raise the question she might have committed this act?"

"No. He would not think you are crazy." *Maybe the idea, but not you personally.* "My guess is, the doctor would want to talk to Grace in person, probably more than once." Father Frank cocked his head to one side. "Don't the Rangers have a doctor they can call when needed."

"Yes. I've never felt the need."

"I think you have the need right now."

* * *

Father Frank watched the Texas Ranger get in his car and leave. *He's seriously considering Grace as a suspect. But how is that possible? She rarely gets out of the house, barely functions. And more important, shows little emotion. Bud Sullivan must have a great alibi.*

The priest headed for the rectory, then detoured by the church. As he walked in the door, a thought popped into his head. *Jane said Grace stomped on the picture of Granet, was clearly upset, angry. Maybe the idea isn't too far-fetched.*

He knelt at the back pew. *Dear Lord, please watch over Grace. She has suffered much in her short life. If she has strayed from the path of righteousness, forgive her and guide her to utilize the talent you have given her.*

He walked back to the rectory, grabbed a Dr Pepper from the fridge and called Norm with Richards's suggestion to get Maggie out of house arrest.

"Well, it's certainly possible. I've seen it happen before. But ..." He paused, and Father Frank imagined him stroking his chin, as he'd seen him do many times before. "The problem here is the Sheriff. He wants to keep her either in jail or on a very short leash. I can't understand why, but it certainly looks like he does. He may try to block us. Still, Judge Hamm didn't seem to feel that way." The lawyer paused again. "Oh, why not? Let's give it a try. There really is no down side to asking."

"Shall I tell Maggie?"

Norm gave a short laugh. "I'd wait. First let me see if I can even get a hearing. No point getting her excited and then nothing comes of it."

Father Frank had just hung up when Maggie walked in. "I made a little progress today."

"Progress? On what?"

"Not yet. Let's just say I've got a little project going. I'll tell you about it if and when things fall into place."

Chapter 48

FRIDAY MORNING, NORM Winters stood before Judge Jimmy Hamm. "I'm petitioning the court to release my client ROR, your Honor, and allow her to return to her home, her husband and her job." Norm Winters sat down beside Maggie, who sat quietly and almost demurely.

Judge Jimmy Hamm nodded and looked at the Assistant District Attorney, who was shaking his head. "You want to comment on this request, Mr. Tamaford?"

Maggie looked over at the ADA. To her he looked too young to be a lawyer. *Probably five feet eight and I'll bet he weighs less than I do. And the crew cut makes him look like a high school kid. I hope he's as inexperienced as he looks.*

Tamaford stood. "I certainly do, your Honor. The Sheriff is opposed to this and the District Attorney agrees with him. She should remain in our jurisdiction, keep the location monitor on, and be readily available when the Sheriff has more questions. This is, after all, a murder case, and Ms. DeLuca is the prime suspect."

The judge looked at the ADA for a moment before speaking. "I understand the sheriff has called Ms. DeLuca in twice since she was released from jail. Is that correct.?"

"Yes sir."

"And did this produce any additional evidence?

Tamaford looked down, swallowed, and then looked back up at the Judge. "I'm not at liberty to say, your Honor."

"Not good enough, Mr. Tamaford. I've been asked to revisit my ROR on Ms. DeLuca. You're objecting, so you must provide some reason."

The ADA studied his note pad, coughed twice, and finally addressed the Judge. "Well, there was some evidence regarding the amount of money that might have been involved."

Norm Winters was on his feet immediately. "Your Honor, the Sheriff was completely confused on the money situation. He misunderstood what was involved. He had made some calculation, on his own, without knowing anything about how it actually worked. We debunked his reasoning and he immediately dropped that line of questioning. And I'd like to add he brought her into the jail in handcuffs, and put her in a cell. If not for her legal representation, she'd still be there. "

The Judge looked from Norm to the ADA. "Is that a fair description, Mr. Tamaford?"

"Well, I wasn't at that meeting. But I listened to the recording. There did seem to be some confusion over the money involved. Nonetheless, the Sheriff —"

The Judge sat up, leaned forward and interrupted Tamaford. "Was the Sheriff reprimanded for harassing the defendant and her brother?"

The young ADA leaned back as if the Judge might reach for him. He stammered for a moment before he managed to say, "Your Honor, I don't see that as pertinent to this hearing. That was —"

"Unfortunately for you, what you think is pertinent is not at issue here." The judge smiled pleasantly as he interrupted. "It's what *I* think is pertinent. So I'll ask again. Is there any new evidence, or any reason why I should not release the defendant ROR, and remove the restriction that she remain in this jurisdiction?" He relaxed in his high-backed chair. "Tell me why I should keep her from her home, family, and job? Go ahead. I'm listening. "

Tamaford shuffled through his papers, knocking several on the floor. He scrounged around, picked them up and stuffed them back in his folder. Winters gave Maggie's shoulder a slight squeeze.

"However," the Judge said, "I'm not going to wait all day for it. Do you have anything else to present?"

"It is a murder investigation," the young lawyer stammered.

"Are you suggesting I have forgotten that?"

"No, Sir, ah, I mean, your Honor."

"Do you have anything else to say? Now."

Tamaford poked in his brief case for a few seconds, then looked up. "No, Your Honor."

"Then, I am removing the restriction that Ms. DeLuca remain in this jurisdiction." He turned to Maggie. "However, you will keep the location monitor on, and you are not to leave the state. Is that clear?"

Maggie nodded vigorously. "Yes, Your Honor."

"Should the court, or the Sheriff, require you to return to Timber County, you will make arrangements to appear quickly, within twenty-four hours."

"Yes, Your Honor."

Judge Jimmy Hamm picked up the gavel and banged it once. "This hearing is closed."

Chapter 49

FATHER FRANK GOT a box of Cheerios out of the cabinet and grabbed the milk from the refrigerator. Maggie had been fixing elaborate breakfasts while she was here, but it was back to reality now.

Probably what I deserve. When she first moved in, he felt his life was being invaded. He loved his sister. But having another person take over your space, even someone you love, could be unsettling. And then that feeling changed. After a week, it felt comfortable. He settled into the routine of having someone else using the shower when he wanted it; remembering to take out clothes for tomorrow before retiring, since he was sleeping in the office; and having someone else prepare meals - always better than he ever made. Now he found himself missing her cooking – and her company.

He had just finished breakfast when the phone rang.

"Prince of Peace Church, this is Father Frank. How can I help you?"

"You already have. This is Dick Richards. Since you got me started on this I thought I'd give you a brief update, and perhaps a heads up. I have spoken with the Ranger's psychiatrist. She is very interested in speaking with Grace."

"I think that's a wise move."

"Thank you. The other thing I wanted to alert you to is Sheriff Bark is bringing in a couple of the earlier suspects to re-interview them. So, don't be surprised if he brings Maggie in again. Just be warned it could happen. I know Judge Hamm allowed her to leave this jurisdiction. But she'd better not mess around if the Sheriff calls her back. She must come. He would use any delay or refusal to return as a weapon to force her back into this jurisdiction and possibly a jail cell."

"She wouldn't do that," Father Frank assured him. "She was excited to get back. So I know she won't jeopardize it. But I'll pass on the warning."

"Just remember, the Sheriff hasn't given up on her. He's looking for anything at all to strengthen his case against her. Be careful."

The priest hung up the phone and sat down to think. Richards had been very helpful to him and Maggie. For whatever reason, he'd decided early on Maggie was not guilty. And yet, he kept hinting at aspects in the case that made Maggie a prime suspect. *Wish he'd tell me what those are. And why he doesn't think either Billy John or Val is as good a suspect.*

He thought about calling Maggie right now and telling her, but decided not to. She deserved a day or two to feel free and enjoy her life with Jeff.

* * *

Saturday morning, Father Frank drove to the auto repair shop. He had gotten a message that his Taurus was repaired and ready for him to pick it up. He inspected the new fenders, windshield and driver's side window. Everything looked well done. He turned in the rental car, settled his account with the body shop and settled into the Taurus. *Nice to be back in my familiar, if old, car. Must admit, though, there were some pretty nice features in the rental. Oh well, I have a luxurious life, if not a luxury car.*

Back at the rectory, Father Frank put the finishing touches on his homily for tomorrow. *We expect God to be forgiving of our mistakes. But how many of us are forgiving of the mistakes of others? I hope this little sermon will help.* He said a quick prayer that he had found the words to help people, then slipped on his tennis shoes and headed outside to his Saturday group of young basketball players.

Today, nine boys and two girls were already gathered, taking shots. When the girls first showed up a few weeks ago, the boys didn't know how to react. But soon, one of the girls, Katie, was dropping in clean shots from twenty feet out. At the time, one of the boys came over and asked the priest if they had to let the girls be part of the Saturday B-Ball.

"Afraid they'll make you look bad?" Father Frank asked.

"Naw. It's just, well, you know. I mean, how do you guard a girl?"

The priest laughed. "I'd say very carefully. She may go around you. Just remember, it is supposed to be a non-contact sport." He gave the boys shoulder a squeeze. "It will be fine. And I'll be here to make sure they don't run you off the court."

For an hour, he worked with a group of teens, coaching each player, pointing out how they could improve their defense, the subtle art of positioning their feet, and how to know when to take a shot and when to pass. He loved doing it and it was good exercise. *I sit in committee meetings; I sit when counseling; I sit in the confessional; I sit while writing a sermon. Without a little basketball, my most exercise is standing out front on Sunday's and shaking hands. Thank you, Lord, for giving me a little basketball. Feel free to take a few pounds off my waistline.*

* * *

It was the Saturday before Thanksgiving so the annual food distribution should have been in full swing. He and two other ministers in town had organized the function two years ago. Last year, three other churches joined in and it had become an important event, particularly for those families struggling financially. Father Frank decided he needed to get over to town park and make certain Prince of Peace was keeping up its share of the drive. Of course, the first person he ran into was Georgia.

"How's it going, Georgia?"

"Great. We've had more people stopping by, needing supplies, than either of the two previous years. And, fortunately, we've had more food donated this year."

"And you have plenty of help, I see."

"Yes. And the good news is, several of those pitching in are new to the parish."

"Excellent. Good to get new people involved in these activities."

He followed Georgia over to the Prince of Peace booth and visited with parish members passing out supplies.

Before leaving, Father Frank made a point to speak with the other ministers whose churches were helping make this year's drive such a success.

* * *

Sunday afternoon, Father Frank got a call from Maggie.

"Can I come bunk with you again? Tonight?"Her voice was only a little depressed.

The priest leaned back in his chair and pressed his fingers against his eyes. *Is the Ranger's speculation coming true?* "Of course, yes. What's the occasion?"

"Old Bark-Bark wants to harass me again. And don't start on me. I've had to almost hogtie Jeff to keep him from coming down with me and attacking the Sheriff."

"I won't give you any problems. Come on. When will you get here?"

"I'll have dinner with Jeff and then head on down. I'm meeting with the honorable Sheriff at 9:00 in the morning." She paused for a second. "Think Mr. Winters could accompany me?"

"I'm sure he would if he doesn't have another commitment. Give him a call."

"I've tried him several times and haven't gotten through to him."

"I'll call him and see if I can have him meet you in the morning. If he can't, I'll be there. Be careful. On the drive down, I mean. I know you'll be careful with the Sheriff."

Chapter 50

AT EXACTLY 9:00, Maggie and Norm Winters entered the Timber County Sheriff's office. At a little after 9:25, she was ushered into an interrogation room. Fifteen minutes later, the Sheriff came in, placed a recorder on the table and read in the basics of the interview.

"So DeLuca, do you want to tell me about your activities on the Thursday night that Rod Granet was killed?"

Maggie bristled. *I've answered that question at least four times.* "I bought a soda at the cafeteria, went to my room and did not leave until after 8:00 the next morning."

The Sheriff almost smiled. "And what time would you say you returned to your room?"

"I don't know exactly. I was upset and didn't look at my watch. But I would guess it was about 9:00."

Now, the Sheriff did smile. "You were upset? I guess if you had just killed a man you would be upset."

Norm immediately leaned over and whispered in Maggie's ear.

"I did not kill Granet." Maggie's voice had risen several decibels.

"It does seem that you have a very quick temper. Do you lose it often?"

Maggie clenched her hands in her lap and locked her jaws. She would not let him force her to say something she'd regret.

After a moment, the Sheriff looked at his notes and then at Maggie. "I have a witness who says it was closer to ten o'clock, not nine."

Again, Norm whispered to Maggie.

She was steaming, but managed to hold her tongue. He hadn't asked a question, so she did not have to respond.

"So, you're not going to disagree with that statement?"

What's best? Should I argue this? I said I didn't know exactly what time. She took a deep breath and tried to relax. "As I said earlier, I don't know exactly what time it was. I do not believe it was as late as ten."

"So, this witness was lying, you think?"

She almost lashed out at the man, but caught herself just as she opened her mouth. She took a minute, then pretended she was talking to Jeff. "No. I'm not saying your witness was lying. I wasn't sure what time it was. Perhaps she wasn't sure what time it was either. Did your witness have a reason to believe it was exactly ten? Maybe her favorite TV show just went off."

"I'll ask the questions, Ms. Deluca. And you did not leave your room after that until the next morning?"

"That is correct."

The sheriff shuffled some papers around, then pulled one out. "Suppose I told you that Granet was killed around nine-thirty."

It's not a question. Do not respond.

"That would actually give you time to slash his throat and then walk back to your room." When she did not respond, he added, "Wouldn't it?"

She opened her mouth, then stopped. *That's a trick question. Be careful.*

Once more, Norm whispered something to Maggie.

"I don't know, Sheriff. I have no idea how long it would take a person to walk over to whatever cabin Granet was in and then walk back. And I have no idea whatsoever how long it would take to kill him."

"I think it would be enough time."

"Well, I don't know. However, there was talk going around that he was killed between eleven and twelve. I was in my room at that time."

Bark puffed up as if he might start yelling. But instead, he said, "You can't believe any of that talk. I'm the one with the facts. Can anyone corroborate that you were in your room?"

Again, Maggie thought there was no good answer. Not good to say no one can collaborate your alibi. And saying yes would require producing a person who knew she was in her room. "I don't know."

"So you have no alibi."

"Yes, I do." It came out louder than she wanted. *Slow down, gal. Don't let him make you lose control.* "My alibi is that I was in my room."

"And no one can corroborate that?"

Another private word from Norm to Maggie.

"As I said, I don't know. I can tell you no one was in my room with me, but I don't know if anyone was watching to see if I came out. But, I did not leave my room until after eight o'clock the next morning. And I did not know Granet had been attacked, killed, whatever, until almost ten o'clock the next morning."

The Sheriff restacked his papers and then looked at Maggie. "Let me explain the situation to you. When I produce a witness who says you were out of your room when you said you were in it, it will mean you are lying to me, hiding the truth. That will make you look as guilty as sin. So, think very carefully before you answer. Even if you did not kill Granet, now is not the time to lie. Are you certain you were in your room between ten o'clock Thursday night and 8 o'clock Friday morning?"

When she did not speak immediately, Bark added, "And I might be able to get that witness in here within fifteen minutes. So think about that before you answer."

Maggie opened her mouth to answer, then stopped. *I was not out of my room. But could he have gotten someone to say I was? There's no way I can know that.* She leaned over and held a whispered conversation with Norm.

Then she sat up straight and took a deep breath. "Sheriff Bark, if you produce a witness who is telling the God's honest truth, that witness will *not* say they *positively* saw me outside my room between ten o'clock Thursday night and 8 o'clock Friday morning."

The Sheriff fixed her with a steely stare. Maggie knew he was trying to intimidate her. This cold, grey, cement block room, the recorder sitting in front of her, the deputy standing behind her, all were intended to make her nervous. And they succeeded.

She could now understand how some people pleaded guilty when they weren't.

"Last chance to change your story."

Maggie shook her head. "No. I'll stick with the truth."

For a full two minutes, neither said anything. Finally, the Sheriff spoke into the recorder," This concludes the interview with suspect Margaret DeLuca." He looked at his watch. "Ten fifteen."

He pulled his papers into a pile and picked them up. Without a word to Maggie, he walked to the door. As he left he said to the deputy, "Show DeLuca and the lawyer out."

                                   * * *

"You'd have been proud of me, little brother." Maggie stood in the rectory kitchen, drinking a cup of coffee.

"Yes, I would have. Because I know you did not let your mouth get ahead of your brain. Otherwise, we'd be speaking on the telephone instead of in-person. Or I'd be talking to Norm and he'd tell me I needed to post bond or something." He took a drink of his Dr Pepper. "Are you staying?"

She grinned. "Nope. I'm on my way home. I just stopped to tell you, and to call Jeff. I didn't want to use my phone while driving. I know old Bark-Bark would have someone following me ready to haul me in if I talked while driving."

"Good thinking. And I'm sure Jeff was glad to get that call."

"You bet he was."

"So, what did the Sheriff want?"

"Nothing, really. I believe he actually thought he might get me to confess, or something. He had no new evidence. Oh, he said someone told him they had seen me entering the residence hall. Which was probably true. But way too early. At least an hour before Granet was killed."

"Nothing else?"

"No. He threatened to bring in the witness and catch me in a lie. I basically said he could try. But Norm kept me from freaking out."

"Be very careful, Maggie. He obviously wants to put you back in jail. "

She took a last sip of the coffee, and put the cup in the sink just as the doorbell rang.

"I'll get it," Maggie said. In a minute, she was back with Mike. Father Frank looked at the detective. "To what do we owe this visit?"

"Remember I mentioned I had a friend who was a deputy over in Timber County."

"You did."

"I think I may have found out why Sheriff Bark doesn't like you or me, or Maggie either, for that matter."

Father Frank put his drink down. "I'd like to hear that."

"Talked to my friend this morning. We had some classes together in criminal justice in college. He said the Sheriff had been unusually angry the last couple of days. He and the ranger had some, uh, *discussions* behind closed doors, and occasionally he could hear them yelling. Actually, he said the Sheriff was yelling. He never heard the Ranger."

Father Frank laughed. "Lieutenant Richards is pretty soft spoken. But I wouldn't want to argue with him."

"Bark said you and I were instrumental in getting Judge McFatage kicked off the bench and almost tossed into prison."

"True enough," said Maggie. "And he should've gone to prison. Bark didn't mention me, though? I had a hand in on it, as I recall."

"Indeed you did, Maggie. And I have to admit, I was a bit uneasy on a couple of things you did. But it worked out. We got the evidence." Mike laughed. "And I got to keep my job."

"Somebody tries to poison my brother, I'm going after 'em."

Father Frank held up his hand. "Okay, Mike, you've piqued my curiosity. So, what does Judge McFatage's problems have to do with Sheriff Bark?"

"Ah. The connection." Mike waited until Maggie and the priest were looking at him. "It so happens Sheriff Sam Bark is married to a little brunette. She's shorter than you are, Maggie. She seems unassuming, quiet. Very pretty."

"Okay. Pretty, petite. What's the punch line?" asked Father Frank.

"First, she leads the Sheriff around by the nose. If she says jump, Bark says how high. But second, and here's the important part, she is Judge McFatage's daughter."

Father Frank's eyebrows shot up and his mouth fell open. "Oh."

"So, Bark doesn't want you around, and he'd love to be able to put you in jail." Mike nodded. "Even for a day or two. It would make his wife happy and that would make Bark happy. I'm dead serious when I say, be careful around him. I certainly am."

Maggie frowned at Mike. "But he can't put Frank in jail without just cause."

Mike pursed his lips and twisted his head to the side. "Obstruction of an investigation is pretty nebulous. My guess is, he couldn't make anything stick. But it might take a day to get it straightened out. Toss you in on Friday evening. Might not get a judge to set you free until Monday morning."

Maggie's temper spiked. "Then he'd have to deal with me."

Mike shook his head. "He's already got you under house arrest. And he thinks he has a real chance of locking you up, Maggie."

Father Frank cocked his head to the side. "If it weren't for Lieutenant Richards, I'm afraid Maggie would already be in jail."

Maggie held up her hand. "No house arrest. I spent the weekend in Dallas and I'm headed back there in the next few minutes."

"The judge let you out of this jurisdiction?"

"He did."

"Well, you'll get out of this scot-free. But if you goof up, Bark can put you back in jail. Be careful. Same goes for you, Father. Do not cross the man."

Father Frank gave Mike a slap on the shoulder. "Thanks. It's good to know what his problem is. Doesn't make it go away, but at least I know what I'm up against."

* * *

After Father Frank and Maggie bid goodbye to Mike, Maggie turned to her brother. "I'll be very careful I promise.

Now, give me a hug for the road. And, sorry Frank, but I hope I don't see you for awhile."

Chapter 51

LIEUTENANT RICHARD RICHARDS sat across the desk from Sheriff Bark. "I asked you not to harass Margaret DeLuca."

The Sheriff's face turned red and for a moment, Richards thought he might explode. "I did not harass her. What did she say?"

"Nothing. But I've heard about it."

"I brought her in, that's it. I had just cause. I have a witness who saw her out of the dorm area later that night."

"How late?"

"Later than the suspect said she was out."

"Give me the times."

Bark shuffled through some papers on his desk, as if he might find an answer there. Without looking up, he said, "The witness suggested DeLuca was out an hour later than she admitted."

"The time, Sheriff?" Richards voice was hard and demanding.

"DeLuca said nine; the witness said it was probably ten, or maybe after."

"And the forensic pathologist said Granet was killed around eleven thirty."

The Sheriff stretched up. "He said he *died* about eleven thirty. His throat might have been cut earlier."

"His carotid artery was severed. The one on the right. Below the split. He probably died in less than two minutes."

"But —"

"Sheriff, I have a witness who tells me Margaret DeLuca was in her room between eleven and twelve. She isn't the murderer. Quit wasting your time."

The Sheriff raised up half out of his chair. "How can you have a witness? She said she was alone."

"So, you believe her when she says she was alone, but not when she says she was in her room? Come on, Sheriff. You *want* her to be guilty. Yes, she was alone. But the walls in those rooms are very thin."

"But we interviewed every person spending the night there." The Sheriff was almost mewling.

"And my men did a better job. Drop it. That's the last I want to hear about Margaret DeLuca. Set up a meeting with the District Attorney, you and me. This afternoon."

"I'll see if he is free," Bark said sulkily.

"See that he is."

* * *

District Attorney Ralph Butts was leaning back in his maroon leather chair, his ropers resting on the corner of his impressive desk. He wore a business suit with a distinct Western cut. His string tie was held in place with a gold horseshoe-shaped clasp with "A & M - 1995" engraved on it.

Richards's first thought was that Butts ate too much Texas barbeque.

Butts removed his boots from the desk and sat up straight. "Grab a chair." He picked up his phone and punched a number. "Tamaford, get in here - now." He put the phone down. "He's my assistant. I want him to hear this."

Richards sat directly opposite Butts. Sheriff Bark sat in an adjacent chair glaring at the Ranger. Within ten seconds, the ADA came in the door.

The DA motioned his assistant to a seat and turned back to Richards. "Okay. Let's get this rodeo started."

"All right." Richards tried to sound agreeable. "As you will have to prosecute this case, let's go through all the possible suspects the Sheriff has come up with, and a few of mine. You should have a sheet on each of them."

"Okay, but I have an engagement later, so let's make this quick."

Richards frowned. "Ralph, this may have a direct impact on your election in a few months. You need to give this however much time it takes."

The DA looked startled and sat forward in his chair. "I don't see how the election has any bearing on things."

"Let's begin and perhaps you will see the relevance. First, Billy John Bartok. He admits visiting Granet shortly before he was killed. Bartok also admits he probably broke the victim's nose. And he has a pretty good motive. Granet tried to seduce Bartok's fiancée. Allegedly."

"And," the Sheriff spoke up, "he got into a fight just a few days ago. Broke another nose. His anger can pop up on short notice."

Richards summed it up. "He has motive, opportunity, and means. Plus the capability of acting on that anger quickly."

"Sounds like a good suspect," Butts said.

Richards stuck up two fingers. "On your next sheet, you have Val Monroe. We have witnesses who saw her at Granet's cabin the night he was killed. Apparently, she was trying to rekindle an affair they had three years ago, the first time Granet spoke at this conference. Another woman alleges she heard Granet tell Monroe he wasn't interested in a, quote, *fat pig*. Several have confirmed she was hurt and angry by that statement, understandably, and I think we have to consider it might be sufficient motive. She certainly had opportunity. And as a member of the conference staff, she would've had access to the kitchen and knives. She also had stayed at the retreat housing that night, though she lives only ten minutes away. But when she was asked to give the police a list of all who stayed at the retreat that night, she omitted her name. And lastly, she was planning to leave this area, with no plans where she was going, until the Sheriff told her not to leave his jurisdiction."

Butts as he looked at his watch."So, two good suspects. Which one are you proposing?"

"Neither."

"What?" The DA sat up straighter and cocked his head to the left. "Why not?"

Richards leaned forward. "First, let me say again that since you will prosecute this case, we want you aware of all the components. So, we are going to give you information on all the suspects we have uncovered." Butts just nodded, so the Ranger continued. "Dr. Haas, the forensic pathologist says there is clear evidence that the killer was shorter than Granet, and left handed. That knocks out Ms. Monroe, who is, barefooted, almost as tall as Granet. And she is right handed."

"And Billy Whatshisname?"

"Bartok. Also taller than Granet. Also he's right handed."

"So, if we rely on Dr. Haas, we eliminate both of those. Should we consult with another pathologist? I know Dr. Haas is well respected. Still, ..." The DA raised his eyebrows and left the unspoken question dangling in the air.

"Since either one of those, the height or the dominant hand, will rule out those two, I'm inclined to rely on his opinion."

The DA pursed his lips, then said, "Okay. Let's look at your other suspects. Who's next?"

Richards looked at the Sheriff and nodded slightly.

Bark leaned forward. "Margaret DeLuca publicly threatened Granet the day he was killed. She is six inches shorter than Granet, and she is left handed."

The DA nodded. "Publicly threatened him? Sounds like a good suspect."

"I thought so," said Bark, with a smug look at Richards.

Richards took over. "Except Dr. Haas estimates Granet was killed between eleven thirty and twelve. Deluca claims she was in her room at the retreat from —." He looked at the Sheriff, then back at the DA. "From about ten that night until eight the next morning. "

"Can that be corroborated?" asked the DA.

"Somewhat. The walls in the retreat's housing are pretty thin. A woman who was in a room next door claims she heard Ms. Deluca thrashing round in the room between ten and somewhat after midnight. She said she would have called someone about the noise if she'd known who to call. This corresponds with what the suspect stated. The woman in the room on the other side also admitted hearing sounds coming from the room during that period. However, she was not as certain of the exact time."

The DA looked down for a moment. "Tell me about this public threat, she made."

Richards explained about DeLuca's claim Granet had stolen her novel, and she intended to go to the publisher with her case. "The Sheriff and I disagree on the viability of DeLuca as the killer."

The DA looked at the sheriff. "Sam, let's hear your side."

"Well, DeLuca has quite a temper. She not only made the threat, but one of my deputies heard her say on her cell phone that he, Granet, deserved it."

"Granet deserved to be killed?"

"Yes sir." Bark looked at Richards, then turned back to Butts. "At least that's how my deputies took it. Granet deserved to die."

Butts drummed his fingers on the desk for nearly a minute. Richards thought maybe there was a pattern to the drumming, but he couldn't quite decide what it was or if it held any significance.

The DA looked at his watch. "I'm going to have to bring this to a close. I have an important appointment." He stood up.

Richards did not move. "I think you'd better cancel it right now. Depending on how this goes, it could have an impact on next year's election.

"Ralph, I'm moving ahead, and I want you to know where this is going and give you a chance to express an opinion. And the sooner the better."

Butts squinted his eyes and gave the Ranger a stern look. "I'm the one who decides *if* and when a case goes to trial."

"Yes, you do. But I decide when it goes to the media. I think you're going to want all the facts before people start calling you."

Chapter 52

BUTTS SAT BACK down. "Make it quick."

"I'll skip the details of how I found this out. But suffice it to say, a canoe was found with the victim's blood on it."

"How'd blood get on a canoe? I thought he was killed in one of the cabins," demanded the DA.

"That's the $64,000 question. He was killed in cabin 2. The canoe was found on Lakota Lake. One side of Lakota comes to within twenty-five feet of the cabin where Granet was killed. The other side of the lake fronts on a nice residential area. The owner of the canoe, Bud Sullivan, lives there. He claims someone might have borrowed it without his permission of course, and just not tied it up when they finished.

Butts broke in. "You said the victim's blood was on the canoe. How about the paddle? Any blood on it? Any fingerprints?"

"The paddle was never found."

"But here is where it gets more interesting. Allegedly, Sullivan's daughter, Grace, was raped three years ago. Again, allegedly, Granet was the one who raped her."

The DA let out a long breath. "Looks like you have two good suspects there, the woman who was raped and her father. Have you checked them out?"

"I said *that* was where it gets interesting. *Here's* where it gets tricky. The father has a pretty good alibi. Grace, the daughter, may have RTS."

"What' RTS?"

"Rape Trauma Syndrome."

"Never heard of it."

"It's a form of PTSD. Grace Sullivan was a vibrant, young woman whom many thought was a gifted writer, heading off to college. Now she's a totally introverted, non-communicative person who doesn't write and looks like she's on strong medication. But, I am told she's on no medication. That has yet to be confirmed."

Butts rubbed his chin, his eyes almost closed. Then he looked up. "Maybe that's how she *wants* to look. Maybe she's faking it."

Richards shook his head. "I don't think so. I've had Dr. Hedley, a highly respected psychologist who's worked with the Rangers many times, evaluate her. Dr. Hedley wants to spend some more time with her, but her initial impression is, the woman is not faking it. That's just the state she's in now. And probably has been since the rape."

"You said this alleged rape was *three* years ago?"

"That's correct. And I explained that to Dr. Hedley before she interviewed Grace. The doctor said there were many documented cases of PTSD lasting much longer than three years. However, she said much less is known about RTS, and she personally has not dealt with an RTS case that extended that long, so she'd like to consult with some of her colleagues who have, and then meet with Grace again."

"Just how strong is the father's alibi?" asked Butts.

"He was up in Greer County, hunting with Sheriff Dudley."

"Sounds like a pretty solid alibi."

"I have to agree. But, I'm going up there and talk to him. I only got his confirmation over the telephone. I'd like to look him in the face and ask again."

"All right. Let me know what happens." Butts looked at his watch and stood up. "I'm late, but you said earlier this could affect my re-election. I'd like to know how."

"I'm convinced the murderer is either Sullivan or his daughter—a man with a sheriff as his alibi, or a woman with RTS. Either way, a conviction's going to be tough. And neither one will win you any votes."

Chapter 53

"HEARD U ALL most got shot. Keep U nose out R may be a nother."

Father Frank read it again. Same as last time. Letters cut out of some newspaper and pasted on a plain sheet of white paper.

He was more careful with it this time, but suspected they'd be no usable prints on it. He called Lieutenant Richards and told him of this new threat.

* * *

Thirty minutes later, Richards knocked on the door of the rectory and Father Frank let him in. They sat in the living room. "The timing is interesting," said the Ranger. "Of course you know the Sheriff called Maggie back in for some questions. But you may not know he also called in Billy John Bartok and Val Monroe. They had each done something to be picked up on the Sheriff's radar."

"Like what?"

"Seems Bartok can't keep is hands to himself. Some guy said something about Holly, and before he knew it, he had a broken nose. Bark put Billy John on notice for that one. Told him that one more such action and he'd be in jail. As for Monroe, the Sheriff found out she was leaving the state. Apparently she had no place in particular to go to. But she canceled her lease on her house and was ready to vanish. Obviously, Bark told her to stay put. Either one of them might have been worried when they had to go submit to another round of questions. And that might have prompted the note."

"Are they still considered as suspects?"

Richards gave a small laugh. "Now you know I can't answer that question. Just as I cannot say whether Maggie is still on the suspect list."

Now it was the priest's turn to laugh. "Well, I can. She's still got the location monitor on her ankle. And Bark feels free to call her back from Dallas because someone saw her go into her room at ten o'clock at night." He paused for a moment. When Richards didn't speak, Father Frank continued. "Do you want to see this note? I've been more careful with this one."

"That's why I'm here. There's little chance there will be any usable prints on it. But The Texas Rangers catch most criminals by paying attention to details."

"Do we rule Monroe out because this is in such poor English?"

"Not at all. It could be a deliberate ploy to throw suspicion on someone else. I've seen a college English professor send an anonymous note using terrible grammar, just to divert attention from herself."

He took the note, placed it in an evidence bag and studied it for a minute. "I'll have the boys in the lab go over it, see if they can come up with anything."

"Did you get the psychologist to check out Grace?"

"I did. She had a good visit with Grace. She believes the young woman is definitely still suffering from RTS."

"Could she have been capable of killing the man who raped her?"

"'Allegedly' raped her. Dr. Hedley is not ready to make that judgment. But she believes the rape did happen. Of course, when the doctor makes her report, you know that will be confidential and I won't be able to tell you anything that's in it."

Father Frank nodded. "Gotcha. But it can be used in court, right?"

"Depends on the judge. What I can tell you is Dr. Hedley will see Grace again, probably more than once."

"How did Bud Sullivan respond to the doctor interviewing Grace?"

Richards laughed. "Not well. He threatened me. Opened the door with an AR-15 in his hand, hanging next to his leg."

Father Frank's eyes opened.

The Ranger smiled. "He didn't know I was a quick draw champion. I had my Sig 320 out and resting on his temple before he realized I wasn't wasting time talking to him. He put the rifle down. We had a nice talk and he agreed the good doctor should visit with Grace. And no, I did not give him his rifle back."

"And this next visit by Dr. Hedley?"

"We've already talked about that. I gave him a choice. Dr. Hedley could visit with Grace in her room, or in a Dallas hospital. He decided in Grace's room would be best. I don't think he'll be any trouble next time." The Ranger worked his lips around like he might be polishing his teeth. "I think he's afraid Grace might reveal something. But whether that would implicate herself, or him, isn't at all clear to me." He paused only a second. "At this point."

Father Frank frowned and cocked his head to one side. "But he has a sheriff providing him an alibi."

"I'll know more tonight. I'm heading up to talk to the Sheriff now." He started to leave, but turned around. "I did ask Bud if he shot at you. He asked me if you were still alive? And when I said yes, he said that was my answer. If he shot at you, you wouldn't be."

Chapter 54

FATHER FRANK WATCHED the Ranger leave. What if Bud's alibi checked out? What if he really was fifty miles away at the time of the murder?

The priest walked into the kitchen and grabbed a Dr Pepper out of the refrigerator, carried it back into the living room and sank into his La-Z-Boy recliner. *How would Grace have known which cabin Granet was in? Of course, maybe he was in the same cabin as three years ago. I could check on that.* He drank a little soda. *No. I won't. Besides, she could have paddled up to the shore, just sat and watched. She might have seen Billy John smack Granet. Or maybe Val trying to rekindle something. Probably not much activity around the cabins that time of night. Granet's would have been obvious.*

For a long time, he sat with his eyes closed, imagining the scene. What would Grace have thought if she saw Bartok hit Granet? Would that have brought a smile to her sad face? And then Val came and was turned away. Would she have cheered? He shook his head. *No. In her RTS state, she probably would have had no reaction to those. They had no bearing on her own emotional state. She just needed retribution.*

Father Frank put his drink down, walked over to the church, and knelt at the back.

Dear God, forgive me. This young woman has suffered so much. It is not for me to speculate if she did this, or how or why. I pray You will help her regain her life and use the talent You have given her. And please help me not judge Grace. Or Bud. Or anyone.

As Father Frank walked back to the rectory a thought popped into his mind. What if neither of the Sullivans killed Granet? Lieutenant Richards had zeroed in on them, clearly believing one of them was the killer. After all, the blood, Granet's blood, was on their canoe. But what if Bud was right? What if somebody really had stolen his canoe? And that person had paddled over and killed Granet. Billy John? Not likely. He'd broken the guy's nose. If he wanted to kill him, why not do it then? Why go poke around until he found a canoe at the right place and then paddle across the lake and kill Granet? Didn't make sense.

So, Val? She lived over on that side of the lake. And she could have known Sullivan's canoe was there for the taking. But she was staying at the conference center. If she had left to go get the canoe, the cameras would have shown her leaving. Could she have tampered with the camera or the recording? Possible. But not likely. She was crushed, and angry. But Father Frank didn't think she was murderous.

He entered his office. *It's time I got back to my day job.* He corrected himself. *No. It's time I got back to **my job**, my only job.* He sat there for a minute, thinking about the murder and his parish. *I hate to admit it, but the Sheriff was right. I should stay out of this investigation.* He smiled. *But Bark was right for the wrong reason.*

He looked at his calendar. He had two counseling sessions tomorrow, and he needed to start on Sunday's homily. Then he frowned as another entry caught his eye: "Work on financial books." He took a deep breath. *I need to say to myself once every day, "Working on financials can be invigorating and even fun." Maybe twice every day.*

Chapter 55

LIEUTENANT RICHARDS DROVE up to Clear River in Greer County, where Sheriff Dub Dudley had his offices. The day had started out as beautiful, but dark clouds were gathering as he approached the Red River. He could hear thunder in the distance. *I hope this weather is not indicative of this trip. The nearer I get to Dudley's office, the worse things look.* By the time he reached Clear River and found the Sheriff's office, it had started to rain. *Bad for his hat, but good for the trees. He'd take that deal.*

He slipped the rain cover over his Stetson, got out and hurried into the building. "I'm Lieutenant Richards. I have an appointment with Sheriff Dudley."

Within a few minutes, the Ranger had introduced himself and now sat in a small office opposite the Sheriff. *He looks like a stereotypical sheriff straight out of an old Western movie. I bet he's got a horse tied up out back.*

The Sheriff appeared at ease. "I don't get visited by a Texas Ranger very often."

Richards smiled. "I'd say that's a good thing. When you are, it usually means you have some serious crime in your county, or a serious problem in your office. Neither is a reason to celebrate."

Dudley laughed. "You're right on that. I don't need any tough problems up here. And truth to tell, we seldom have any in this jurisdiction. And my office runs as smooth as a well oiled windmill. So which is it? Crime or office problem? Can't say as I'm aware of either one."

The Ranger took a few seconds to get out a small brown leather notebook and a pen, each with the Texas Rangers logo on it. "When I talked with you on the phone the other day, you told me Bud Sullivan was up here with you on Thursday, October 29." He looked at his notes.

"That's right. Went deer hunting. Got myself a four-point that night." He gave a small laugh. "Bud got nothing."

"You're sure of the date? And the time?"

The smile came off the Sheriff's face. "Well, I was when you called. But let me check." He reached over for a pair of glasses. "Can't read anything without my cheaters on." He pulled up a file on his computer. "I guess it was about maybe five thirty in the morning when I shot it. I field dressed it immediately, of course. Took it to the processor that morning. We'll have venison for the rest of the winter. Hell, probably all year. You do know that Axis is the very best venison."

"I've heard that. You were hunting on private land?"

"Yeah. Family land. We've been there near a hundred years, I guess." He studied another file on the computer. "Here it is. I took it into the processor on October thirtieth" He looked back at the Ranger. "So, yeah, Bud came up the night of the twenty-ninth."

Richards's eyes never left Dudley. "Good. Matches what I have. What time did you say he got here? And where did you meet?"

"We met at my house."

"Was anybody else there - at the house?"

"No. I live alone since Irene passed two years ago." The Sheriff's relaxed posture stiffened a little.

Richards noted the slight change in Dudley. "What time did he get there - at your house?"

The Sheriff looked down at the top of his desk. His lips stretched out into a thin line. After a moment, he looked up. "I'd say about ten o'clock that night. Maybe ten-thirty."

"And the two of you went right out to the hunt?"

Dudley gave a nervous laugh. "No. We're gettin' too old for all nighters. We slept for a bit. I'd say we left the house about four."

"So, you had a couple of beers, then slept for awhile before leaving at four."

"No. No beer. We —"

"Sheriff, think about this before answering. What time, approximately, did you first see Sullivan that night? If it comes to it, these are questions the D.A. will have to ask you in court, under oath."

The muscles in Dudley's arms tightened. His jaw locked tight. He swallowed. "I don't know exactly what time that would be."

"Would you say before one or after one?"

When the Sheriff didn't answer for a minute, Richards asked, "Were you awake when he arrived?"

The office was so quiet Richards could hear the electric clock ticking off the seconds.

"I'm not sure." Then he looked up. "I just remember he called earlier in the evening and suggested we go deer hunting. I said, yeah. Come on up. And he said he'd be right up in a bit, but don't ..."

"Don't what?"

Dudley looked down. His eyes blinked rapidly. He looked at the Ranger. "Don't wait up for me."

"So you don't really know what time he arrived?"

He took a deep breath. "Not really. But from his phone call, I expected him to be here before midnight."

"But you don't know."

Dudley just shook his head.

"And yet, he's using you for an alibi in a murder case."

Now Dudley looked anxious. "But he did call and set it up. And we did go hunting. I've known Bud for many years. He's a good man. There's just no way he'd be involved in a murder."

"How about attempting to destroy evidence?"

The Sheriff said nothing, just staring into space. Richards let the silence drag on.

"I might have seen him near midnight," the Sheriff said finally." I kinda remember hearin' a noise and half waking up. I think that's when Bud got here. I probably saw him and went right back to sleep." He nodded vigorously, sending his message: this is what happened.

"Did you actually see him?"

"Maybe. I know I heard him. No one else would come into my house at night without being invited. It was Bud. Had to be."

"Did you look at the time?"

"Not really. Now I think on it, I remember. It was Bud. And I'm pretty sure it was near midnight."

"Was it raining when he got there?"

"Raining? I don't know. I was asleep."

Richards let silence work on Dudley. Finally, the Sheriff asked, "Does that make any difference?"

"I don't know. Does it?"

Again Dudley looked down at his desk. His muscles were tensed. and he was breathing heavily. "I don't think it was raining when Bud got there. I remember waking sometime later and it was raining then and I thought we might not go hunting after all. I went back to sleep and when Bud woke me around four, it had stopped." He took a deep breath. "There wasn't any water on the floor by the front door. If it was raining, Bud would'a brung in some water. He'd 'a parked a good distance from the house." When Richards didn't say anything, the Sheriff continued. "I honestly do not know when he arrived. I think it was before the rain, whatever time that was. And my thought is, it was around midnight. But I'm not going to swear to that."

He looked up at the Texas Ranger.

His breathing had settled down.

He's not hedging the truth now, and it's easier not to stretch things.

* * *

Dick Richards climbed into his car, shook the rain off his hat, and started the engine. *Not much of an alibi. But I imagine it will get stronger.*

Chapter 56

FATHER FRANK CAME out of morning Mass and looked over at the bench, not really expecting to see Richards. But sitting there, white Stetson in his lap was the Ranger. And sitting next to him was a lady Father Frank didn't recognize. The priest spoke to one of his parishioners, then headed toward Richards.

"Good morning Lieutenant Richards. I missed you inside today. And who is your friend?"

"I knew you weren't preaching today. This is Dr. Patricia Hedley, a clinical psychologist who is assisting the Texas Rangers today. Pat, this is Father Frank DeLuca, whom I've been trying to recruit for the Rangers."

The attractive African-American woman held out her hand. "Glad to meet you. Dick speaks highly of you."

Father Frank took her hand and chuckled. "You see. It *is* possible to fool a Texas Ranger. Would you like to come into the rectory and have some coffee?"

"That would be nice. But we've only got a few minutes, so perhaps another day for the coffee."

"Any time." Father Frank turned his attention to the Ranger. "What's on your agenda today?"

"Dr. Hedley wanted to ask you a few questions."

Father Frank sat down on the ground in front of his visitors. "Fire away."

Dr. Hedley wrinkled her forehead. "We can sit closer together. You don't need to sit on the ground." She started moving closer to Richards.

"No. Really, this is fine. This way, I can see both of your faces."

"Okay. From what I have gathered from Dick, you may have been the only person Grace has talked to recently. When I visited with her two days ago, she said... well, basically nothing. I was lucky to get an occasional nod or a shake of her head. Words seemed reluctant to come out. How was your visit with her?"

"I have spoken with her twice. The first time, she said only four words. 'I don't go anywhere.' That, and like she did with you, a few nods and head shakes were the only signs she even heard me. Mostly, she looked at the floor. But when I asked her if I could come again, she indicated that would be okay. One other thing. I asked, 'Do you still write?' Her head snapped back as if I'd slapped her. Then she looked back down and was back in her catatonic state. I'm sure Dick has told you she had been a gifted writer. Then, three years ago, she just stopped."

Hedley nodded. "The time of the alleged rape?"

"Yes. My second visit didn't produce much more. Again, she only said one sentence during our entire visit. 'I'm trying to start.' That was in answer to me asking if she was writing again. But her manner was basically the same. Head slumped down. Appeared as if she was heavily sedated. I'm told, although I have no opinion of my own, that she is not on any type of medication or drugs."

"I appreciate the information. She is so uncommunicative, anything helps. And it's not likely I will be able to have a long series of visits with her."

Father Frank looked at Richards. "You've talked with Jane. My guess is, she's the only person who gets anything out of Grace. Would a visit with Jane help Dr. Hedley? What do you think?"

Richards rubbed his chin. "I can't see how it would hurt. She's the only person we know of who worked with Grace shortly after the ... incident, whatever caused her withdrawal." He looked at Hedley. "What do you think?"

Before she spoke, Father Frank held up his hand. "Jane apparently spent a lot of time with Grace after her mother died five or six years before this incident. Jane said she was sort of like her grandmother. So when this happened, and Grace didn't eat or talk, the father called Jane and asked her to come. Apparently, she spent a lot of time with Grace after this happened. From what little knowledge of the situation I have, I suspect Jane is the only person Grace has really talked to - about anything, but certainly about the rape." Father Frank smiled a little. "Now Jane is a little different. But I think, if we can set it up, you'd find it helpful."

Both Father Frank and Richards looked at Dr. Hedley.

"I'd be happy to give it a try. I'm not too proud to accept help wherever I can get it."

"I'll see what I can do this morning. I'll let you know the moment I know. I assume sooner is better?"

"Absolutely. This morning would work for me. I'm scheduled to meet with Grace this afternoon. I'd like to talk with Jane before then, if at all possible."

Chapter 57

AS SOON AS he got back in the rectory, Father Frank called Georgia and ask if she might set up a meeting between Dr. Hedley and Jane.

Twenty minutes later, Georgia called back. "She said she could meet with Dr. Hedley in one hour. But she reminded me of her conditions and the psychologist should know those, and agree to them, before the meeting."

"I'll pass it on. Where shall they meet?"

"At the Dairy Queen. Just to remind you, she only does one-on-ones. Can't be both the Ranger and the psychologist. And don't forget the Dr Pepper."

Father Frank called Richards and gave him the message. "We'll be there."

"Remember, you and Dr. Hedley go inside the Dairy Queen and buy a Dr Pepper, then go back to the car. Jane will be there. You introduce Dr. Hedley. Then disappear."

"And what am I supposed to do while they talk?"

"I'd suggest a Turtle Pecan Blizzard. Inside the Dairy Queen."

Richards laughed and disconnected.

* * *

An hour and a half later Dr. Hedley had finished her visit with Jane and she and Richards were driving to the Sullivan's. "So, what did you think of Jane?"

A grin came over Hedley's face. "I loved her. Straight forward. She says what's on her mind and doesn't care what you think about it. And she has no problem saying she won't answer a question or address a subject. Refreshing. Although, I still don't understand all the secrecy."

"I don't either. I asked her about it. She said people trust her. They feel like they can tell her anything and trust she won't pass it on. I guess she feels the secrecy is needed if she's going to protect that."

"Makes sense - a little. She confirmed that shortly after Grace's mother died, Bud called her. Said he didn't know how to deal with a girl about to become a young woman. Jane became Grace's surrogate grandmother. But three years ago, suddenly Grace was completely changed. Even Jane couldn't communicate with her. Jane said it took her over a month to find out what happened. She said Grace cried, slept and stared at the wall. That was her day. Jane claims that sometimes she would sit and hold Grace for two or three hours without the girl saying a word."

They stopped for a red light. Richards looked at the psychologist. "That had to be very tiring and emotionally demanding for Jane as well."

Hedley nodded. "I personally can't even imagine going through something like that. And I deal with disturbed young people all the time. In some ways, Jane thinks Grace is better now. She can function a little: cook, keep herself clean. But other than to Jane, she still doesn't talk, not even to her father. Not that she blames him in any way. And Jane says she has to work to get anything out of Grace."

They drove in silence for a few minutes. "I did talk to some of my associates. None had had a case of RTS that lasted quite this long, but of course everyone responds in their own way. Nobody seemed surprised that Grace was having such difficulties. Several had seen cases as long as two years or more. And a few cases that seemed as difficult as Grace." She stared out the window, watching as they drove beside Lakota Lake. "Anyway, I'm hoping what Jane has told me will help me have a better session today."

"I see you brought lunch."

Hedley laughed. "It might help her open up some, as least a little. And it will help me. I'm ready to eat."

"And two blizzards."

"Well, that ought to improve anybody's mood. We'll see."

They pulled up in front of the Sullivan's home. "You're sure you'll be okay if I take off for a couple of hours?"

"I'll be fine. And I'm sure I can use that much time and probably more. If the need arises, I'll call you. You have your cell phone?"

"Always."

* * *

An hour later, Dick Richards had checked at two stores in Clear River that were open until midnight. The woman on duty at the first store said the man who worked the late shift was currently on vacation.

Richards lucked out at the second store. The man said yes, he had worked the night of October 29. and he did remember the rain. "We'd been praying for rain for weeks and then it came. We're getting some rain now. But September and October were as dry as a bone in the Sahara. So, we were excited to get some, and it was a good down pour for a couple of hours and that was it. I was hoping it would hold off 'til I got home. I'd closed the doors, closed out the register, checked the refrigeration, and almost made it. But, on the way home, it hit and I got drenched getting in the house."

"And what time was that?"

"I'd say about 12:15. Maybe 12:20."

"And where do you live?"

"Right here in town, over on Mimosa street."

* * *

Richards made another stop at the local radio station, where the station manager directed him to Wendy Wilson the nighttime DJ.

"October 29? Yeah I was here. My shift goes until six in the morning when the farm show comes on."

"By any chance, did you notice the time when the rain started?"

"Well, you're in luck there. Another few days and I wouldn't have a clue." She pulled open a drawer. Inside was a small frame. Dick guessed there were probably two dozen compartments, each holding a small USB disk. Wendy thumbed through the collection of disks. "Aha, there you are." She plugged the thumb disk into the computer on her desk and began searching. "I record each of my shows. Keep them for a few weeks. Then write over them. This one would have been erased next week."

"Pardon me for asking, but why do you keep those?"

She laughed. "You'd be surprised. I get calls every week. 'What was that song you played last night. Around 2:30 or so.' Or , 'You mentioned such and such last Wednesday night. Can you tell me what it was?' They just expect I have total recall. So, I keep recordings." She kept searching through the computer files. "There's a window in the studio and ..." She stopped. "Here it is."

From the computer's speaker, Richards heard a musical number stop, and then Wendy's voice. "Well folks, we knew it had to happen sooner or later. It's actually raining right here in Clear River, Texas. All you people who said it would never rain again, and that includes my father, are proven wrong. Here it is, October twenty-ninth at 12:18, I guess it's now October thirtieth, and it's just starting to provide some much needed moisture for our little piece of paradise. Wow. It's really picking up. Glad I'm in here and not out riding my Suzuki home. I'll keep you posted on how the rain goes. But for now, how about a little rain music."

She stopped the recording and turned to face the Texas Ranger. "There you are. And see, you're another person who wanted something from one of my broadcasts."

Chapter 58

DICK RICHARDS AND Dr. Hedley sat in Ralph Butts's office. Buzz Tamaford, the ADA, was there also.

"Mr. Butts, I'm very skilled at this. I've been working with disturbed people for twenty-plus years. And I've worked with the Texas Rangers for maybe eight years. In the most relaxed setting, as safe and nonthreatening as possible, Grace is still inside herself. She's as damaged as any soldier from Afghanistan with PTSD. If you want to know if she would understand the nature of the charges against her, I seriously doubt it. But, if you want to know if she can help her attorney in her defense, the answer is a definite no."

Butts leaned forward. "Is it possible she's faking this state she appears to be in?"

"In my professional opinion, based on more than a thousand cases over the last two decades, the answer is no. She is not faking anything. What you see is what she is. Plain and simple."

The DA leaned back, placed his finger tips together and closed his eyes. After a few moments, he opened his eyes and looked at Richards. "What do the Texas Rangers think?"

"I have not discussed this with my superiors yet. But I can give you my opinion. I've investigated seven suspects, and another half-dozen persons marginally involved.

"The two most likely candidates, in fact, the only viable candidates, are Bud Sullivan and his daughter, Grace. A canoe they owned was floating in the lake that night. And once we recovered it, we found the victim's blood on it."

"And how did the blood get on the canoe?"

"That's the question. No prints. Nothing to indicate how it got there. Bud claims people, unknown, sometimes borrow the canoe and have been known to fail to tie it up properly.."

The District Attorney looked skeptical. "Paddled over and killed a man and then paddled back and didn't tie it up? Sounds pretty farfetched to me."

"I agree. And Bud appears to have a good alibi. Not perfect, but it comes from the Sheriff of Greer County."

Ralph cocked his head to the side. "Why not perfect?"

"He's a little uncertain about the exact time. And my guess is, his certainty will increase as time goes by. Bud visited him the night of the murder. If the Sheriff becomes certain of the time of Sullivan's arrival, then it's entirely possible Sullivan could not have been at the Lakota Retreat Center in the window of time the pathologist says the murder was committed."

"And he's the father of the girl allegedly raped."

* * *

"There are two other things that discourage the case against Bud Sullivan. First, When I asked him, casually, where I should sit if I were paddling a canoe by myself, he said that in such a case, he always knelt with his back against the bow seat, facing the stern. And when I mentioned that his canoe looked like someone sat in the stern seat, facing toward the bow, he said that was because −. And he stopped abruptly. I think he was about to say that's where Grace sat. But he caught himself and said probably somebody borrowed it."

"So? What does that prove?"

"It doesn't prove anything. But the blood was on the stern seat. Less likely that Bud transferred it there."

"So, it proves nothing." Butts leaned back and folded his hands over his ample belly.

"Right. Doesn't prove a thing. But it's another piece that does not point to Bud. Then I verified at what time it started to rain in Clear River, where Sheriff Dudly lives. A pretty strong case it was 12:18 a.m. Sheriff Dudly believes Sullivan arrived before the rain started. So, if Sullivan got to the Sheriff's house before 12:18, he must have left his house by 11. I made that drive twice to check it out. If he had to paddle across the lake, get hit by the speed boat, hide while the man driving the speed boat looked for anybody, then swim to shore, get into his house, dry off, clean up, change clothes and leave by 11 o'clock, he would need to have killed Granet by 10:30. That's an hour or more before the earliest Dr. Haas believes the murder occurred. And we have a witness who says Granet was alive at around ten-thirty."

"Who is that?"

"Billy John Bartok. He admits he broke Granet's nose between 10:20 and 10:30. But he left Granet alive and cursing. And Dr. Haas says Granet's nose was broken an hour before his throat was slashed."

Richards paused. "Again, not conclusive. But making the case against Bud Sullivan more difficult to prove."

"Right."

When the DA offered nothing more, Dick continued. "Grace Sullivan, the alleged rape victim, has no alibi. She was home alone. The family canoe had the victim's blood on it. She had motive. She fits the profile of the murderer as given by the forensic pathologist. "

"What does that mean?"

"She is the right height and she's left -handed. Everything points to her."

"So, what's the problem?"

"As Dr. Hedley stated, she may not be competent to stand trial."

The D.A. looked at the psychologist.

Dr. Hedley leaned forward. "Mr. Butts, I've testified in many trials. And every time I've testified that a person was not competent to stand trial, they were not put on trial. As you well know, competency involves the ability to understand the character and consequences of the proceedings against her, as well as her ability to assist in her defense. Grace Sullivan fails both of these requirements. I believe these are facts. I am confident there is no subterfuge. And I will testify to those statements in court, if necessary."

"I've brought in the best in the area," Richards said.

Ralph let out an exasperated breath. "So, I'm back to my question. What do the Texas Rangers think? Shall we bring her in for trial or not? I'd like your opinion."

For the first time, Richards looked uncomfortable. He stared at his Stetson sitting in his lap.

"Dammit, Richards. I need some firm commitment. I'm not about to bring in a young girl, who appears to be damaged, and try her with thin evidence, a young, pitiful looking girl. There's no way a jury will convict her unless you have some pretty strong evidence. I'm not looking to be the ogre right before election. Either get me some solid evidence or drop it. You Rangers are supposed to be the best. Act like it."

He stood up and headed for the door. "This meeting is over. No evidence, no trial. Call me when you get your act in order."

Chapter 59

FATHER FRANK ALMOST dropped the chalice. He blinked, not sure he was seeing correctly. There, in the back pew was Texas Ranger Richard Richards.

The priest recovered and finished the service, then quickly divested himself and walked out the front door of the church. Sure enough, there was Richards, sitting on his favorite bench under the huge Southern Pine.

"Hello. I was surprised to see you in church this morning," Father Frank said as he approached the lawman.

"Well, I may need some guidance. Have you any house guests today?"

"No. Why?"

"Let's go have some coffee and I can explain my problem."

* * *

In the kitchen, Father Frank started a pot of coffee and popped two frozen cinnamon rolls in the microwave. "Okay, what is today's subject?"

"Before we get on that, let me address another matter. The gun shot through your car."

"Did you find out who shot?" asked Father Frank.

"No. And we're not going to. If we had recovered the slug, we'd have had a chance. Without it, no chance. We searched the bridge. No slug. Most likely in the lake and we'd never find it. Bud had been hunting a week or two before that, so nothing could be determined from his AR-15. I've returned it to him, but with a strong warning about shooting it in town."

"Okay. And thanks for that. What is the main topic today?"

"What else? The Granet case."

"And why is today different?"

Richards folded his hands on the table. He looked troubled. "We're at the end and I don't know what to do."

"Sounds like an ethical dilemma," the priest said gently.

"You could say that," Richards confirmed. "The blood." He paused, shook his head, then continued. "The blood on the canoe tells me that one of the Sullivans killed Granet. Both father and daughter have a strong motive. Bud has an alibi. I've tried to disprove it, but I haven't been able to. And other things make it harder to prove Bud is the killer. So that leaves Grace. She has no alibi."

The Ranger thought of Bud's statement that he'd kneel against the bow seat, facing the stern. But the blood was in the stern. Someone was sitting in the stern, facing the bow, a position more likely used by Grace.

He took the cup of coffee Father Frank offered, spooned in sugar and added a little milk. "Much as I hate to say it, I'm absolutely convinced Grace killed Granet. Motive is clear. And while she seems to be oblivious to the world around her, according to Jane, she reacted very strongly to seeing Granet's picture in the paper the day he was killed."

"Yes. Jane said Grace stomped on the picture. But that's pretty weak evidence for the crime of murder, I would think. Did Dr. Hedley pursue that?"

"Actually, she did. She even showed Grace a picture of Granet."

"And?"

"Nothing. Hedley said Grace took no notice of it, showed no emotion at all."

"Interesting. What did the doctor have to say about that?"

"She said it could go either way. Grace had no feeling for this man, maybe didn't even recognize him. Or, he was no longer in her life. At this point, Hedley didn't feel she could make any judgment on what it meant. She doesn't know Grace well enough to say."

The priest pursed his lips. "So it might help make the case for motive, or maybe not."

"It's just part of the total picture. She had the opportunity
- he was right there, just across the lake. She had a canoe."

"Which got smacked in the middle of the lake."

"Not really in the middle of the lake. But not a problem
for Grace anyway, if she was in that canoe. She had a swimming
scholarship to T.C.U. So she would have had no difficulty
swimming to shore. Her father was gone. She could come in
sopping wet, dry off. Dispose of any bloody clothes, or just run
the washing machine."

Father Frank fixed his coffee. "Sounds pretty calculated
for someone in Grace's state. Did Dr. Hedley think she could pull
that off?"

"I haven't posed it to her that way, but I will. And then
we have means. According to the forensic pathologist, the
murderer was shorter than Granet, probably five foot, five inches
or less. And left handed. Grace matches those physical
characteristics. Neither Billy John nor Val Monroe does."

"Based on the opinion of a pathologist."

"A forensic pathologist. And he's good. I trust his
opinion. Grace fits both of those."

"You're talking about the fact that Grace is shorter than
Granet and left handed." Father Frank found himself wanting to
defend Grace, at least in his mind. "Lots of people fit that
description."

Richards smiled. "True. Like your sister."

"But Maggie didn't have a canoe, or access to one."

"So, I'll dismiss Maggie. Grace not only had access to a
canoe, she probably used that particular one all the time. In fact,
her father accused her of leaving it unsecured, sometimes."

"Okay. But others had motive, means, and opportunity,
not just Grace. How about O'Reilly?"

"Only the Sullivans really had easy access to that specific
canoe - the one with Granet's blood on it." He wiggled his head
left to right and back again. "The blood on the canoe speaks loud
and clear. Granet wasn't in that canoe after his throat was slit.
The murderer was."

Father Frank reached over and pulled the rolls out of the
microwave, put one on a plate with a fork and handed it to

Richards. He fixed the other one for himself. "Of course, Billy John's bike has Granet's blood on it."

"True. But he told us he'd punched Granet in the nose. And sure enough, Granet's nose was broken. And again, the forensic pathologist determined Granet's nose was broken an hour before his throat was cut." Richards took a bite of the cinnamon roll. "This is really good."

"Yeah. I love 'em. But Maggie gets on my case for eating them for breakfast."

"But she's not here."

"So, we're having cinnamon rolls. Shall I put some more in the microwave?"

"Not for me. But I'm really enjoying this one."

Father Frank wiped a little cinnamon off his mouth. "So, what is your problem with the case right now? It sounds as if you've settled on your suspect—Grace. I can't deny the thought saddens me, but what exactly is your problem now?"

"I don't like to leave a case open. I always solve them."

"Good. And you have this time also."

"But I'm not going to get a conviction."

Father Frank put his coffee cup down and stared at the Ranger. "Is that necessary? Does that affect your status or a promotion?"

"No, it does not affect status. But yes, it's necessary."

"Why? Another notch on your belt?"

"No notches. Justice. It's important to get justice."

For nearly a minute neither man said anything. "Justice." Father Frank repeated the word as he finished his cinnamon roll. "What is justice?"

"Surely as a priest, you know what justice is."

"I have my definition, but what is it to you as a lawman?"

Richards drank a little more coffee. "Grace took a life. She must pay for that."

Father Frank caught Richards's eye and held it with his laser focus. "And has she not paid a lot already? Has she not, in essence, lost her life for at least three years, and who knows for how many more?"

The lawman stared into his coffee cup, then drank some of it.

"Dick, I'm not saying it was right for her to kill Granet, if in fact she did. I'm questioning if we, society, need to punish her some more."

"But, we know —"

"That she had motive, opportunity, and means. What is it we tell the jury? You must be convinced beyond a reasonable doubt. If you convinced the DA, beyond a reasonable doubt, that Grace was guilty, he would prosecute her. And you might, or might not, convince a jury."

Richards busied himself finishing off the cinnamon roll.

"Are you, in your role as an investigator of this crime, one hundred percent, without the tiniest, slightest doubt, absolutely certain that Bud Sullivan did not, or could not, have done it? Is it *possible* that his alibi is false?"

In all his dealings with Richards over the last few weeks, this moment was the first time Father Frank saw even a hint of doubt, the smallest grain of uncertainty.

When Richards did not say anything immediately, Father Frank continued. "Let me ask one more question. If the DA knew somehow, with certainty, that he could win the case, right or wrong, but get a conviction, would he prosecute it?"

Richards thought a moment. When he answered, he did not look at the priest. "Yes."

"But your evidence, right or wrong, does not give him that certainty."

"No."

Father Frank turned around, grabbed the coffee pot and refilled their cups as he let Richards think on his own answer. Then he said, "You've done an incredible job in a very difficult case. There were over a hundred people who had means and opportunity. You've sifted through a dozen who could be considered real suspects. You've found all the possible evidence. And you've honed in on the most likely of your suspects. But, the evidence is still not sufficient. One might even call it thin. There is doubt. Can you, with absolute certainty, place her in the canoe that night at the appropriate time?"

Richards shook his head slightly. "No."

"Can you, with absolute certainty, place her at the scene of the crime?"

Again the Ranger shook his head. "No."

He reached over and put two more rolls in the microwave. "I understand you are torn over what to do, and let me say I agree with you on one point: whatever Granet did, he did not deserve to have his life ended. But I don't think Grace deserves to have her normal life ended. Putting her through a trial in her current state, even if she is found not guilty, might obliterate *any* chance she has of returning to a normal life. At best, it would surely delay it more years. And in my opinion, which really doesn't count for much here, a good defense attorney would destroy any chance the DA had of a conviction. All a trial will accomplish is to further damage a young woman's life."

The priest looked out the window at the maple tree near the road. The falling leaves signaled winter would be arriving soon. Father Frank loved spring, with new life popping up all around. Truth be told, he didn't much like winter. But to have an inspiring spring, he understood that winter was necessary. "Justice."

The Texas Ranger nodded.

Father Frank folded his hands and rested them on the table. "There's a famous Ivy League professor who gives a series of lectures every year. Hundreds, maybe thousands, of students jam the auditorium *every* week. The topic is justice. The talks are amazing. I've managed to hear a couple. You should try to catch some of them. Check around on the internet. Justice."

Without looking at the lawman, Father Frank continued, "Justice, it turns out, is very difficult to define adequately." Now, he looked Richards in the eyes. "Compassion is not."

He retrieved the plates from the microwave and placed them on the table. The Ranger and the priest ate the warm roles in silence.

Chapter 60

MAGGIE AND JEFF had come for a Thanksgiving visit. She had some exciting news to share, so Father Frank had invited Georgia and Mike to join them for the holiday dinner. Dick Richards was coming too before returning to Tyler.

The six sat around the table. Father Frank said a brief prayer and thanked the Lord for all the incredible ways He had enhanced their lives. And he asked the Lord to help each of them to be kind to those they came in contact with.

Maggie looked at Richards. "I'm saving my news until after dinner. So why don't you tell us the state of your case? That way, it won't spoil my amazing dessert. And no, it isn't pumpkin pie. This is way better."

She started the sweet potato casserole around. Georgia passed the turkey in the opposite direction. Mike took some asparagus and passed the dish to Father Frank.

Richards laughed. "I don't think this will ruin anybody's appetite. First, there will be no trial. The case is closed."

Maggie jabbed her fist in the air and let out a loud "Yeah." Father Frank smiled and said a silent prayer of thanks. Jeff yelled "All Right." Mike slapped the table, which shook several glasses but none turned over, and said, "That's good news. How did that happen?" And Georgia said, "Wow."

"Basically, we just couldn't put together enough verifiable facts. Our case, which Father Frank called weak, by the way, was not sufficient for the District Attorney to pursue it. I had brought in a specialist, Dr. Patricia Hedley, to study some of the aspects. She concluded the DA couldn't win in court, and explained as much to him. The best case we could put together was a certain loss. So, as of now, it has been closed."

"Does this mean there's a killer on the loose and we need to be careful about opening our doors?" asked Georgia.

"It does not." The Ranger assured her. "Your lovely community is as safe as always."

Jeff said, "So what I get from this is, this was a killing related to, and perhaps brought on by, Rod Granet."

Richards smiled. "Well put. And accurate. This was not in any way random."

"Well, I for one, am certainly glad it's over," said Maggie. "That ankle bracelet was definitely not my style. I almost jumped up and down for joy when they took it off. But they did not tell me that the case was closed, just that I was no longer a suspect and the location tracker was not necessary."

"And in other news," Jeff said, "we got an excellent report on the baby just yesterday."

That brought a round of cheers from everybody at the table.

The Texas Ranger tapped his spoon against his glass a few times to get everybody's attention. "I'd like to say one other thing. This case would have gone nowhere without the help of Father Frank. I owe him a huge debt of gratitude. He guided me through the investigation, and was extremely helpful in concluding the case. And I'll tell all of you what I told him. If he ever decides to leave the ministry, the Texas Rangers will gladly take him on."

Again, everybody, except the priest, cheered.

"One last thing, since I know several of you are concerned. With considerable help from Dr. Hedley, we convinced Bud Sullivan to get Grace into some serious counseling. I convinced him that if he really did love Grace – and I think he does – he will get that started immediately." Richards nodded as he said, "And I will check in a month to see how that's going."

* * *

The dishes were cleared and dessert plates and silver placed on the table. Then, with Jeff providing a triumphant entrance (using a paper towel tube for his horn), Maggie brought in dessert. Everyone sat forward to study the delicious looking concoction.

"Okay," said Georgia. "What is it?"

"It's called a devil's food pudding cake and strawberry delight with vanilla ice cream. And if you don't like it, Jeff and I will eat it all."

"Not going to happen," Mike said. He reached for the serving spoon.

Richards stood. "In the name of the Texas Rangers, I must commandeer this dessert."

"And why is that?" asked Father Frank.

"As evidence."

Mike stood. "As the only other law enforcement officer here, I have to ask in what case is this evidence?"

Richards looked around the group. "In the case of the devilish strawberries.

Father Frank stood. "I'll bless it and drive all evil spirits out of it." He waved his hand over it. "Lord, bless this dessert. Ah, now it looks like a heavenly dish."

Maggie stood. "Okay, guys. Have a seat or the cook will take it away." Everybody laughed and the men sat down. "I'm going to pass it around. But anyone stealing too much *on the first round* gets put in solitary confinement in the kitchen until the rest of us finish all the dessert."

Maggie sat down. "Now, for my news. For a while, I've been working on a little project of mine. First, I have to say I had a lot of help on this. May Ellison, this year's conference director, was actually the assistant director three years ago, when Rod Granet spoke here the first time. She managed to dig up records from that conference and allowed me to contact a number of the women who attended that conference. I got on the phone and started contacting them, asking if any of them remembered Shannon O'Reilly. Some did, and some passed me along to other people who might know her. Long story short, after two hundred seventy-five thousand calls - well it seemed like that many - I found a couple of women who not only knew Shannon, but had stayed in contact with her."

"Incredible."

"Fantastic."

"Good work."

"Thank you, thank you. All praise accepted. So eventually I found her and contacted her. Three days ago, I put her back in touch with her father."

"I'm curious," Richards said. "Did you ask her if Granet followed through on his promise to help her in New York?"

"I did and he did not. She lived with him for awhile, until he found someone else and kicked her out. But by then, she liked New York, had found a job, and so she stayed. Only then, she was too embarrassed to call her father." She stopped and helped herself to some dessert.

Her brother put his hand on her fork before it got to her mouth. "No you don't. You got our attention. No dessert for you until you finish the story."

"Spoil sport. Okay, so O'Reilly called his daughter after all these years, and ..." She took a big bite of dessert.

"Maggie was mean to me all the time I was growing up. Why am I surprised?" Father Frank sighed.

"Okay, little brother. At this very moment, he's on his way to see her. They had a good visit on the phone and she was excited that he would come visit her. A happy ending."

* * *

After the meal, Richards took Father Frank aside and thanked him again, privately, for all he had done. "I was smart enough to quickly recognize what a perceptive person you are. And I can't express my deep gratitude to you, not only for your help during the case, but for your help with my personal conflict about it. Thank you for opening my eyes to a much larger picture."

"You're welcome. The way I see it, though, is - you did your job and I did mine."

"By the way, it was Billy John who sent the threatening notes to you. We brought him in, raked him over the coals, and put him on a year's probation. He won't bother you."

The priest looked perplexed. "Can a sheriff put somebody on probation?"

The Ranger laughed. "Very good, Father Frank. No, he can't. But Billy John doesn't know that. We kind of shook him up. He's not a bad kid. Just a very short fuse. He's got to learn to control that temper or he'll get in serious trouble."

"Thanks. And I think it is fair to say you *did* solve this case. But the suspect was not competent to stand trial." He put his hand on Dick's shoulder. " I hope we can ... visit in the future." He gave a small laugh. "I almost said work again. I hope we can *visit* when it's not related to a murder trial. "

They shook hands and Father Frank watched the Ranger leave.

* * *

Later, after Georgia and Mike had left and Maggie and Jeff were preparing to leave, Maggie pulled Father Frank aside. "Before we go, I have to tell you something, and I don't want this to go to your head. You recommended I read Granet's book carefully and see if he had done something to improve on what I had written."

"Did you?"

"I did."

"And?"

"Not much different. But I found a few places where he had cut out a scene, or a description, or some useless action. Most likely, it was an editor who did those things, not Granet. And, I hate to say it, but it was better. It moved more smoothly. Was a little tighter."

"Great. It's always good to learn."

"Agreed. But remember, he won the Austin Benedict Award for plot. And it was *my* plot all the way. No variance there. It should have been me getting the Award."

"But, big sister, Granet has shown you that you *are* an Austin Benedict winner and you *can* be a *USA Today* bestseller." He cocked his head to the side. "Did you really know that before?"

She frowned and shrugged. "Probably not. I wanted to be. But did I really believe?" She raised her eyebrows. "Maybe not."

"So, some good came out of it. Now you know."

* * *

Father Frank saw Maggie and Jeff off and headed over to the church. He knelt in the back and looked at the cross hanging behind the altar. *Dear God, thank You for all the great things You have done for me and those around me. Please help Maggie deliver a beautiful baby. And thank You for introducing me to Dick Richards. He's a good Ranger, and I think he'll be a good friend. Please keep him safe in a dangerous job, and guide him to a blend of justice and compassion.*

And lastly, but far from least, help Grace find her life again. Let her gift for beautiful words inspire others. Amen.

He got up, left the church and started toward the rectory. As he passed under the basketball hoop, he said aloud. "And this week, I'll find some time to shoot some baskets. Got to keep my shooting eye sharp."

The end

Thank you for reading ***A Plot for Murder, A Father Frank Mystery, Book #3.***

Please read the next page.

From the Author

I hope you enjoyed *A Plot for Murder*. If you did, it would be a great favor to me if you would leave a brief review on Goodreads or the site where you purchased the book. It can be as little as two or three sentences - what you thought of the book, any particular character you liked, or any particular scene or situation you found enjoyable or well-done. Reviews are very important to writers. They can make a big impact on the success of a book, or a writer.

If you did not like the book, please email me at: jim@jamesrcallan.com and tell me what didn't work for you. Of course, feel free to write me directly if you liked it also.

If you will write and provide me your email address, I can keep you updated when I have another book released I think you will enjoy, or some free book or short story I'm giving away. Just drop me an email to: *jim@jamesrcallan.com* and say "Send me a free story." And I will. I promise I will not sell, rent, or give your email address to anyone, nor will I spam you with many emails.

A Plot for Murder is a Father Frank Mystery, Book #3. A brief peak into each of the first two Father Frank Mysteries, *Cleansed by Fire, Father Frank Mystery, Book #1*, and *Over My Dead Body, Father Frank Mystery, Book #2*, will follow on the next few pages. I hope you will take a few minutes to take a look at those.

Most of all, thank you for reading A Plot for Murder.

Cleansed by Fire, **A Father Frank Mystery, Book #1**

Here are some reader comments on this series.

I started Cleansed by Fire this past rainy Sunday afternoon...couldn't put it down, and read it straight thru till I finished it late that night .
—Bob Hostler, published review

I really enjoy cozy mysteries when they're this good. And when a writer makes a crime-solving priest as interesting to a Southern Baptist reader as James R. Callan has done, he's really accomplished something.
—Roger Bruner, published review

Move over, father brown, there's another temporal avenging angel in town! when father frank deluca learns through confession that his confessor knew in advance that a church was going to be burned, he is anxious to find this arsonist.
—ELIZABETH ERIKSE, published Review

What a delightful mystery! Father Frank is clever and an all around great character. James R. Callan is a terrific writer who makes all his characters interesting and realistic.
—Bonnie Engstron, published review

Chapter 1 starts on the next page.

Cleansed by Fire

~ ONE ~

"Bless me Father for I have sinned."

Father Frank DeLuca waited in the dark behind the screen of the Prince of Peace confessional. The voice sounded familiar, like he should know the person but he quickly wiped that thought from his mind. He did not want to know who it was.

When nothing more came, he said, "How long has it been since you last took the Sacrament of Reconciliation?"

"Ah, I don't remember. Kind of a long time."

"Is there something in particular that has brought you back today?"

Another silence.

Finally, "I knew about the fire Thursday."

Thursday. Father Frank's mind searched through the events of two days ago. "You mean the Pine Valley Baptist Church? That fire?"

"Yes, Father." Then he quickly added, "I didn't set it or nothin'."

When the boy did not continue, Father Frank said, "But …?"

"I knew it was going to happen. And I didn't tell nobody, uh, anybody. I mean, I didn't tell the police."

Father Frank furrowed his eyebrows and ran a hand through his black, curly hair. He hadn't heard if the fire had been classified as arson or an accident.

"Do you mean you knew someone was going to set fire to the church before it happened?"

"Yes."

Father Frank's mind raced down several paths at once. As a rule, the priest tried not to recognize any penitent. Tonight, with news of the arson, his mind inadvertently associated the voice with a name—Sammie Winters. Did someone tell the boy they were going to burn a church? Did he have a vision or premonition? Sammie didn't seem the type. Had he heard someone talking about it?

"How do you know this?"

The teenager remained quiet for a moment before answering, almost in a whisper. "I, uh, I heard someone say they were going to burn a church."

"Why didn't you tell the authorities?"

"I couldn't. Uh—you don't understand. I just couldn't."

The priest closed his eyes and rested his forehead in his hands, suddenly weary. Could the fire have been prevented? He took a deep breath. He was supposed to give guidance. He raised his head.

"You're right, I don't understand. But God will. Talk to Him. Tell Him you're sorry for your sins, and say a Rosary for the people who lost their church."

"Yes, Father."

"I absolve you from all your sins." Father Frank made a sign of the cross. "In the name of the Father, the Son, and the Holy Spirit."

The priest cleared his throat. "There is one other thing. Since you know who committed the crime, you really should tell the police. Now. If you don't, this is going to weigh on you like a lead warm-up jacket. You have information that can help the police solve a crime, and an obligation to tell them."

The boy said nothing but Father Frank heard the door

open and close. Sammie was gone.

The priest sat in the darkness, eyes wide open, as he hoped no one else came into the confessional tonight. Sammie Winters knew Pine Valley Baptist had been arson. He probably also knew the name of the arsonist. Why wouldn't he tell the police?

The priest sighed. Maybe Sammie was more involved than he indicated. Maybe he pushed someone into setting the fire. What *was* the extent of his participation?

Sammie didn't seem like the type to be involved in serious crime. He seemed like a good kid, and attended mass every Sunday with his parents. Yet, some connection existed between Sammie and the arson. Father Frank shook his head. Maybe he didn't know Sammie that well since he wasn't involved in any church activities. Nice looking kid, about fifteen. What had he gotten himself into?

~ * ~

Even now Father Frank could see the inferno—red and orange flames with yellow tongues flickering, roaring, stretching upward, trying to reach the tall pine trees that towered over the white frame church. He could feel the heat, pulsing on the breeze. First hot, then warm, then hot again, lest you forget it was consuming a building. He could hear the frustration of those trying to save something—firemen who were losing the battle, parishioners who were losing their church, and Reverend Fisher, wringing his hands, almost in tears. Just a month ago, he had celebrated his twentieth year as the minister of Pine Valley Baptist.

The church burned to the ground.

At least no one was killed. Allan Moore, one of the volunteer firefighters, had sustained serious burns when he tripped and fell on live coals. Maybe all of that could have been avoided if Sammie had told the police what he had known before the fire was set. Father Frank said a quick prayer that Pine Valley Baptist would rebound, rebuild, and use this misfortune to draw closer to God. And the priest prayed that Sammie would go to the police and tell what he knew.

Father Frank guessed the crowd of gawkers to be over fifty. He'd been there too, watching the firemen struggle to put out the fire and work to see it didn't spread to adjoining properties. He had felt a deep loss, watching a house of God being destroyed, not knowing what he could do.

He felt the same way now. What could he do? He shook his head in the solitude of the confessional. Nothing. The seal of confession prevented him from telling anybody, even the police, what he had heard from Sammie. And yet, how could he do nothing? Someone had destroyed a church. Not his church but a Christian church, and that was like a cousin being attacked.

Cleansed by Fire is in paperback, e-pub, mobi formats, and in audio (narrated by Five-time Emmy Award-Winner Jonathan Mumm).

On the next page, you can read the first chapter of *Over My Dead Body*. It will only take two minutes. I think you'll enjoy it.

Over My Dead Body

Chapter 1

Syd snorted and thrust his chin toward his adversary. "Over my dead body."

The man almost smiled. "If you insist," he said easily.

Seventy-two year old Syd Cranzler squinted against the bright Texas October sun and scrutinized the well-dressed man in front of him. Syd was probably six inches shorter than the man, but Syd's voice had more iron in it. "Was that a threat?"

"No sir, Mr. Cranzler," Duke Heinz said.

Syd didn't like this city slicker, wouldn't have even if he weren't trying to steal Syd's homestead. Even Duke's clothes irritated him. The conservative black pinstriped suit, power-red tie and black wing-tips polished to perfection made the man look like he was posing for a magazine picture in New York City. And what was this "Duke" bit? Did he think he was John Wayne? "Why don't you just mosey on down the road a mile?" He jerked his hand up and pointed. "Lots of land there."

They stood on pine needles under three towering trees. Forty feet behind them was Syd's small, frame house, looking like a giant, square tumbleweed.

Bud Wilcox, Pine Tree's City Manager, pushed his straw hat back a little and took a step forward. "Syd, Pine Tree wants this shopping center *here*, inside the city limits. Think of all the tax revenue we'll get."

"So's you can waste even more'n you do now? It ain't your house and land, Pipsqueak."

Bud reddened at the nickname Syd often used on him, but kept his mouth shut.

A mud-caked '92 Camaro rattled to a stop half off the black-top road. A man got out and started across the yard to where Syd was shaking his finger at Bud.

Duke started to speak, but Syd cut him off. "And don't tell me again it's twice what it's worth. You don't know what it's worth to me. And what's this 'fee simple' bit?" He cocked his head to the side. "You think I'm simple? Take your money and go back to Jersey."

Bud waggled his balding head. "It's a lot of dollars."

"He don't need your money," said the man from the Camaro. "He stole enough from me."

"Stay out of it, W.C.," Syd snapped. But his focus never left Duke. "You keep your money; I'll keep my land."

Duke spread his hands. "Mr. Cranzler, the Supreme Court says eminent domain can be used to obtain land needed for a project in the public interest."

"I know all 'bout the Supreme Court, and how they trampled all over people's property rights. I'd like to see some private company try to take the land *they* live on. They'd change their tune right fast. But that case was decided for a Yankee town. This is Texas. We still believe in property rights down here. And this ain't in the public interest. It's in Lockey Corporation's interest."

Duke smiled as he pulled a folded paper from the inside pocket of his coat. "Here's the court order, and it's signed by a judge right here in Texas." He held the paper out to Syd.

Syd ignored it. "Judge McFatage, right? He'd sign anything for a price."

Bud Wilcox leaned in. "Now, Syd, you shouldn't talk about the Honorable McFatage that way."

"Honorable, my foot. He's for sale. Common knowledge. You know what they say: he's the best judge money can buy. And it looks like Lockey's the buyer."

"Look, Mr. Cranzler," Duke said. "We're going to start dirt work in three weeks. I'd like to have all the paperwork in order by then. You've lost this fight. You might as well recognize that. You can delay signing. But by fighting this, you may end up getting less money and paying a lot of it to lawyers. You can't stop it. This project *will* be built. And it starts in three weeks."

"Three weeks?" Syd pulled on his chin and a sly grin crept onto his leathery face. "I'm bettin' my lawyer'll have my appeal filed before then. And I'm thinkin' I can tie this up for years. You sure Lockey wants to wait that long?" His head bobbed up and down as he continued. "Be a lot faster to go somewheres else." Now he laughed. "Bet they're gonna cut you loose when this don't happen. Can your butt."

Duke's smile faded and his eyes turned hard. "Two months from now, this will all be asphalt."

"Like I said, over my dead body."

Duke put the paper back in his pocket. "Old man, you'll hardly make a bump in the pavement."

* * *

Over My Dead Body is in digital and paperback formats, plus in audio, narrated by five-time Emmy Award winner, Jonathan Mumm.

Again, consider joining my email list and I'll send you a free short story that's just fun. Email me at: jim@jamesrcallan.com and say, "Send me a free story." I won't spam you, and I will never sell, rent or give your email address away. And that's a promise.

About the Author

James R. Callan took a degree in English, intent on writing. But when writing didn't support a family, he returned to graduate school in the field of mathematics. He pursued a career in mathematics and computer science. Along the way, he received grants from the National Science Foundation, NASA, and the Data Processing Management Association. He has been listed in *Who's Who in America*, *Who's Who in Computer Science*, and *Two Thousand Notable Americans*.

But writing was his first love. He has published fourteen books and picked up a number of awards along the way. ***A Plot for Murder,*** the third Father Frank mystery book, is his latest mystery/ suspense book.

Callan and his wife split their time between homes in northeast Texas and Puerto Vallarta, Mexico. They have four grown children and six grand-children. His website is: **www.jamesrcallan.com**. If you enjoyed this book, sign up to receive *occasional* updates on Callan's books email me at: jim@jamesrcallan.com and say, "Send me a free story." *I absolutely promise NOT to spam you, or give, trade or sell your email address.*